WAVERING JUSTICE

WAVERING JUSTICE

ANNE KANE

This is a work of fiction. Names, characters, places, and incidents either are the product of the author's imagination or are used fictitiously. Any resemblance to actual persons, living or dead, events, or locales is entirely coincidental.

ISBN: 0692681345
ISBN 13: 9780692681343
Library of Congress Control Number: 2016909362
Anne Kane, Aledo, TX

PART I

Chapter 1

1942

"You have just contaminated the whole surgical field, Miss Black," the nursing instructor bellowed. "Start again—from the beginning," she said, trying to be patient.

The student, Gennie Black, her hands quivering, removed her contaminated gloves. She opened a new pack of sterile gloves, regowned, and went through the sterile surgical procedural test again. The educator remained silent.

Gennie exited the basement classroom and hoped that no admonitions and a nearly imperceptible nod of the instructor's head meant she had passed. Beginning to climb the stairs to the fourth floor where the freshman nursing students lived, she heard someone yell her name from above, in the stairwell.

"Telephone call for Gennie."

"Tell them to hold on," she called back and pulled her uniform skirt above her knees, taking two steps at a time. At the top of the four flights, two phones hung on the wall: a direct line to the hospital and a pay phone.

She picked up the dangling receiver and said hello. Breathless panting followed.

"Hi, Gennie?"

"Hey, Will. What's up?"

"I need to talk with you. When is your next day off?"

"This Saturday. I get off at noon."

"Okay, I'll pick you up at the train station and take you home."

"Is anything wrong?"

"Hell yes. There are rumors that President Roosevelt is lowering the draft age to eighteen any day now. If we have to go, Herb and I don't want to wait until we're drafted and instead want to go into the navy."

"I hate that. How soon will you have to enlist? Can you two finish the semester? What are you going to do?"

"That's what we need to discuss. This phone bill will be astronomical if we start talking now. I think we should wait until Saturday."

"You're right. I'll see you then. I love you."

"I love you too."

She hung up the black receiver on the wall phone and walked down the students' dorm hall, pulling off her nurse's cap and unbuttoning the waistband of her pinafore apron. On either side of the long corridor, she passed closed doors. Behind each one a small cubicle contained a single bed, a dresser, a wall-mounted lavatory, and a closet. Maybe this residence hall had appeared luxurious after the 1906 earthquake, when it was built, but now the rooms seemed austere, with only a central bathroom for the whole floor.

Once in her room, Gennie perched her cap on the corner of the mirror and hung her apron on a hanger. Only then did she allow herself to be dramatic, flinging her body on the bed and fingering the promise ring that hung around her neck. "The unfairness of it all," she thought. "Our hopes and plans for the future are being exploded like those US ships at Pearl Harbor."

Two months had passed since the Japanese had bombed the Hawaiian Islands. The fear that this enemy would attack the West Coast of the United States had caused air-raid siren alerts, blackouts, and new rules that forbade streetlights and driving after dark. The people in small towns near military bases felt vulnerable. A sighting of a Japanese submarine off the coast of San Diego had made the foreboding real.

Following their June graduation from high school, Gennie and Will had both started their fall semesters: Will at Stanford to study business and Gennie at All Saints Hospital in San Francisco for nurses' training. Their parents had given approval to these plans, especially because Will's dad hoped the family grocery chain would be passed to his son. The kids had gone steady for the past two years and planned to marry after college. The imminent threat of military conscription into a war zone jerked their complacency.

On Saturday afternoon Will waited for the train to arrive at the station. He paced along the tracks in front of the new art-deco building with its terra-cotta carved chevrons over the door. When the steam engine slowed and passed him, he stopped and scanned each of the hunter-green commuter coaches. His light brown hair, slicked back with hair gel, and pointed nose hinted at his Germanic heritage. With a stiff stance, hands clasped behind his back, he looked like a commander reviewing parading troops marching by.

The conductor stood on the bottom stair as the train came to a stop, and then he put the step stool down and helped Gennie with her big suitcase—stuffed with dirty laundry to be done while home. The suitcase looked huge next to Gennie's petite stature and surely had challenged her strength and agility to get it on and off the streetcar and onto the train.

Will's rigid posture immediately dissolved when he saw Gennie. He loped to her, grabbed the suitcase, and put his arm around her shoulders, pulling her to him. They exchanged a brief but urgent kiss. Starting for the parking lot, they walked, still wrapped together, their smiles exuding joy. Will bent down and sniffed at her hair.

"You smell like a hospital."

"That's ether. I scrubbed on a T and A—a tonsillectomy—this morning, and they used ether for the anesthesia. When it vaporizes it gets into everyone's hair, skin, and clothes. As soon as I shower, I'll be good as new."

"Well, I'm glad it's fixable."

Will helped Gennie into the car and started the motor. "I thought we would drive around and talk before I take you home."

"Okay, but I haven't had any lunch. Can we stop somewhere to get a Coke?"

"Do you want to get something to eat?"

"No, I'm not hungry, just thirsty."

Will drove to a corner drugstore, going in and bringing out two cold bottled Cokes before he headed the car toward the city park. He stopped at the curb and lowered the windows a little to air the interior of the pungent odor of ether. Switching the ignition off, the tune on the radio, "Amapolo," came to an abrupt end. He turned to face Gennie. She had never seen him look so grim.

"I need to make a decision and hope you will agree with me. As I told you, I want to enlist in the navy before I am drafted. Herb does too. 'Cause it sure looks like all of us guys will be inducted." He halted, searching her face for a reaction. "After hearing all the stories from the vets about the First World War and the horror and mayhem in the trenches in Europe, I don't want to be in the army."

"How soon do you have to enlist?"

"I don't know. Dad, Herb, and I are going Monday to the navy recruiter to ask him all the details."

"I guess it's ultimately your decision. Can you avoid going into the service somehow? Are there any excuses—ah, deferments—that are acceptable?"

"Yeah, if I take a note from my momma to the president, I'm sure he will say, 'Will, boy, you don't have to serve.'"

"Don't make fun of me." Her face fell into a pout. "I'm afraid for both of us. All our hopes and dreams seem to be disappearing in front of our eyes."

"Well, there is one part of our plan I want to carry out right now. I want us to get married before I enter basic training."

Gennie looked at him with complete disbelief. Of all they had talked about, one thing they had agreed on from the beginning included finishing their education before marriage.

"You know I would wait for you whether we were married or not. I can't remain at the nursing school if I'm married. I'd have to drop out."

"Not if you don't tell them."

Gennie looked into his eyes to see if he was teasing her. No, she gazed into an intense and serious face.

"Obviously you have been thinking about all these options for days. I didn't expect this. The ether vapor is getting to me. I need to get home and shower," she said.

"I've just suggested we get married immediately, and you want to shower."

"I love you and want to marry you. But it's more complicated than that. There's just so much to consider. Give this smelly girl a kiss, and let's go home."

Will revved the motor as he left the curb, squealing the tires. They drove to Mayfield, a couple miles south of Palo Alto. Gennie's parents lived beyond the few short blocks that represented the core of the town with its dozen or so stores. The house sat on thirty acres of gently rolling hills studded with huge oak trees. Native grasses proliferated and were harvested into hay bales in the summer. Palm trees that Gennie's grandfather had planted years ago bordered the short driveway in front of the two-story house. The stucco exterior with a red tile roof reflected the Mexican influence on California architecture.

Will followed Gennie up the walk to the kitchen door, carrying her suitcase.

"Come on in. I'm sure Mom will be glad for you to stay for dinner. You can tell both Mom and Dad about your plans."

They entered the kitchen, where Gennie's mom stood preparing dinner. Will perched on a kitchen stool while Gennie raced upstairs to shower. He had an easy relationship with Gennie's folks, Erma and Bob Black. He was actually more relaxed with them than with his own parents, who had high expectations for their only child. He often balked at their demands. Erma continued chopping salad ingredients, and Will proceeded to recite his proposed plans. She listened, commenting only that she anticipated this development after reading about the draft in the newspapers.

In a few minutes, Gennie came downstairs dressed in a slim skirt and pullover sweater, her short blond curly hair still damp. Will went to her, bent down to inhale the improvement, and said, "Wow, now you smell super."

"It's that Blue Grass talc you gave me for Christmas. I love it."

The back door opened, and Bob Black came in after his day at work as a building contractor. He went to Erma and kissed her on the cheek. "What a nice surprise to see you two kids here. You staying for dinner?"

Erma rolled her eyes at him as if to say, "Have you ever known them to turn down a meal?"

He placed his metal lunch box on the kitchen counter and went in the downstairs bathroom to wash up. He came out and went to the cabinet, withdrew two wine glasses, and poured sherry in each one.

"Do you guys want anything to drink?"

"No, thanks. We just had a Coke on the way home," Gennie said and Will shook his head.

They went out to the glassed-in porch that overlooked the vast meadows at the back of the house. As they sat facing the west, the winter sun descended behind the distant purple mountains, and the birds ceased their chirping. Erma said, "Will has been talking about some important choices he is facing." She then went on with a synopsis of his conversation with her, and Will added some thoughts from time to time.

"We'd like your opinion," Gennie chimed in, looking at her dad. He took off his glasses and pulled out his handkerchief from his back pocket to dust the lenses.

"Well, your mother and I have already discussed this, since it appears obvious that all our young men will be drafted. I dare say that the parents of your classmates are having this conversation too. Of course, Will, it is your choice of what branch of service you go into, and I agree that the army infantrymen faced some horrible experiences during the last war. The navy seems a good choice to me." Will nodded in agreement, and Bob continued, "As for marrying beforehand, I understand a man's desire to go off to battle with a wife at home. It's not a question of Gennie's loyalty but your desire to be married in an official ceremony and share the joy of a marriage bed before you leave. It may make the many lonely nights far away from home easier to bear."

Will's look at Gennie seemed to say, "See, *he* gets it."

"But as Gennie's father, I have to be concerned that she would have to give up her dream of becoming a nurse. Also, if she continued and—God forbid—something happened to you, Will, she would have a profession and a way to support herself. Otherwise, she might have to look for a husband to survive financially."

The bluntness of his answer stunned the younger couple.

Erma added a softer perspective. "Whatever you decide, we will support you. And we think you'll make it work, regardless."

The oven timer went off, signaling that the meatloaf was done. Erma stood and asked Gennie to set the table for six because her sister, Susan, and a girlfriend were studying together and would join them. She asked Bob to call the girls to dinner and said to Will, "How good are you at tossing a salad? Follow me, and let's see."

Susan and her friend, both juniors in high school, carried the spirited dinner conversation. Their words ricocheted like machine-gun bullets. They made fun of the school officials, who were trying to find a way to keep the students safe during possible air raids.

"Last week they told us to crawl under our desks and hide our heads, but this week we are expected to be on streets walking to a 'safe room,'" they recited. "Our homeroom is assigned to a designated building with a basement in the neighborhood, but we are only in our homeroom first period. When the air-raid siren sounds, what a scramble it will be to get to your homeroom so you're not left behind. And they are canceling our Spring Carnival at night because it's under floodlights on the football field. Now it will be in the afternoon. Won't that be an exciting date? And did you hear that no one can drive after eight p.m.? Our senior year will stink. It's not fair."

Erma murmured, "That's not the last time I am going to hear those words: 'It's not fair.'"

After the guests left and everyone had headed to bed, Erma readied the house for sleep, locking doors and turning out lights. When she saw the slit of light under Gennie's door, she knocked softly, went in, and sat on the edge of the bed.

"Are you okay? I know it's been a long day."

"Yes, there is one thing that is bothering me. Will didn't mention to you that he thinks we shouldn't tell the nursing school when we marry, did he?"

Her mom, shaking her head no, reacted just as her daughter had: with a look of disbelief.

"Gennie, living a lie is no way to live." She reached for Gennie's hands and held on to them as if that would make her transmit her message stronger. "Living a lie will torment you with always expecting someone to find the truth. Your freedom would be stifled."

This passionate response surprised Gennie. Did it spring from one of Erma's own experiences? This rekindled Gennie's longtime curiosity about her mother's past. When questioned, Erma never divulged any information about her childhood. All she would say is that her life began when she met Bob. That subject was closed.

Her mom continued, "Two and a half years is a long time to keep a secret, especially when there will be family members who know you are married. And what if the nursing school learns right before you graduate, or right after? Will they take away your diploma?"

She paused for a moment and then said, "If you marry Will now, you must give up your dream of becoming a nurse and decide that your marital happiness is not only pleasing him but also fulfilling your dreams. There are other medical careers that don't require students to be unmarried. We can look into them. And if you marry now, do it without feeling that it is a sacrifice."

She bent down and kissed Gennie on the forehead. "Think about it."

Gennie reached up and turned off her bedside lamp. It had been a busy and exhausting day. Yet her mind would not rest. She thought, "Why can't I be joyful on this day that Will suggested an immediate marriage? Every other girl in our senior class last year would have traded places with me. After all, he's tall, athletic, and gentlemanly to girls, and he has a great future in business. Even college coeds enroll in school just to snare a husband and obtain their MRS degree. We've all been told since childhood that girls are placed on this earth to be dutiful wives and mothers. Now, just because I don't have a suitor on bended knee, a huge diamond ring, and that dreamed-of gorgeous silk crepe wedding gown that skims the body to the hip and then flounces out to a voluminous skirt, can't I be thankful I have Will? But I could have both: a nursing education and a wedding after the war. Once the United States entered World War I, it lasted two years until the armistice. If Will came home in two years, he could finish his education, and I could do the same. If I say no and Will gets killed"—she shuttered at the thought—"I would have to live with the guilt that I denied him his one wish—his one memory of happiness. He is going out to the unknown, but I will be here in the cocoon of my family and friends. Who is really sacrificing?"

She turned on her side and closed her eyes.

The next morning, Gennie awoke to the luscious smell of home-brewed coffee. She had just recently become a caffeine fanatic and even tolerated the hospital cafeteria brew. In the kitchen, her folks were at the breakfast table, and she went in to join them.

After a glance over her dad's shoulder at the newspaper headlines, she said, "I sort of have a tentative plan." He put down the paper and took a sip of coffee. "I will make an appointment with the director of nursing and ask her if there is a possibility of being a married student, since we are at war. This would be my first choice." She poured herself a cup of coffee. "If that's not possible and Will is insistent about marrying now, we will."

Gennie darted her look to both of their faces. "I hope I can come home to live after he deploys, until I decide on another career course."

Her dad stood and hugged her shoulders. "I am so proud of you," he said, choking up, with tears welling up in his eyes. Her teary eyes met his, and the three embraced.

Chapter 2

Lem Mueller, Will's father, didn't relish the job of taking Will and his roommate, Herb, to the navy recruitment office. He knew that Will, at eighteen, embodied few coping skills, had a quick temper, and would be challenged by authority. Only since he had been in a relationship with Gennie had he mellowed. Lem appreciated that she had that effect on Will, but away from her, would he lose his control?

Lem drove his 1939 Buick Roadmaster to pick up the boys at their college dorm. He liked the car but wondered whether it would survive throughout the war. Already all car manufacturers had been forced to manufacture war machines.

Will and Herb Jordan were at the curb, waiting for their ride. Both were tall and lanky and on the cusp of their best years. Will had passed his father in height about two years ago. Approaching middle age, Lem had added girth and a balding pate. Every day he dressed in a three-piece suit with a tie befitting a prosperous businessman.

"Hey, boys, jump in. Are you ready for this? Do you have cold feet?"

The answers—"Yeah" and "Nah"—didn't sound convincing.

Lem liked Herb, who seemed more mature and had a good work ethic, since he was raised on a dairy farm up in Oregon. In the few months since the two boys had met and roomed together in college, they had found camaraderie;

Herb most likely missed his brothers, and Will had never had a sibling relationship. They both shared the dream of wanting to be business owners. Will's idea of introducing grocery supermarkets to these central California communities appealed to Herb.

At the recruiting office in downtown Palo Alto, Lem listened as the boys learned that they should join the navy before they received their army draft notices. If the boys signed up together now, the navy would allow them ten days to get their affairs in order and also guarantee that Herb and Will would go into basic training together. After basic, there were no promises.

Lem told the navy recruiter, "I have concerns about our German surname. I remember the anti-German sentiment during the First World War. Many people showed their anger by boycotting German-owned businesses and changing German-named street signs, and the Metropolitan Opera no longer performed music by German composers. Even my brother changed his surname to Miller, but I'm proud to be a third-generation owner of Mueller's Grocery Store."

As it turned out, his family's loyalty to the small community of Mayfield proved to shield him from the discrimination. Now, though, his son would be enlisting into an unknown group of men. The family reputation couldn't protect him.

The recruiter tried to assuage Lem's fears and said that the boys would learn in basic training how to report any discrimination or hazing. "I know there's a lot of anti-German sentiment that can be directed at our own citizens, but I understand the political climate isn't the same as in World War I, and I would hope we are a little more tolerant." Looking at Will, six feet tall and muscular, he said, "I think this kid will take care of himself."

Will smiled. "Yeah, Dad, I'll be fine."

Lem thought, "This arrogant son can show his youthful bravado, but may God protect him."

On Monday, back at the nurses' dorm, Gennie called the office of the director of nurses and made an appointment with the secretary to see the director that afternoon. At two o'clock, Gennie appeared, dressed in her full uniform: blue dress, white pinafore apron, white cap and stockings, and polished shoes. The secretary went into the inner office to let Mrs. Hadley, the director, know Gennie had arrived. Motioned in by the secretary, Gennie stood in front of Mrs. Hadley's desk.

"Miss Black?"

"Yes, ma'am."

"What brings you in today?"

Gennie had her proposal memorized. "My boyfriend is enlisting in the navy, and we want to marry before he deploys. I would like permission to stay in training while he is away fighting for his country. I respectfully request a special dispensation, since we are at war."

Because she had not been offered a seat, she stood in front of the desk, facing the director.

Mrs. Hadley paused a moment before answering. To Gennie it seemed like waiting for a long freight train to pass a grade crossing.

"Miss Black, there is a reason for this rule. This is an intense educational curriculum. It is felt that marriage would detract from your studies and work experience. It is not only our board who believes this but most nursing schools in our country."

"Is there a chance the board would reconsider because of the war conditions?"

"No, this ruling will stand." She rose from her chair, the meeting completed.

"Thank you, Mrs. Hadley," Gennie said and turned to go.

"And Miss Black, may I remind you not to try to deceive us. Remember: our nursing creed includes honesty and integrity."

"Yes, ma'am."

"Good-bye, Miss Black."

The office door closed behind her automatically, and Gennie walked swiftly across the hospital foyer and out the side door to the parking lot. A torrent of tears appeared that she could not control. She ran across the parking lot to the nursing dorm, bumping into some upperclassmen on the way to the stairs. The other girls exchanged a knowledgeable look—just one of those emotional breakdowns that training seemed to provoke. Every student had two or three.

Once inside her room, the phrase "Good-bye, Miss Black" resonated in her head, and another stream of tears erupted. Amid her sobs, she blubbered, "You old biddies. You think that a married woman would taint your pristine virgins with titillating information about married life and distract them from their precious, pure nursing careers." She thought, "You don't trust your students to understand and be discriminate." Not usually vindictive, Gennie resented the sudden and complete loss of her dream.

Most of her classmates were either at work or in the cafeteria. She went to the phone, plunked in a nickel, and gave Will's number to the operator. No one answered. When the coin returned, she called her folks' number.

"Momma, Mrs. Hadley said no, there isn't any chance of changing the rule. And then she said, 'Good-bye, Miss Black.'" Gennie choked down new sobs. "Will's not in his room, so I can't talk with him. I need to now." She sounded like a frustrated seventeen-year-old child—which she was.

"You'll just have to keep on trying. He might be at his cafeteria. He knew you were going to talk with Mrs. Hadley, didn't he? He'll most likely try to call. Do you have to work this evening?"

"No, I worked this morning." Just then an alarm bell sounded, meaning more coins needed to be inserted. "I'll call you when I know something."

Gennie couldn't help having a thought creep into her mind: "Isn't Will being selfish wanting to marry now and depriving me of a career? He would be traveling far away from home, wanting memories to carry with him through the rough times, but knowing that I continued to pursue my nursing dream should count for something." She did not remember when she had been so conflicted, when she hadn't gotten her way.

Will did phone and suggested he drive up to see her. If he left immediately, he could be up there in an hour, giving them some time to talk before the eight o'clock government curfew on unauthorized driving. Streetlights had been capped with black tape so aircraft could not see them, and the top third of headlights were taped and looked like they had droopy eyelids. The darkened streets challenged drivers.

They went to the donut shop around the corner from the hospital and exchanged the news of their interviews. The boys were going to sign up the next day. They had waited because Herb wanted to talk with his family about his choice. They both were going to drop out of school immediately.

Gennie knew she needed to write a letter of resignation if she planned to leave. Will still thought they could have kept their nuptials a secret and did not offer to postpone a wedding.

"You're the one who won't try to do both," he told her. "Then we would both have what we want."

Back at the dorm, she again called home and asked someone to come and pick her up in the morning. She wrote her letter of resignation in longhand and walked across the bridge that connected the dorm to the hospital, sliding the envelope under Mrs. Hadley's office door. All this time, Gennie had avoided her classmates and any maudlin display of sadness. Her decision had been made. Instead of participating in the usual evening visiting and mingling in the hallway, she closed her door and began to pack.

At home the following day, Erma offered to help Gennie make wedding plans, saying "There isn't time for melancholy thoughts." It reflected her mother's obvious philosophy of "Don't dwell on the past; look to the future." They decided on a small home wedding performed in front of the living-room fireplace by a justice of the peace, with a few friends and relatives as guests. Mother and daughter rode the commuter train to San Francisco, where they shopped for a wedding outfit and trousseau. First they went to The Emporium on Market Street but were disappointed with the selections. Next they walked up to the City of Paris. Here Gennie chose a peach silk suit with generous lapels and an accordion-pleated skirt. A filmy blouse, just a shade darker, peeked out of the jacket that had only one button at the waist. A small hat with a modest veil completed the outfit.

"All brides need new undergarments for this special day," the saleslady purred. "May I show you our selection?" She brought out matched sets of slips, panties, bras, and garter belts—exquisitely embroidered. "These are the latest from Paris and unfortunately may be the last for a while." Gennie picked out a set adorned with white silk flowers and a seed pearl center. "Now has Mademoiselle purchased her nightgown yet?"

After Gennie tried on many and chose a white lacy nightgown and peignoir, the saleslady shifted her attention to Erma. "Has Madame chosen a mother of the bride dress? May I show you our collection?"

Erma paused before answering and then shook her head.

"Momma you need something special, too," Gennie said. "Daddy would want you to have a new outfit,"

The saleslady asked Erma, "What is your favorite color?"

"It's light blue." Gennie answered for her mother. "It shouldn't be too frivolous. She'll want to be able to wear it later to parties at the Elks Club." Erma chuckled as her daughter was suddenly taking over the decision making.

After trying on several Erma chose a white collared short-sleeved dress, The skirt had four deep pleats which the saleslady observed would make a graceful silhouette on the dance floor. As the purchases were wrapped in tissue paper and boxed, the lady asked if Erma and Gennie would each like to purchase a pair of silk stockings. "They are the absolute last shipment from Japan and we are limiting them to our best customers." They accepted the offer with enthusiasm.

A store employee helped them down the elevator with their purchases to the front entrance where the doorman hailed a taxicab for them. When Erma and Gennie were settled in the back seat of the cab, Gennie said, "Now this is what I call a colossal shopping trip."

At home after giving a fashion show of their purchases for Bob, he told Erma, "Gennie will be a beautiful bride and all grown up."

"They are so young though. It's hard to imagine, since we were so much older as newlyweds."

"Kids are fearless. They don't see any of the possible pitfalls. We had so many doubts. Remember the discussions we had? But, see, it's all worked out." He reached for Erma's hand and gave it a squeeze. "And it will work out for them too."

While the Black females occupied themselves with clothes shopping and reception ideas, Bob went to the Elks Club and borrowed folding chairs for guest seating. Margaret offered blossoms from her blooming camellia tree for

Gennie's bouquet. She brought over a sample blossom for the bride's approval. "It's perfect," Gennie exclaimed looking at the creamy white petals with a pale yellow center.

Will telephoned Gennie one afternoon and suggested they go out to their old high-school burger hangout.

"I've called my football teammates to join us, but some of them are already in basic. I guess I never realized I was one of the younger guys."

Between the early curfew and the absence of some of their key guys, the usual boisterous antics were subdued.

On the next Sunday afternoon, a small group assembled in the Blacks' living room. Erma had ordered tall, white gladiolas for vases on either side of the fireplace, and Bob had gathered some newly blossomed almond branches to tuck in between the glads. Almond trees exploded with white wispy petals and peach-colored centers in spring. They were among the first to blossom and announce the end of winter weather.

"These blossoms are the harbinger of a new season," Bob declared to Erma, "appropriate for the children's fresh beginning." Each spring, he snapped the first flowering twig off one of the random almond trees in the meadow and brought it indoors, placing it in a vase on the kitchen table as a sign of renewal.

Herb arrived after visiting his folks in Oregon to be best man and Susan excitedly fulfilled the maid-of-honor role. Will had recruited one of his football buddies to operate the Victrola. His assigned job was to start the turntable and at the precise moment Gennie and Bob appeared at the back of the living room, to put the needle on the spinning record. He did it perfectly and the wedding chorus of Lohengren accompanied the bride down the aisle.

After the ceremony and during the reception, Bob looked at his wife and two daughters as they lined up for a photograph. "No doubt that they are related," he thought. All three were small and trim. Only their hairstyles set them apart: Erma's silver hair was twisted into a chignon; Gennie's curly hair had been cut very short because of her surgical rotation, and Susan's sun-streaked shoulder-length hair included a fringe of bangs.

"That's going to be a great photo," Bob said to Lem, who was the photographer. "We've never had an occasion for all of us to be so gussied up at one time."

Will's parents, Margaret and Lem, had bought the newlyweds a five-day honeymoon at the St. Francis Hotel in San Francisco. After cutting and serving the wedding cake and punch, the young couple left for the adult world of marriage.

Their room overlooked Union Square. They could hear the cable car clang in the distance. Gennie removed her jacket, hat, and shoes. She stood at the window and gazed at the block of park below, its geometric paths crisscrossing the grass. Twilight arrived early in February, and they watched as the streetlights came on, their brightness dimmed by war regulations. She turned to the bed and lay across it on her back. Will joined her and lay on his side. He touched the contours of her face with a gentle caress and then kissed her—a calm gesture.

"You know, for the first time in our lives, no one can tell us what to do or what is expected of us," he said. "Our choice is to please each other. Not anyone else."

She smiled, and Will traced his fingers from one of her dimples to the other. She closed her eyes and dozed. An hour later, when she awoke, she went in and unpacked her nightgown and matching peignoir. The lingerie saleslady had assured her that her groom would be dazzled. Will too had rested; he denied sleeping, but when he saw Gennie, he reached for her. She started to dance away, evading his grasp. The diaphanous swirls of the nightgown gave her a delicate quality. She let the filmy peignoir slip from her shoulders and then slowly allowed it to slip to the floor. Will went to grab her again, but she stepped back.

"Not yet," she said, avoiding his reach. She again twirled and swayed until she was sitting cross-legged on the floor. Her gown fluffed up around her, and the yards of soft organza encircled her. "Okay, my prince, come get me."

He took her offered hand and brought her body next to his. "You are so beautiful."

When he untied the satin ribbon on each shoulder, the nightgown slid down to her waist. He started kissing her breasts. She felt sensations, new and exciting, and guided his hands. They collapsed on the bed. Youth and inexperience did not deter their ardor.

For four days, they explored each other but took time out to also see the city. They parked the car in the hotel garage and went on foot and by cable car and streetcar, finding popular attractions and some obscure nooks and crannies in old neighborhoods. They experienced adventures in their hotel room and out of it.

On the last night of their honeymoon, coming in from a movie, they heard the band in the bar area off the lobby of the hotel. It felt good to be inside after their wet and dark walk from the theater; scary shadows had loomed out of each building's entrance in the darkened city. They shed their damp coats and walked to the bar's entrance to listen.

"Let's go inside," Gennie said. When Will seemed reluctant, Gennie pleaded, "Please, let's just listen to the band."

They found an empty table in the dim room, and the waiter immediately appeared.

"Can I get you something to drink?"

"Two Cokes," Will replied.

"Are you guests at the hotel?"

"Yes."

"Room number?" With their credible answer, he said, "Thank you."

The drinks arrived with paper parasols embedded in maraschino cherries. They clinked their glasses. "Cheers," Will said, and Gennie giggled.

They watched the few couples on the small dance floor in front of the bandstand. When the band finished one tune, the clarinetist came down a few steps to the microphone, and the beginning notes of "Stardust" resounded. Gennie grabbed Will's hand and said, "Let's dance this one."

Out on the dance floor, Gennie said into Will's ear, "We've danced together at sock hops, proms, and now on our honeymoon." That pleasant thought helped blot out the memory of the newsreel they had just viewed at the movie. Seeing the graphic photos of battleships being exploded had unnerved her. She rested her head on Will's chest, and he held her tight. The tune made her misty-eyed; music could be the conduit to emotional fears and tears—and joy.

The next morning they drove home for one last day together. They opened their wedding gifts and, at Bob's suggestion, went to the bank and opened a joint account. Will and Gennie spent the night in Gennie's old room, but they were conscious of the thin walls, and the small bed with its squeaky springs impeded their enjoyment. The next day Will faced the emotional challenge of saying good-bye to his parents—especially his mother. Although their relationship had been difficult, no one had foreseen this forced departure with its inherent danger. Herb had spent a few days with his family and then returned to Mayfield. Both Herb and Will had asked their parents not to go with them to the ferry in San Francisco, where they could cross the bay to the Oakland railroad terminal. There they'd board a train to the East Coast. To where they did not know.

The trio—Will, Gennie, and Herb—headed for the ferry building on the Embarcadero in Will's car. They parked and joined a crowd waiting for the ferry to arrive. Herb stepped away from the couple, giving them a moment alone.

"Damn this war," Will said. He cupped Gennie's face in his hands. "How can I be away from my baby's chocolate puddin' eyes for eight weeks?" He kissed her with an intensity that took Gennie's breath away.

She gasped and said, "From our heavenly honeymoon to this sudden separation—it makes it so hard to part. I will miss you so." Gennie joined his lips again.

The ferry had docked, and the crowd started moving toward the boat.

"I love you. Stay safe," Gennie whispered into Will's ear. It took effort for them to disengage their embrace.

Most of the departures now included soldiers going off to training or war, and the emotional angst was palpable. Gennie had planned to be the brave one sending her man off to basic. She'd vowed no tears, but when she looked up and saw Will's eyes watering, filling up, and spilling over onto his cheek, she too could not stop the sobs. They parted, and she grabbed Herb, hugged and kissed him too. The passengers piled onto the stern deck of the boat and crowded together. She stood and waved until the ferry turned and she could no longer see the boys.

Gennie had had little experience in big-city traffic in her two years of driving, but as a married woman, she needed to accept these types of challenges. Will had given her explicit instructions for how to get back on Highway 101. Once she found it, she continued south until the main street of Mayfield intersected the highway. It helped that traffic had thinned since the war. Tires for civilian use were no longer being manufactured, and gas was being rationed.

Once home, Gennie finished unpacking and wrote a letter to Will. She had promised a daily letter, even though she knew he wouldn't get it for days, but the newspapers, government, and radio broadcasts all encouraged letters from home—cheery ones, no sad news or complaining. She went downstairs, walked down the driveway to the road, and put the envelope in their mailbox, raising the red flag. She made a list of their wedding gifts to write thank-you notes for, but she needed to buy appropriate white stationery first. She felt aimless with no classes to go to and didn't feel ready to socialize with old friends yet. Actually, she had not cultivated female friends in high school, because she and Will had always been together. Could she be wallowing in self-pity, or was her mind trying to catch up with all the recent rapid changes? She preferred the latter possibility.

Chapter 3

A week later, Gennie was home alone when the telephone rang. She ran to answer it, lifting the bell shaped receiver off its cradle and talking into the speaker of the candlestick phone. It was Lem and he asked his new daughter-in-law, "Are you staying busy?"

"Not really," Gennie answered.

"Any thoughts on getting back in school?"

"I haven't figured out what I want to pursue, and anyway, I can't get into any programs until next semester."

"I'm wondering if you would consider working in the grocery store. We are losing employees to the draft and are having a hard time finding ladies who don't have young children at home. You could work part time—just a few days a week, or more if you want to. It sure would help me."

"That sounds great, but I have no retail experience. In fact, I haven't worked at all."

"It's really not that difficult. Do you want to talk it over with your folks?"

"I'm a married woman now, you know, so I think I can make my own decision. When do you want me to start?"

"Is tomorrow too soon?"

"No, what time?"

"How about meeting me at nine a.m.?"

"I'll be there." Gennie did a short pirouette in the hallway in front of the phone alcove. It would be good to do something useful besides waiting for a letter from Will.

Gennie reported for work a few minutes early, eager to have a purpose. Doris and Fred were already there. Doris clerked behind the counter, and Fred, who was past the draft age, had been the store manager for a few years. Once introductions were exchanged, Doris gave Gennie an apron, plain and utilitarian, to protect her clothes.

Lem had told the two that his new daughter-in-law would be reporting for work, and they greeted her with enthusiasm. They were engaged in small talk when a stocky young man entered the store. He appeared comfortable being there and approached Gennie.

"My name is Mario." He extended his hand to her, and a wide smile spread across his face. "I sell produce to the store."

His Italian family had truck farms in the deltas of the coast and provided fresh merchandise to most of the independent food stores in the area. He also bought from other local farms. He considered Lem, with three local stores, a good customer.

"Mr. Lem is hiring an attractive staff," he said to Doris. Mario liked to flirt and considered himself good-looking—even though he was married and over thirty.

Doris cautioned him, saying, "This is the boss's new daughter-in-law; you'd better be careful."

In his usual suave manner, he said, "Well, his son has good taste too."

Lem strode in through the back warehouse door. He smiled at everyone and walked over to give Gennie a hug. "I guess you all have met? Gennie, Doris is an old pro at teaching new employees the ropes, so I suggest you follow her around today. I need to get an order out to Mario first, and then I'll check back with you."

Mario had a clipboard under his arm with the day's prices on produce. He and Lem went to the two short aisles of fresh fruits and vegetables just left of the front door. As they went from one type of produce to the next, Mario recited prime and current prices for each and made a prediction about the price and availability in a week. His delivery trucks came out twice a week because no refrigeration existed in the stores. When Mario had secured the order, he asked if they could go to the back of the store and talk. It wasn't a usual request, but Lem said, "Sure."

The two men walked towards the rear door to the warehouse. Cardboard boxes filled with unpacked product stood in the aisle. Here they stopped to talk.

Mario said, "There's a Japanese family who owns property near the naval airfield close to Mountain View. Their farm grows strawberries, asparagus, and tomatoes for us. Their land doesn't abut the airfield but evidently is too close for the government's comfort in this new war effort. President Roosevelt signed an edict that all Japanese must leave the West Coast. They have been told they must sell the land immediately and be relocated inland."

"Why are you telling me this?" Lem asked.

"The family, the Nakamuras, came to my relatives hoping we could buy the property, but we don't have that kind of cash. I told them I would try to find a buyer."

Lem nodded, seeing where this conversation was going.

"This family has been here—American citizens—for three generations. They are peaceful and hard workers. It is ludicrous what is happening to them."

"What are you suggesting I do?" Lem asked.

"Do you have enough cash to buy them out? The government forbids them from owning any property. They need cash—now. The land has great potential, and they are willing to sell it at less than normal value. When they evacuate, they feel they need the cash in hand."

"Geez, Mario, I'm going to have to think about this. I know time is short, but that's a big investment."

"Yeah, and just think—a Dago and a Kraut trying to help out a Jap." He chuckled, adding, "Our own axis benevolent league."

Lem smiled. Mario could always put a funny spin on any transaction.

"I'd like to see the property, Mario. Why not make my Mountain View store your last stop this afternoon, and I'll meet you there at two? We'll talk to the owners, get their ideas on price and conditions, and see if it's possible. There are some things in life that are unfair, and this is one of them. I never thought our government would be so punitive against innocent people."

Lem came to the front of the store and told Gennie he had some unexpected business but he felt sure she was in good hands and would try to return before she left in the afternoon.

Mario's information left Lem with a deep uneasiness. The government's heavy-handed approach to Japanese citizens—some even native-born—alarmed the bejesus out of him. It seemed that the executive branch of government felt heady with power. "Just plain scary," he thought.

He drove the grocery truck to his house, went inside, and realized that his wife, Margaret, must be coffee klatching with her neighbors. He went to his desk to retrieve the folders about each grocery property. He studied each one for a few moments to refresh his memory with the figures and left for the bank. His family had been frugal for generations, and the three stores were free of debt.

Arriving at the bank, he walked into the president's office. They were long-time friends. Without revealing his purpose, he asked for an estimated figure of what he could borrow. They reviewed the figures, so Lem ascertained what he could propose for the property. If the Nakamuras were offering it at a rock-bottom price—as Mario had claimed—he wouldn't be risking anything.

At two o'clock he met Mario, and they drove out to the property. The land stretched out from the tree-surrounded house with long rows of low strawberry plants and was bordered by high bushes of boysenberries on fences. Mr. Nakamura greeted them and asked them to come inside. He wanted them to say hello to his elderly father, whom he respected and wanted to be part of the decision. When they went outside again, their host lamented about how this move seemed to be destroying his father.

"We are going through very difficult times," Mr. Nakamura said. *His* father had sacrificed his whole life to be able to purchase this land and pass it on to future generations. The original money had come from back-breaking panning for gold, which his grandfather had cunningly hid and hoarded. "Now we are losing it without a fight."

They toured the property but not all of it; it covered four hundred acres that had been part of a larger Mexican land grant. Located near the southern end of the bay, it had been considered of little value years ago. Besides the flat cultivated areas there were fenced pastures leased out for grazing cattle and open grassy lands that were harvested for hay each fall. The three men came upon the foreman in the fields, and Mr. Nakamura introduced both Mario and Lem to him.

Lem asked Mr. Nakamura, "Can I be a good steward of this land even though I won't live here at first? Do you think the laborers are capable of keeping the crops going without hourly surveillance?"

"Hands-on supervision is best, but I think you can make a modest profit with the laborers we have. They love the land and are happy to be able to make a decent living. If you treat them right, they will do a good job. Of course, if your family lived here and worked the fields, your profits would be better."

"I expect there are others looking at the property. Have you had any offers?"

"Yes, there are some who want to take advantage of our situation. It is rumored that some landowners with large properties have influenced the government into getting our land first—at a very low price. I would rather sell to an individual like you."

"Okay, Mr. Nakamura, before I give you an offer, let me say that if we clinch a deal, I will make you a promise: when you can return, I will sell one half of the property back to you—the part that has your house on it—for the price per acre I am buying it. When I retire from the grocery business, I've wanted some land I could cultivate and live on, so I don't want to sell it all back to you. If you would be willing to have me as a neighbor, I would be honored."

Mr. Nakamura's usual inscrutable expression crumbled when he heard this offer, his eyes filling with tears.

"I have to put my pen to paper to give you an exact offer," Lem said. "I'll call you tomorrow."

When they got back into the car, Mario said, "Boss, I think you could have offered him ten cents an acre. When he heard that you would sell it back to him, you had him in your hand."

"Damn it, Mario, can you only imagine what he and his family are going through? Now my question is, are we German Americans next? If they see the name Mueller on the deed of sale, will they want me off the land too? I thought since we are born citizens, we would not be suspect. Now I see this Japanese family, who are all American-born, being herded up and shipped to who knows where."

"It could be the same for my family. I hear they're rounding up and questioning the Italian Americans back East."

They drove silently back to the Mountain View store, where they parted. "Thanks, Mario, for this opportunity. I hope I can make it work."

Lem continued along Highway 101 to Mayfield. Already, in an effort to conserve gasoline, the national speed limit had been lowered to thirty-five miles an hour, but Lem's brain revved up to overdrive. The past few years, he had followed the real estate prices on acreage in the Sunday papers. They had plummeted during the Depression and just now seemed to be stabilizing. He had announced that he eventually wanted to turn his stores over to Will and get out of the daily grind of retail. With the experimentation of using mechanically refrigerated railcars and trucks instead of icing down foods the way they did now, there would be more opportunities to ship to distant communities. Fresh produce could be shipped anywhere in the United States. He wanted to investigate the feasibility of growing crops and shipping them back East.

Lem pulled up into the store's back parking lot and came through the rear warehouse door. It was nearly five o'clock, and Gennie smiled when she saw him.

"They're making you work every minute of your shift, aren't they? This is a tough establishment you are working for," he said. He grinned and winked at Doris. "How has your first day gone, Gennie?"

"Well, I've learned a lot...I just hope I can remember it all tomorrow."

"Why don't you call it a day? I'll help Doris and Fred close up in about an hour. We'll see you tomorrow."

When he returned home, Lem expressed to Margaret how he hated to be suspicious of his own government. Granted, spies posed a possible problem during a war, but to warehouse a whole ethnic group seemed preposterous.

To punish the whole because of suspicions of a few challenged his pride in his country.

He posed questions to himself: "Can I deliberately put my family in harm's way because of a business venture? Wouldn't it be best to lie low and be inconspicuous at this time? Mr. Nakamura will sell his land to someone even if he or she is less than ethical and wants to take advantage of him. Do I need to be a savior? No, but what I do need is to find a way to buy this property without drawing attention to my name."

When Lem told Margaret of his plans, she nodded. He knew she wasn't interested in moving to a farm. She had been raised on one and didn't want to return so this was his own project. He had promised her that they would keep the house in town so she could continue her social contacts—her club work and bridge. She acknowledged, though, that the farm would challenge him, and that would make them both happy.

After dinner Lem telephoned Bob Black. Young Susan answered because most of the phone calls were for her. Lem asked Bob if he could visit with him in a few minutes.

"Sure, that will be fine. Come through the side door. No need to knock; you're family now."

When Lem arrived he exchanged some pleasantries with the family and followed Bob out to the back porch.

"Can I offer you something to drink? Coffee? Beer?"

"No thanks. As you might guess, I came over for a reason. I would like to propose an idea. It might sound a little strange. I have an opportunity to buy a farm near the airfield. The government has notified the Japanese owners that they have one week to sell all of their property and belongings and be ready to evacuate to an internment center. I would like to help these people, and also my long-term goal is to own some farmland for my retirement. The hang-up comes because of my suspicions about our leaders. I am afraid that if my German surname appears on the deed of sale, my family might also be targeted."

Lem paused and cleared his throat. "I would like to ask you to be my agent and put your name on the deed. The Nakamuras need cash, so that is how I will pay them. You and I can sign an agreement between us that we can have notarized, but it will not be for public view. I will keep the deed in my safe. It will have to be filed with the county, and you will be billed for the taxes, which I will pay. That will be part of our agreement."

"Whew!" Bob leaned back in his chair. "That's a lot to think about."

"And there's not much time to think. The Japanese must get out in two days."

"Can I talk with Erma about this? Or do you want it just confidential between you and me?"

"No, talk with Erma. I don't think we need to have family secrets. Eventually, it may become evident that I own the property, but no one has to see our agreement. And unless someone wants to snoop, I don't think anyone but the government will care. Right now I'm not going to tell Will; I think he has enough on his plate with basic training."

Bob went out and got Erma, and they sat down again. Lem went through the explanation, and an hour later, the Blacks decided to acquiesce to his request. Now that Gennie belonged to that family, Bob was protecting her too.

Lem planned to go out to the Nakamura farm in the early morning, and if they accepted his offer, he'd withdraw his money and secure the loan. He would compose the agent-owner agreement and make copies for Bob and himself.

Lem got up to leave and said, "Looks like I'd better get an early start in the morning; I have a lot to do. Can you be free by midafternoon so I can pick you up and you can give the Nakamuras the money and sign the deed? If they're asked, I want them to be able to say you were there and handled the transaction."

"Give me a call when you know what time. I'll be ready." The three shook hands, and Lem went out the side screen door.

When Lem arrived home, he called the Nakamuras and asked if he could come by with his offer shortly after dawn. They agreed, and he headed for bed.

When he reached the farm before eight o'clock, both the father and son were waiting for him.

"Before I make you an offer—I know you could get more for this place if you had more time to market it to more prospects. I also know that this is the best offer I can make with my available funds," Lem said. With this, he handed them a paper with his bid written on it.

The Japanese men exchanged looks without discernible expressions on their faces. Then the father nodded. The son apparently agreed. "We will accept your offer. It is most gracious. We will forever be indebted to you."

"I will bring you the money this afternoon. Shall I telephone before I come? My son's father-in-law is going to act as my agent, and his name will be on the deed. His last name is Black, so I don't think that should draw any governmental suspicions."

As he moved to leave, the elderly man got out of his chair and came to Lem with his head bowed and his hands together, palm to palm. Without even thinking, Lem bowed back, turned, and exited the door.

The rest of the day, banks and offices filled Lem's time. When he returned home in the evening, all transactions accomplished, he found Gennie at his house in the kitchen, reading to Margaret. A letter from Will had arrived, and Gennie had offered to share it.

Margaret looked up at Lem and said, "Oh, Gennie, start at the top. Lem's going to want to hear this too."

Gennie returned to the first page of the letter and began to read.

Dearest Gennie,

First of all, *I miss you*. The trip on the train was crowded and hot, and all I could think of was that each mile took me farther away from you. Three long days. I wanted to write you, but the bumpy ride made it impossible. (As if my handwriting isn't bad enough.)

Boy, once we got here, the pace increased. We immediately lined up and got shots, and they buzzed our heads. No more hair. They gave us each an empty cardboard box and told us to put our shoes in it. Then they proceeded to have us totally undress until we stood there in our birthday suits. We put the boxes in front of us and waited until every last guy had his box filled, closed, and addressed to his home. (Please call Mom and tell her, or else when she gets this package, she may think I croaked or something.) Anyway, there we were, standing around nude with no talking. I never minded being with the guys in the gang shower in the gym, but this was different, with the

> drill officers walking back and forth looking at us. What do you do with your hands? The guy next to me is from Texas, and he drawled, 'Makes you wish God gave our bodies pockets.' I, of course, snickered and almost got into big trouble.

In the margin of the letter, Will had drawn a bald, nude boy with his hands covering his private area. He had been a cartoonist for their high-school paper, and Gennie stopped to show the drawing to his parents. They exchanged smiles. Then Gennie continued reading the letter:

> Maybe they were checking to see if all our vital parts were accounted for. Finally, they passed out our uniforms, underwear, socks, and shoes. My shoes didn't fit, but no one seemed to care. We lined up and trotted to the parade grounds, where we marched for the next three hours. I got blisters on my feet, and they just got worse. The next day, I went to the drill officer and told him my feet were bleeding. He said, 'Pull off your socks.' When I did the skin went with them, and my feet were raw, so he sent me to sick call. The doctor gave me salve, wrapped them, and told me to stay off them for one day. He also sent me to the commissary to get fitted for shoes. Now, with a couple of Band-Aids, I am doing fine. So that's the highlights of this week.

Gennie looked up and said, "The last couple of sentences are gushy and romantic, so that's basically the news."

All during their courtship, Will had come to her house to hang out. Gennie had a cordial and formal relationship with the Muellers. She was getting to know Lem at the store and now would need to work on a friendlier kinship with Margaret, whose kitchen seemed to be the neighborhood meeting place.

"Gennie, thank you for bringing this over," Margaret said. "You are a dear to share. Sounds like he is having his challenges, but at least we know he is okay."

"I need to get back home to write him a letter," Gennie said as she headed to the back screen door. Margaret stood too, straightened her skirt over her ample figure, and followed her guest to the door.

"Say hi to your mom and dad for me. Come by anytime."

That night, down the road at the Nakamura property, the lights in the house stayed on until the early-morning hours. Inside the women and girls ripped out the seams in the linings of the men's and boys' coats and sewed in the paper bills.

The next few weeks, Gennie wrote daily of her adventures working at the grocery store and all the people she saw. Because Gennie had attended all twelve grades of school in the community, she knew most of the customers by name or face and learned where their servicemen kin had deployed. From Will's letters, she learned that boot camp lasted either eight or ten weeks. At that time, they would graduate, learn where they were assigned, and come home for a week of leave.

Anticipating Will's furlough, Gennie asked her parents if she could get a bigger bed in her room, which is where she thought they would stay; she thought a nonsqueaking box spring would make them less self-conscious. Bob and Erma had already talked about swapping out Gennie's upstairs room for Susan's, which was downstairs. When Bob had constructed it after Susan's birth, he'd thought they might use it as a downstairs master suite after the girls left home. Now it would give the young couple a chance for privacy. When Susan learned she could redecorate her new room, she acquiesced.

Erma and the girls were looking at paint samples and making plans when Gennie mentioned that she had missed a period. Immediately, she said she guessed that stress had caused it. Erma smiled and said, "Two healthy youngsters could quickly make babies."

The newspapers promoted victory gardens and the warm weather of spring was the time to plant. Bob did the heavy spading of a small square of the backyard with Erma and Gennie buying the seeds and planting. On her days off Gennie worked in the garden, weeding, watering and watching for predatory insects. The sun bronzed her skin and lightened her hair to the color of straw.

The weeks went on, with Gennie continued working three or four days a week at the store. She filled her evenings perusing the "Monkey Ward" (Montgomery Ward) catalog and old copies of the *American Home Magazine*, looking for a bed and mattress and décor ideas. Instead of the dark woods of the '30s, the trend she chose featured blond finishes with modern, straight lines. "Won't that be fun?" she thought and wrote to Will about the developments in redecorating.

As the days filled with sewing, painting, buying and gardening, Gennie realized she had missed her second period. One morning Erma met her at the breakfast table with her usual cup of coffee, but a pale and wan Gennie refused.

"Are you queasy?" Erma asked. "Methinks you are expecting a baby."

"Yeah, it looks like it."

"You don't sound excited."

"Oh, I'll be fine with it. It's just one more event I can't control. So much has changed in the last couple of months."

"Let me get you some saltines. Maybe that will settle your stomach."

Later, when Gennie saw Lem at the grocery store, he looked at her and asked, "Are you all right?"

"Yeah, but I suspect you are about to become a grandfather."

"What? Really? That's wonderful!" He put his arm around her and gave her a gentle hug.

"I don't want to tell Will until he is home on leave. If I tell Margaret, do you think she will keep it a secret? I thought I would come by this evening after work and tell her."

"It will be hard. She'll be so thrilled, but I know she can."

In the weeks since she had been working at the store, Gennie never saw any glimpses of the father Will had previously described to her. *Dictatorial*, *tyrannical*, and *inflexible* were words Will had used to describe his father. Instead she observed a boss who cared for his employees, and they talked of him with respect and friendship.

One night, during one of her visits to her in-laws' house to share her letters from Will, Gennie had asked if she could call her in-laws something other than Mr. and Mrs. Mueller or their given names. They'd decided that Mama M and Papa M would be good choices.

That same evening Gennie gave her news to the expectant grandma, who couldn't contain her joy. Yet enthusiasm evaded Gennie. Maybe it would occur later, but not now.

Chapter 4

March and April can debut some beautiful days in central California. The oak-tree branches shoot out leaves the color of green apples. Spring rains prompt the grass to sprout through the earth's dry mat. Bushier poppy and lupine plants get ready to bloom. Early in the morning, the fields display hundreds of carats of sparkling dew, reflecting the prisms of sunlight—in a brief moment before the droplets evaporate.

Gennie stood at the kitchen window watching her dad walk down the front driveway toward the road to pick up the newspaper, which was thrown there each morning. He had lived all his life in this house, which his father had built. Gennie watched him stop and admire the landscape and listen to the chirping birds. She poured herself half a cup of coffee and took a tentative sip. It had recently become her nausea barometer; this time it smelled and tasted good. She put a slice of bread in the toaster, poured her dad a cup of coffee, and put it at his place on the table. He came in, greeted her, and placed the front section of the paper next to his coffee. He gave Gennie the second section. He attempted to shield her from the headlines and bad news from the war front, especially in the Pacific, where a skeleton naval fleet was retreating and losing battleships often.

"Is this your day off?" Bob asked his daughter.

"Yes."

"Do you have plans for the day?"

"Just laundry and maybe going shopping with Mom."

"I'm going out to Old Grist Mill Road to check on some rumors that they are planning an army camp there. Do you want to go with me? It will only take about an hour."

"Sure, I've always been good about procrastinating when it comes to laundry."

Within an hour they were driving on the country roads toward the coastal foothills. He drove his truck in his usual work clothes: overalls and shirt sleeves rolled up to reveal tan, muscular arms.

"I want to see if I can get a contract for building these barracks," Bob said. "The raw materials are drying up for residential construction, and I hope to retain all my carpenters, if I can. They can easily get jobs at an assembly plant, but most have said they'd rather work out of doors."

"Yeah, everything's changing for everyone."

"This brings up a subject I wanted to talk to you about."

"Sounds like a lecture coming on." Gennie smiled when she said this, because she and Susan had endured his sermons all their lives.

"I know this morning sickness is not pleasant and can sap your enthusiasm. But I have observed that you are thinking negatively and sighing a lot. I detect some self-pity. I think you need to put this all in perspective."

Gennie did not interrupt. She knew the rules: Bob would listen to her rebuttal at the end of his discourse.

"You have repeatedly complained about being a victim of others' decisions. You are correct that no one could stop the events of the war. Will and the other boys had to go into the service; after all, the enemy attacked our country."

He saw some army jeeps parked on the side of the road, and he stopped behind them.

"I want you to realize that some of the decisions made since then are yours to own. You chose to marry Will and leave nursing. You and Will decided not to try to prevent a pregnancy on your honeymoon. I am not saying they were wrong decisions. I just want you to realize you were not powerless. You made your determinations, and you will have to live with them—not acting persecuted but as an adult who recognizes that all preferences have consequences. Even good choices can have untoward outcomes. Try to find joy and contentment for your baby's sake and well-being.

"Now I need to find these army guys before they get away. You can give me your side when I get back." He walked across the road and headed for the group of men in the field.

Gennie got out of the passenger side of the truck and walked along the ditch. A walking trail fifty feet behind the truck went up a knoll, and she followed it and viewed all of the countryside. "Dad's right," she thought. "He usually is. He thinks through these lectures beforehand. I can't go through life blaming others for the consequences of my decisions."

When Bob returned to the truck, Gennie said, "No contest. I will work to be more positive; after all, negativity never leads to progress."

He nodded, showing his satisfaction, and replied, "I also have the name of the army officer who will award the contract. It's been a worthwhile drive."

A young general practitioner who had recently set up practice in Mayfield had been drafted, so Gennie called the Palo Alto Clinic for an appointment. Since she made the appointment for ten days later, Will might be home and able to go with her. She felt excited by that thought.

Finally, Will telephoned that he had graduated that afternoon and hoped to catch a train that night. Once in Oakland, he would take a ferry over and then either catch a train or thumb a ride. The patriotic fervor of the country made "thumbing" an easy way for men in uniform to travel. All drivers picked them up, feeling it was their small way to support the troops.

Gennie didn't want to stay at the front window at home waiting for a sign of him, so she went to the grocery store. It made the time go faster. Whether she did anything productive or not—well, Doris seemed understanding.

Will's timing turned out to be fortuitous because he was able to catch the lone train from San Francisco to Mayfield. It stopped at the station just a block from the store, so Will headed there first. Gennie couldn't believe it. She had her hair pinned back and the grocery apron on—not at all how she had envisioned she would appear for his homecoming. He wore navy blues and a cocky sailor's cap over the burr cut hair. He was slimmer than she remembered, and he carried his duffel bag over his shoulder. Doris watched their embrace and kissing with tears in her eyes. Fred started sniffling over in the fruit department and then extracted his handkerchief from his pocket, wiped his eyes, and blew his nose. When Will stepped back, he went to hug Doris and shake Fred's hand.

"Is Dad around?"

"No, he went on an errand," Doris answered.

"Can Gennie have the rest of the day off?"

"She sure can." Doris went around and untied Gennie's apron strings.

"The car's in the back; let's go through the warehouse," Gennie said, tugging at Will's sleeve. Will got into the driver's side, and his knees hit the steering column.

"They told us that many things would be changed at home. Damn, even the seat's been changed." He smiled. Without putting the key in the ignition, he kissed her again. How great to be together. The urgency of their separation and reunion suddenly rushed in. They had not been prepared for the avalanche of emotion their reunion would bring. They parted and just looked at each other.

"Where do you want to go first?" Will asked.

"Let's go to your folk's. Your mom has been as anxious as I have to see you home."

"Okay, but we aren't staying all evening. I want to take you out to dinner, just the two of us."

As they got close to the Mueller house, Gennie said, "Let's stop first a block away from the house. I have something to tell you before we get there."

"Have you and Mom had an argument?"

"Oh, no. On the contrary, we're enjoying each other's company. We even go together to the Red Cross one night a week and roll bandages." Gennie took a deep breath and, without a preamble, blurted out, "You are going to be a father."

Will's eyes went blank. No joy, no anger, no nothing. When Will didn't respond, she asked, "Will, did you hear what I said?"

"Yeah, you sure do know how to shock a fellow. Are you certain?"

"I haven't been to the doctor yet, but I have all the signs and symptoms, so I'm pretty sure. You don't sound happy. You know we always talked about having a family."

"I'm happy for you, Gennie. But I'm not going to be around to enjoy our firstborn. At the graduation ceremony, the commanding officer told us that the war would certainly last two years, maybe three or four. I may be able to come home once a year. That's not how I saw us having a family."

Gennie felt a cold cloud descending on their car. "Well, I didn't get pregnant by myself," she pouted.

"Honey, I'm not blaming you. Coming home, I thought about how I could possibly leave you again for such a long time. Now I will be leaving you with all the responsibilities of raising our child, while I will be out there somewhere wishing I were with the both of you. Of course I'm happy. It's just unexpected. Boy, when they told us to be prepared for changes on the home front, they weren't kidding. Let's go home and see Mom."

"She already knows. There were a few mornings when I was sick at work, so I had to tell your dad. So I decided to tell your mom too. She's really thrilled."

They drove the block to his house. By this time Lem had heard from Doris that Will had arrived, so he'd raced home, and his truck sat in the driveway. The young couple walked inside arm in arm, smiling. The parents embraced their son, their joy contagious. Will started to tell his dad some more graphic parts of boot camp, and his mother listened. Gennie told her that Will knew about the expected baby. Margaret jumped up and embraced her son in a hug and gave him a kiss—an unusual display of emotion for her. After about an hour, Will announced that he and Gennie planned to go out to dinner and needed to go to her house to clean up. They drove to Gennie's house. Gennie snuggled next to Will, inhaling his scent; she was almost in his lap. Only the floor stick shift prevented her from getting closer. She visualized them being naked and then her having him inside her. Her face flushed with such an erotic thought.

Will felt challenged to drive and keep his eyes on the road.

The Blacks greeted their son-in-law with genuine affection and talked for a few minutes. When Gennie rushed the exchange, explaining that they wanted to go out to dinner, Erma said, "We'll have plenty of time to chat in the next few days; you two skedaddle."

Gennie had written in her letters about the progress of redecorating their room, so Will was prepared for the blue morning-glory wallpaper behind the headboard of their new bed and the newest fad in bedspreads: blue chenille. They undressed quickly and went into the shower together, basking in the privacy of their "suite." They headed to the restaurant to enjoy their first date in two and a half months.

The next few days they wandered around town and the parks, went to see Lem's berry farm, and traveled to the proposed Old Grist Mill Road army camp with Bob. There they stomped around, tracing the very apparent San Andreas fault line. Already stakes were in the ground delineating the barracks, and Bob hoped to start in a few days.

When the time came for Gennie to go to the obstetrician's appointment, Will went with her. If nothing else, this would be a reality check. The doctor interviewed them both in his office and took Gennie in for her exam. When they returned, he confirmed to Will that he indeed would soon be a father. He asked if Will would be stationed nearby, and when he heard that he was to be assigned to a ship, he frowned.

"I'm hearing this much too often," he said. "I recommend a parenting class at the high school to all my new parents, but I will especially want Gennie to take it." Looking at her directly, he said, "It will give you confidence, since you are doing this alone." He gave them some other informational sheets and then directed them to the business office. "Make an appointment for four weeks from now, and I'll see you then." He shook Will's hand with a firm grasp and added, "And good luck, sailor."

The joy of this confirmation, when juxtaposed with the sadness of their impending separation, prevented the giddy, jubilant euphoria of most newly pregnant couples. The war had robbed them again of a lighthearted memory.

Once Bob heard of the doctor's confirmation, he showed the couple his plans for a nursery off the hall, next to their bedroom. Later it could be used as a library or office, so he justified building it.

The remaining days passed quickly, and again the time to say good-bye arrived. Gennie accompanied Will in the car to San Jose, where he would catch an express train to San Diego. Once there he would learn his ship assignment. This time their parting seemed more desperate. They didn't know how long it would be before they would see each other again—or if they would *ever* see each other again. Neither dared to think about the latter.

Gennie arrived home and collapsed on the bed, crying and drenching the bedspread, the dark-blue circle of her tears ever widening on the light-blue chenille. It had been a difficult visit for both of them. In contrast to the ebullience of the honeymoon, they now realized their new responsibilities, and their feelings became raw. Neither one wanted to express inner concerns or confront the other. They did not want an argument in their memory banks.

Chapter 5

Gennie enrolled in the evening child-development classes and started a few days later. The classroom held twelve couples and one other girl attending by herself. "I'll go over and talk to her at the break," Gennie thought.

The pediatrician from the clinic introduced herself and started the evening.

As she listened Gennie felt strange being in a classroom at her alma mater less than a year after she'd graduated—especially considering the subject matter.

The doctor said, "We are not here to criticize your parents and how you were raised. How many were raised with paddling and spankings?" Gennie looked around to see all hands up except for hers. "We want you to understand that children are constantly growing up in their capabilities but cannot conquer tasks until their muscles and minds are ready. For instance, we know that the newborn cannot talk. But what if you as a parent decide that it would be convenient if he did because it would make your life much easier? So over and over, you say words to him, and when he doesn't repeat them back, you spank him."

She paused to let the group absorb that thought. "Okay, now think about toilet training. You really get tired of changing those dirty diapers, rinsing them in the commode, and then washing them. It sure would be nice if this kid were toilet trained. You plop him on the potty chair, and nothing happens. Two minutes later, he has a wet diaper. You spank him. Right? We want you to think about this differently."

There were nods of agreement in the group.

"About this time in every session, someone will pipe up with 'I was spanked, and I turned out okay.' And I say, 'Good for you.' But often the child is angry and belligerent after a spanking, not in a learning frame of mind."

Gennie thought, "Well, that's how Will felt about his authoritarian upbringing. He still has resentment about how his parents treated him. I wish he were here to hear this."

"Your parents did the best they could with the knowledge they had. That's all we are asking you to do. Absorb these lessons, and go home and apply them.

"Now take a short break. Restrooms are down the hall to your right." The ladies giggled, recognizing that important information. "After the break one of nurses will pass out the first lesson and speak with you. Thank you." Polite clapping followed the doctor as she exited.

Gennie worked her way over to the other single student. "Hi, I'm Gennie. Looks like we are the only singles in the group."

"My name is Sandy. Is your husband in the service?"

"Yes, navy."

"My husband graduated from West Point and is now stationed in England. I'm a Smith graduate,

"Whoops," Gennie thought. "I'm already in over my head. I think she's out of my league."

"My husband and I graduated from here last year. He just finished boot camp and is on his first ship."

Sandy replied, "Oh, my, I thought our lives were changing, but yours is even more challenging."

Gennie wondered, "Is that pity or commiseration?"

"Since I am pregnant, I couldn't follow my husband to England, so I'm living with my folks in Atherton. Do you, by any chance, play bridge?"

Gennie shook her head. "All the cards I've ever played were hearts with my folks."

"I am looking for three other players. Hopefully, one other will have some experience, but if not, I am willing to teach everyone the rules. Would you be interested?"

"Sure. I may not be your best candidate, but I will be happy to try."

"Okay, give me your phone number, and I will call you. Otherwise, I will see you here next week." They both went back to their original seats and Gennie hoped that their shared first pregnancy experiences would forge a friendship.

It had been only a week since Will had left, so a letter from him in the mailbox surprised her. She tore open the envelope as she walked down the driveway pausing to read what he wrote:

> Dear Everyone,
>
> They just announced last call for all letters in fifteen minutes and said they will be mailed before we set sail. I guess I had not realized we could send one before we left. So this is a fast scribble. I have been assigned to a supply freighter. (If I give you the name, I think it will be censored.) It has been here in San Diego since being hit by a torpedo shortly after Pearl Harbor. We will deliver food and supplies to all combat ships in the Pacific. The older hands say this is a good assignment. We will be in dangerous waters but will not deliberately engage in a confrontation. Usually there is a convoy accompanying us. I'm running out of time.
>
> I love you all.
>
> Will

Gennie quickly went to the phone and read the letter to Mama M. She agreed that it sounded like good news—maybe the supply ship would be less vulnerable than a battleship—and was glad to hear he had arrived safely.

The weeks fell into a routine for Gennie: going to work, her classes, the Red Cross, and bridge. Some afternoons she and Sandy enjoyed going to an afternoon matinee or shopping for their nurseries and layettes sharing their plans for decorating their babies' rooms. Sandy's due date preceded hers by two months.

With only Sundays to work on the nursery, Bob promised that as soon as they finished the army camp, he would send his crew to the house to complete the addition.

Chapter 6

Lem went out daily to confer with the foreman, Joe, at the Mountain View farm. Joe had migrated with his family from Oklahoma in the early 1930s, fleeing the drought, dust, and decimated crops during the height of the Depression. They'd come to the Nakamuras' place six years earlier after following the crops and living in a tent. Joe had heard rumors that the Japanese would only hire their own people, but when he'd showed up with his three young boys, ready to pick berries, they were hired.

As Joe told the story, his speech drifted in and out of his Midwestern accent.

"When we first got here in thirty-four, there was decent work for everyone, but when folks lost their farms, more families followed us. Soon there was fights between the men because the new guys worked for less. I went to Mr. Nakamura and tol' him what the entire ruckus was about. We had a meetin', and the men agreed that if we all worked but stopped at a certain dollar amount per day, we'd have enough food for our families. No more fights, and the crops got picked. Someone said it was communistic. But it worked that time, and because it did, Mr. Nakamura asked me if I'd be a fulltime foreman."

Joe stopped and chuckled. "Now, with the draft and defense plants, we're goin' to have a hard time findin' help. One thing's fer sure: the world's always changin.'"

A couple of days later, Lem asked, "Where are you living now?"

"We found an old store; it use'ta be a saloon. It's on a side street a couple of blocks off Castro Street. It had a toilet room, and the owner and me put in a steel shower. We strung up clotheslines and hung quilts on 'em to make rooms. My family was happy to be in a building and not in a tent, but now the boys get teased at school about bein' Okies and not livin' in a house."

"Well, I've been thinking. A vacant house doesn't age well. Do you think you and your family would like to live in the Nakamuras' house?"

Joe appeared embarrassed by such a generous offer. He looked down at the dusty path and kicked at some pebbles. He reached out and grabbed Lem's hand and shook it, "My family would like that."

"Let's walk over there now and look at what condition it's in. I'm sure they left some furniture behind. What you can't use we could store in the garage. If you think this might be a possibility, your wife could come by tonight and see what she thinks."

Joe's wife had finished high school and now worked as the school secretary in the boys' grammar school. With their one car, she dropped Joe off in the early morning and then went back and picked up the boys for school. She picked Joe up each evening.

Lem and Joe found the record books, but they were all written in Japanese. Lem had to rely on the foreman's memory about the crops. He offered the house rent-free. This, he hoped, would be additional insurance that Joe wouldn't be tempted to go to the war factories and their higher salaries.

After Joe and his family moved in to the house, he approached Lem about getting some chickens. With the proposed rationing of meat, he thought the protein needs of his family could be met with eggs and chickens. Joe also wanted to plant a vegetable garden, which he would share with the Blacks and the Muellers.

Lem recognized what the Nakamuras had most likely appreciated: Joe's ability to access a situation, figure out a solution, and then work with intensity until it was accomplished.

While the two men were walking around the area that would be a vegetable garden and discussing the best place for a chicken coop and run, Joe said, "My two older boys want bicycles, and I told 'em they'd have to earn the money. I told 'em to plant a flower garden for cut flowers and sell 'em up on the road on weekends."

"There's not much traffic on that road—perhaps the produce department in my grocery store would be better," Lem said. "With a sign—'Two boys earning money for bikes'—I'll bet they'll sell quickly."

"They'd like that idea. We were talkin' 'bout zinnias, daisies, and maybe some gladiolas."

"That sounds good. I plan to go down to the *Sunset* magazine headquarters. Why don't you and the boys come with me? We can ask them what other flowers might work. Also I've been thinking about planting evergreen shrubs. With the anticipated building boom after the war, people will need plants for their new homes. Next I plan to call a surveyor to help divide this land equitably for the Nakamuras and myself."

Chapter 7

At the end of August, Gennie bowed to pregnancy etiquette and public opinion, retiring from the grocery store. The heavily starched apron hid the early paunch, but a few older female customers' comments hinted that now she needed to be semisecluded. At home, she and Erma stitched white batiste baby day gowns and picked out wallpaper and paint for the nursery.

The first week of November, Gennie went into labor. The cramps came erratically, and because they started after midnight, she drifted in and out of sleep. In the morning she went to the kitchen and stayed with Erma. She didn't want to be alone. The contractions had increased but still weren't occurring five minutes apart, which was the magic number to go to the hospital. By late morning her water broke, which was also an indicator to go to the hospital, so Bob and Erma drove her there.

With Turkish towels between her legs, Gennie said, "Who knew this would be so messy so soon?"

The custom—actually an ironclad rule—stipulated that no one except the expectant ladies were allowed in the labor room. To call it a "room" actually flattered the massive space, divided like horse stalls with curtains drawn to provide some modicum of privacy. Built in the 1920s and not updated since, the cavernous area allowed all the sounds and odors to be shared. Fortunately, as labor progressed, the mother focused on her challenging task, and little outside seemed to be of her concern.

Gennie's obstetrician had had his early training in Canada, which had exposed him to the teachings of a British doctor who advocated minimum drugs, insisting that relaxation techniques resulted in less sedated and groggy newborns. All of his patients attended classes in the theory and techniques of this ideal. Gennie had a nurse to coach her in the breathing and relaxation. The staff stayed ready to give pain medication at any point, but the longer the mother went without it, the better for the baby.

Finally, Gennie asked for some relief, and moments after receiving the injection, she felt the need to push. Willem Mason Mueller IV entered into the world moments later. The thrill of the accomplishment; the joy of seeing her son all purple and screaming but intact, with the correct number of fingers and toes; and the rush of motherhood encompassed her whole being. "Oh, Will, I miss you now more than ever," she thought. "You have been robbed of a most precious moment for yourself but also for us to share." But her elation soared too high to let her dwell on such thoughts.

"Baby boy, I have enough love for both of us until your daddy gets home," she whispered in the infant's ear.

By the time Gennie went to her postpartum room, her parents had seen Mason in the nursery and telephoned the Muellers about the good news. Their response: they were on their way.

Gennie sent them to the post office with a note to Will (to be sent with the now prevalent V-mail) that she had preaddressed, telling him that his son—all seven pounds and six ounces—had arrived and was beautiful.

Gennie had to stay the recommended ten days in the hospital before going home. The avant-garde clinic doctors also were bucking the popular idea that artificial formula feeding equated to breastfeeding. They believed breast milk to be much more advantageous. However, during the 1920s and '30s, as canned evaporated milk had become available, the milk companies had touted their products to the modern mom. They found the effectiveness of advertising in the ladies' magazines like *McCall's* and *Ladies Home Journal.* Women were ready to be unbridled from the breastfeeding and to share the chore of bottle feeding with their husbands and others. Gennie's pediatrician preached the benefits of breastfeeding, even for six to eight weeks, so Gennie diligently worked at this project. At this time what else did she have to do? "Giving my son the best" would be her motto.

A few days after Gennie came home from the hospital, when it seemed that all activities—including sleeping and bathing—revolved around Mason's schedule, Lem called. "Are you sitting down, Gennie? Will just called. They've docked in San Francisco. He will have a seventy-two-hour leave. I'm on my way to pick him up on the Embarcadero. He hadn't received your letter about the baby, so I told him. I guess I should have let you tell him, but I just blurted it out."

"Hey, that's okay. What a surprise! Do you think you'll be here in two hours? Just get going, and be careful. Love you for calling."

"Margaret is going with me, so we'll have a chance to talk and bring him to see his son. See you soon."

Gennie ran to the front of the house and found her mother in the kitchen.

"Guess what? Will just called his dad. He is in San Francisco and has leave for seventy-two hours! He'll be here in two hours. I haven't been in any clothes except my pajamas. Do you think there is anything I can fit into?" All these sentences peppered Erma in fast succession, and she replied equally as rapidly.

"Who would have thought? What a surprise. One of those skirts you bought to continue working at the grocery store should fit. It's just your waist that most likely isn't back to its size. And one of your sloppy-joe sweaters over it will look great. When is Mason's next feeding?"

"In about an hour."

"Why don't you jump into the shower now and find something to wear? I'll listen for the baby and keep him content—or at least try—until you are ready. Oh, Gennie, this is just the happy lift you needed." Erma gave her a quick hug and then a pat on her bottom. "Get on with you, now."

Gennie fed and bathed Mason before Will's arrival. Gennie had lipstick and mascara on for the first time since Mason's birth and already felt better. With the bed quickly made, the room no longer looked like a convalescent's haven, and Gennie suddenly felt that she had turned the corner on the way to normalcy.

Will sauntered up the walkway with a big bouquet of red roses, as if he were there for just another date with his girlfriend. Gennie ran out the door, grabbed him around his neck, and kissed him.

"Gennie, you look great!"

"I've missed you so. Come in and meet your son."

Erma stood in the foyer, cradling the baby in her arms. She handed the baby to his father, and Will quickly gave the flowers to Gennie. The emotions flooded in, and tears came to his eyes.

"Hi, young man. You are one handsome dude."

Just then the Muellers came up, Lem holding the camera. "I just want to take a few quick photos to document the occasion. Will, come out on the porch where there is more light. Gennie, you move in close to him. Now, Bob and Erma, gather around. You too, Margaret." *Click, click, click.* "Okay, Margaret, let's be on our way and let the kids have their privacy."

Erma called out, "How about coming over for breakfast in the morning? I know we'll all be up. Mason doesn't let anybody sleep in late."

"I'll call you in the morning," Margaret replied. "We'd like that."

Erma asked, "Have you had lunch, Will? None of us have. I can heat up some soup and make sandwiches. Come into the kitchen while I do that, and we can all chat."

Gennie went over to Will and said, "Why don't I put Mason in his bassinet. He'll rest better, and in a couple of hours, he'll wake up and want attention." Will, who had been holding Mason like a breakable object, did not protest.

Erma poured everyone a cup of hot coffee, which on this cloudy November day tasted so good. When Gennie went back into the kitchen, Will grabbed her hand and just sat holding it as if he needed some tangible evidence that he was really home. Then he answered all their questions that he could not write in letters.

"Our ship is the USS Azure Ice, one of two food-supply boats in the Pacific. We follow the fighting and recently were staying close to the Solomon Islands. Other ships rendezvous with us after placing their orders. A huge crane on our ship lifts the crates of food in a sling and delivers them to the other ship. Usually we can make about fifty deliveries before going back to port to get new supplies."

He looked at their faces: He definitely had their attention with this information. "Our usual supply ports are San Diego and Seattle—San Francisco is a fluke destination this time. The Japanese try to target our ship because if they sank the supply ship, it would cripple much of the fleet. But our ship is usually accompanied by a convoy to protect us. One of our convoys took a hit a couple of months ago and was sunk, but most were rescued off of it."

Will paused to sip his coffee. "We are on constant alert, and that is nerve wracking. My specific job is to keep the boilers going so all our electricity and refrigerators stay working, but others are risking their lives to keep us going, and that is reassuring. The best part is that it is good duty because of the great food we get." He smiled as he delivered this positive tidbit of information.

After lunch Gennie and Will went back to their bedroom, where a small sitting area looked out on the garden. They kissed with intensity and passion. Gennie pulled back.

"The doctor said not to have any sexual intercourse for six weeks because of infection."

"Mom already told me on the drive home. It is so out of character for her to acknowledge that we might have a desire to do that." Will laughed and added, "It was an uncomfortable conversation for her."

When Mason started to whimper, Gennie went to change him, with Will shadowing her. As Gennie sat down and positioned the baby, undoing her blouse, ready to breast-feed, Will looked incredulous.

"I thought breastfeeding went out of style twenty years ago. Isn't it more modern to feed with bottles and formula?" He seemed repulsed by this primitive activity.

Gennie proceeded to tell him all the pluses of breastfeeding for the baby and said that although she would do it for the minimum six or eight weeks, she doubted that she would continue. They passed the baby back and forth, talking to the baby, cooing, and burping him.

Gennie wasn't sure how they could cram all their thoughts and experiences of eight months in such a short time. They talked, they hugged, and they talked some more. They kissed. They laughed. They went out to walk in the park, leaving Mason home with Erma. Chilly with overcast clouds that threatened rain, the weather prompted them to take a brisk pace instead of strolling. With Will's arm around her shoulder, Gennie could forget for a moment all her cares and responsibilities. To have him home again permanently could not come soon enough.

The next day Erma sent Bob out to a nearby farm to get two large roasting chickens. She decided they would have a quick Thanksgiving feast because the holiday was just five days away. At breakfast, she told Margaret of her plan, and they decided on the menu, with Margaret volunteering to make Will's favorite sweet-potato casserole. Before Will had to leave at six o'clock in the evening, Mason enjoyed his first Thanksgiving with his daddy. Lem photographed the occasion. The joint effort to make a festive celebration seemed to make the imminent separation more poignant. "How many times do I have to say good-bye to Will?" Gennie wondered.

This visit had served a purpose: it had jolted her out of her routine and lifted the cloud of melancholy. "From now on, I will get up, dress, and leave this room each day," she thought. "I will wean Mason to a bottle, since I am not fond of breastfeeding, and participate in other activities. I need to find a balance in my life. Once he's on the bottle, the grandmothers can care for Mason—which they have been anxious to do—and I can return to playing bridge once a week and perhaps take a cooking class."

Saying good-bye is never easy. This time, however, Gennie felt a clearer direction. She could control her destiny.

Lem felt the challenges of the war affecting his grocery businesses. As the defense construction complex ramped up, more and more civilians were lured into factory jobs with higher wages and a sense of patriotism. Each store had only a skeleton crew of workers, many of them piecing together part-time hours. When rationing started, customers needed to have not just enough money but also sufficient ration stamps. That doubled the time it took to check out customers. The first food stamps were for sugar and coffee and issued in November 1942—a shock for the housewives who liked to bake for the holidays. The following spring, the purchases of all meat, cheese, canned fish, processed food, butter, and margarine were controlled by rationing stamps.

In order for the grocer to get his wholesale grocery order filled, he had to present sufficient pages filled with the used ration stamps. Half the size of a postage stamp, each ration stamp had a different color for different foods. The task of affixing two hundred individual stamps to the government-supplied sheets added hours to a grocer's day.

Gennie started taking Mason over to the Muellers' house on Sunday afternoons to give the grandparents a chance to see him. Each time, on the dining-room table would be cigar boxes filled with the individual ration stamps. Lem, Margaret, and a neighbor diligently worked on segregating the stamps by color and affixing them to the proper sheets. Gennie helped, and soon she suggested that her parents join in too. Mason cooperated by either napping or being happy in the company of others. The gathering became a weekly routine for the duration of the war.

PART II

Chapter 8

1945

In January 1945, President Roosevelt proclaimed that the Japanese internees were no longer a threat and could return to their homes. Unfortunately, most of the families did not have homes to return to, having been told that they could not own their property. Given twenty-five dollars for each family member, they were ordered to buy railroad tickets and leave the camp. If ever a family thanked another human being, the Nakamuras were thankful for Lem Mueller. In more than three years, there had not been any communication between Lem and the family. The internees had been discouraged from contacting anyone outside the camp. With faith in their hearts, they returned to Mountain View without their elderly patriarch. He had died of pneumonia—and maybe despondency.

Before he died, he'd said, "I believe in Mr. Mueller's promise. He is a good man. Trust him. You can work together and both be successful on that land." It is with this spirit that the Nakamuras returned: no anger, no reprisal, just hope for the future.

However, the internees had adequate reason to be annoyed at their circumstances at their Montana camp. The assigned shacks in cold Montana had had only cardboard separations between families, and they'd had to petition to get water for irrigation to raise crops. The first year had been difficult, but they'd learned to create a community with schools, scouting, and an ambitious agricultural program. They had also sent their young men to the US Army. As the word leaked out about what they had endured, many citizens began to find a new admiration for their efforts.

Lem had anticipated that the government would close these internment camps before the war was over. The hysteria of moving the Japanese away from the West Coast had diminished. Many Japanese had been living in the Midwest and East without ever being relocated. The threat that the Japanese army would invade the West Coast appeared nonexistent.

In June 1944, Lem went to Bob and asked him if he knew how to get building materials for a house so that Joe could vacate the Nakamuras' homestead.

Bob told him, "There are some old homes being auctioned by the government when bomber plants and naval yards are expanded. Most of the houses are dismantled rather than moved. I'll let you know when I hear of the next one, and we can go together." In the next few weeks, they found two small homes and in the meantime bought water pipes and waste lines when possible.

Bob said, "I'm glad I have old-timer experience. This takes me back to when we had no power tools at all." Joe helped them when he could, and his boys pitched in too.

When the property had been surveyed, Joe and Lem chose a spot for his future house. Taking advantage of Bob's experience, they began working. The materials from the two houses were consolidated, and although not modern, the home would be livable, with used appliances.

Ben Nakamura—now the family patriarch—consulted with Lem. His family wanted to ease out of the berry business and establish a retail nursery company. As soon as building supplies became available, they planned to build a retail store on the main road with parking in front and sell small flowering annuals and perennials. Because Lem sold his shrubs and trees wholesale only, they could complement one another. Ben would buy from Lem and resell them at retail price.

Recognizing a wind-down of the European conflict but escalation of the warfare near Japan, Will's ship had come into port in June to load for the final push. With less than thirty-six hours in San Diego, Will knew he could not get home and back, so he had to be content with telephone calls to Gennie and his parents.

He said, "The scuttlebutt circulating is that we're preparing for a D-day–type assault on the Japanese homeland. More ships are coming through the Panama Canal from the Atlantic and joining in the assault. It won't be pretty, I'm afraid. But that's why we are in such a rush to fill up with supplies and get back out there."

A few weeks later Gennie received an upbeat letter from Will. Lately his letters had dwindled to fewer than one a week, and they reflected his war-weary resignation about his life.

> Dear Gennie,
>
> Surprise, surprise. Guess who came aboard at San Diego? Herb Jordan! I couldn't believe my eyes. He had gone to radar school after basic and has been stationed off Newfoundland the whole time. He was one of a bunch of transfers we got from the Atlantic seaboard. Herb and I have talked long and hard, and both of us want to pursue our dream of building supermarkets together; neither one of us wants to go back to school. We're having a damn good time making plans...Oh, and he's hoping to marry this girl from the East Coast who he met at a USO dance. Then they will move to California.

Gennie ran to the telephone to call Margaret. They had both been concerned about the downcast tone of his letters. This news would make both parents happy that the boys wanted to come back and go into the grocery business.

When the atomic bombs were detonated on August 6 and 9, and after the surrender on August 11, Will's supply ship still had to stay out in the Pacific filling the other ships' requests so that they could return to the US mainland. Finally, the week before Thanksgiving, Will returned home. Mason had just celebrated his third birthday without his father, but now both families were ready to enjoy the holidays together.

The whole country embraced a festive mood as Christmas approached; strings of colored lights hung over the downtown intersections, and light poles supported wreaths and ribbon bows. The ban on outdoor lighting had been lifted, and the lyrics "When the lights come on again—all over the world" intermingled with Christmas songs and carols on the radio. Both the Black and Mueller households planned for celebrations around Mason, who knew about Santa and that gifts were about to arrive.

Amid all this elation, Will showed unexpected outbursts of anger. He confronted his father about his agreement to sell part of the Nakamuras' land back to them and said it amounted to coddling the enemy.

"Why are you treating those yellow-bellied Japs with kindness? I've given three years of my life to save our country from them, and you are handing them our land on a silver platter." He spat the words out as if they tasted bitter. "We should ship every one of those slit-eyes back to Japan, where they belong. They were Emperor Hirohito lovers then and always will be."

Lem allowed his son to continue to rant and bark out racial epithets; Lem had to take some moments to calm himself. He did not want to respond with equally inflammatory remarks.

"Following your thought process, then we, of German ancestry, are responsible for all the atrocities that Hitler did. We should be forced to give up everything we have accumulated through hard work and be returned to Germany?"

"That's different."

"How so? The Nakamuras were on that land for thirty years. They had no part in the emperor's decision to bomb Pearl Harbor, just like Hitler didn't ask for our opinion. Just think about it. Yes, you sacrificed your young years, but you came back physically intact and not in a pine box. Be thankful for that. Many Japanese have returned and resettled here since January, when Roosevelt rescinded the internment law. If you are going into the grocery business, you will have to accept them as customers and even hire them as employees. Vent if you must to me, but do not take this attitude outside of your house."

Will's eyes still glowered. He never had liked his dad to admonish him, even as a small child, when he'd often stomped out in a huff. This time he took it like a man: maybe the navy had taught him some self-discipline.

Trying to clear the air, Lem said, "Our wholesale organization sent out a bulletin about a prototype supermarket being constructed in San Jose. I don't think it is completed, but do you want to go down and take a look?"

"Okay, but let me call Gennie and tell her I won't be around for lunch."

They drove to San Jose along Highway 101. The new store sat on a large, vacant lot that would be paved later for parking about one mile from the large downtown area. The concrete building had high windows on two sides, a warehouse area at the back, and large floor-to-ceiling windows in the front around quadruple doors. All three of Lem's grocery stores could fit into this one store. The aisles were built wide to accommodate customer-navigated grocery carts, and long cold-storage modules filled the large space. Not only would the fresh produce be refrigerated, but large cases held dairy products and freezers held ice cream and small boxes of frozen fruits and vegetables. The availability of home electric refrigerators instead of iceboxes made mass purchasing a new way to shop for most families.

"This is sure a huge investment in machinery per store," Lem commented as they walked along the aisles. "Before, years ago, we constructed a shell of a building; hammered some shelves, produce bins, and a counter out of wood; and then hooked up a refrigerator for milk and butter, and we were in business. Just like that. We built on a city street with sidewalks already in and a paved street out front with diagonal parking.

"Right now I plan to continue the grocery store in Mayfield until you and Herb take over the other two. Then I'll vacate the building and lease it to some other type of business. I couldn't compete with supermarkets—even if they were a mile or two away. But I'm nostalgic about that building; it's the original family store that Grandfather built."

"I got a letter from Herb this week," Will said. "He went up to see his folks for a couple of days and then headed back east to see his girlfriend, Alice. They're getting married the week after Christmas. Then they'll take a short honeymoon, load up her car and a trailer with all her stuff, and head here the end of January."

"Are you and Gennie going to the wedding?"

"No, Gennie vetoed it. Besides the expense, she didn't think we should take Mason and that it's too long for us to be gone. We're talking about giving them a party when they arrive. Herb wasn't sure if his folks would go either, because of the time they would be away from the dairy. Maybe a couple of brothers will. Anyway, maybe the Jordans can come down here for the party."

"Next time you write, tell Herb that he and Alice are welcome to stay with us until they can find a place to live. He's lived with us before, so he knows the accommodations. Places to rent are hard to find."

"Yeah, I've been asking around for a place to rent for Gennie and me, and there isn't much. Stanford has moved in some Quonset huts for their married students going to school under the GI Bill—but they aren't available to nonstudents."

Gennie also hoped to find a place for their little family to live—by themselves. She wanted to buy a house, but properties were scarce. Tension between Will and his in-laws continued to grow. He showed resentment toward the close relationship between Bob and Mason. Grandpops (shortened to Pops) and Mason were big buddies. Bob had reveled in his grandson's company every morning and evening since Mason was born. He no longer worked late. He wanted to be home to play with Mason before the child went to bed. Bob often had a tall tale to tell Mason, who listened, mesmerized by these original stories; his eyes grew large and intense as he absorbed it all. They went on walks and fished in the small creek that ran at the back of the property. They watched tadpoles grow into frogs.

Each spring the two would tromp over the wet and muddy terrain looking for the first almond blossoms. The volunteer trees were isolated, scattered all over the property. Usually Bob and Mason had to bundle up against the seasonal chill. At each tree, Bob would announce, "Not on this one, not yet."

When they returned after blossom hunting, Erma would ask, "Any luck?"

Mason, the consummate nature boy, was proud to share his knowledge. "Nope, not yet," the young boy replied, mimicking his pops. "We need one sunshiny day, and the blossoms will start."

Bob smiled at Erma, obviously feeling blessed to have these adventures with Mason.

Will's envy festered. While in the service, he must have visualized a son ready to welcome and include him immediately into his life. Gennie had told stories to

Mason about his father while he was overseas—even had him kiss Will's photo every night—yet the child did not have any concept of a father other than Pops. It didn't take long for Will's jealousy to affect the child, who seemingly realized that Will challenged his beloved pops. Instead of patiently building a friendship with his son, Will demanded that he obey him and show him respect. Unsurprisingly, this little intuitive child stiffened his back and refused.

Will told Gennie, "You are raising a brat."

Gennie's momma-bear instinct also reared its head. "You cannot appear in a child's life and demand that he love you," Gennie retorted, her eyes flashing anger. "He has seen you three times in his life, and you tell him you are more important than his pops. You are going to have to earn his love—slowly."

"I don't know this person who is attacking me; you have always agreed with me before."

"Before I wasn't a mother protecting my child. He doesn't understand why you were gone and why you are back. Show him love instead of demanding it. Please don't undermine Dad either. Mason can love both of you. Once we are in our own house and have set up a routine, he will learn to love you. After all, you are a loveable guy." Gennie went over to Will and kissed him on the lips, saying, "Please just give it time."

The search for a house proved to be a challenge. Hundreds of discharged military men who had visited the West Coast while in the service wanted to return to this beautiful terrain and delightful climate. The demand for homes outweighed the supply because building materials remained scarce. Many billboards announced new developments coming "soon," but the homes did not appear.

They found a house in a new subdivision in far south Palo Alto, which would take two months to be completed. Bob looked at it from a builder's prospective and shook his head.

"Not very high quality of construction. They are cutting corners, but I think that's the norm for the times. Hopefully you'll be able to afford something nicer in a few years."

For Will and Gennie, it represented a palace—just to have their own place and be a family in their own kitchen and backyard. They shopped for furniture together, and their excitement soared. Gennie hoped this would soften Will's attitude. He seemed angry with life in general. Even their sex life had changed. Will demanded and was gruff, seeking only his satisfaction. She realized they couldn't remain naïve, groping youngsters forever, and she didn't expect that he had been chaste during his navy career away from her. She hoped they would find the passion and desire together and share it. She wondered if something specific had occurred while he was gone or if it could be that he felt the war had robbed him of three vigorous years to do as he pleased.

When Gennie had asked about any military skirmishes his ship may have experienced, Will had answered that they'd had close calls but the convoy had taken the hits. Upon further questioning, he said he did not want to relive those days. That explanation did not satisfy Gennie's curiosity. "There must have been something else that caused all this anger," Gennie thought. "I can't harass him about this, but if he doesn't talk and share, will he ever lose his resentment?"

"Do you remember how we talked of our hopes to enjoy each other and pledged to be able to talk about it if we didn't?" Gennie asked one evening.

"That just shows how childish we were," Will answered. "Life isn't all fun and games; the war taught me that."

She didn't reply but thought, "I didn't wait for three and a half years for my husband to return, only to be used as an object for his sexual gratification. I have needs too." Knowing that Will did not tolerate criticism, she kept quiet—for now. She used a diaphragm for contraception, not certain if their marriage would survive their long separation and less-than-stellar repatriation. Yet there were moments in that afterglow of sexual satisfaction that Will would grab her hand and plead, "Don't ever leave me, Gen. I can't live without you."

Chapter 9

The honeymooners, Herb and Alice, arrived at the end of January during a cold and blustery week. Alice laughed when she reported that everywhere she went, people heard her Eastern accent, apologized for the nasty weather, and promised it would get better. Because she had just left a place where snow and ice covered the ground, she found these defensive statements humorous.

They stayed with the Muellers and started looking for a house to rent or buy. Both Herb and Alice wanted an older home, perhaps of the Arts and Crafts era, that they could remodel. She wanted to be reminded of her Upstate New York neighborhood with towering trees at the curb and a sidewalk leading to a front porch.

Alice had graduated from Vassar in June with a degree in library science. She had lived in New York State all her life. Her fair coloring and good looks reflected her Scandinavian heritage with serene, cool beauty similar to Ingrid Bergman's. Although pleasant, she seemed reserved.—perhaps due to her Northeastern background that stressed family lineage. Out West, the people often moved there to escape the law back East, so no one asked who you were or where you came from. California would be an enormous change for her. She hoped to pursue her master's degree at Stanford. Because the winter semester had already started, she visited and got advice from the postgraduate faculty about starting in the summer. Gennie decided they would have little in common.

Bob and Erma hosted a small dinner party welcoming the newlyweds. Lem and Margaret, Herb's parents, Gennie, Will, and Susan attended. Susan came from across the bay, where she attended an all-girls liberal-arts college. She and Alice compared East and West Coast women's colleges and found a lot to talk about.

Alice and Bob bonded because she showed knowledge and interest in antique furniture, which Bob collected, repaired, and restored. By the end of the evening, he'd decided he would be the perfect guide to the older neighborhoods of Palo Alto, close to Stanford, to help them find their home.

One day, when Bob shopped at his favorite hardware store, the owner asked if he knew that a certain house was going up for sale. "You know the place. You did the remodel about fifteen years ago."

"Are the owners in poor health?" Bob asked.

"Nah, they just said the yard work was getting too hard to keep up with. I think they're going to live with a daughter."

"That's a nice house. It'll need remodeling again, I'll bet."

Bob couldn't make his purchases fast enough and get over to that address. He went up and knocked on the door. The older man answered. When he saw Bob, he said, "Well, business must be pretty slow if you're coming over here looking for work." Then, grinning, he said, "How in the world are you?" He stepped forward and shook Bob's hand. Bob explained that he'd heard a rumor that the house would be for sale. The man affirmed it. He said they wanted to get a few things moved first so it wouldn't look so cluttered before they put it on the market. He invited Bob in; they discussed a possible price and exchanged telephone numbers. Bob explained why he was looking for a house, and they parted, promising to talk that evening.

Bob could hardly contain his excitement. This equaled the thrill of winning bingo at the Elks Lodge's Friday-night game. He went home and called Alice at the Mueller house.

"Do you have time to drive by a house I've found? If you like how it looks from the outside, I'll call and make an appointment for you and Herb to see the inside this evening."

Alice was waiting on the Mueller porch when Bob drove up. Bob told her the story of how he'd found out about the availability of the house and assured her of its sound construction.

They stopped in front of the prospective house. A roofed porch stretched across the front, a picture window faced the street, and the exterior walls were covered with brown shingles.

"Years ago, when these homes were first constructed, the slang name for this street was 'Professors Row,'" Bob said.

Alice caught Bob's excitement. That evening, after Herb saw it, they made an offer, and the owners accepted. They had bought a house and could move in about three weeks, pending their financing.

What an exciting time for both couples! Will had already started working full time at the Palo Alto grocery store in January. Now Herb started to work in Mountain View. Lem paid them a nominal salary for two months, but then they had to buy him out with their saved navy salaries and loans. They both had a lot of learning to do. The concept of the super "grocerteria" had been conceived on the East Coast, and many chains were slowly migrating across the country. The massive influx of young families challenged the boys to find the best locations first. The wholesaler who serviced the independent grocer felt the competition from the chains and was eager to teach and counsel the boys. Herb and Will put in long hours apart and met to compare their ideas. They decided to rename their stores the "Super M Stores," with a tagline of "Carrying on the Mueller Market Tradition."

Lem mentored the boys as well as he could. He felt keenly about an insurance policy for a partnership. He stressed that if they consented to a partnership, they had to draw up a legal document that would include a buy-sell agreement that was backed by an insurance plan: each partner owned and paid for an insurance policy for the other. If one partner died, the surviving partner would collect the insurance money and buy the widow out. Lem knew of too many partnerships in which one partner had died and the surviving partner had had to work with the widow. It seldom succeeded. The widow had minimum business knowledge and usually did not have any natural symbiotic relationship with the surviving owner. The wrangling that followed often destroyed the business. Also, the insurance money assured the widow a way to provide for herself. Lem wanted Gennie and Alice to understand that, with this policy, the men were protecting their families.

Lem stepped back and watched the two partners work closely for the first year, both being involved in the acquisition of the bank loans for the land for their original supermarkets. As time went on, Will became the one who negotiated the land deals and the contracts with outside providers, and Herb found, hired, and supervised all the help. They developed different philosophies of business: Will loved the challenge of price wars with their competition, wanting to build volume as a means to profit. Herb believed in providing service and maintaining a reasonable margin of profit. He wanted to fashion the food products they carried according to the ethnic makeup of the neighborhood. Will wanted all products standardized in each location. The conversations often grew heated as they tried to protect their positions.

Chapter 10

Once Gennie and Will had settled in to their home, she suggested they have another baby. She hoped Will would participate more fully in the family activities with a new infant. She had also decided to do everything in her power to make this marriage work. "You always complained about being the only child—that you were lonesome."

"Yeah, but this baby will be five years younger than Mason. There won't be much companionship there," Will replied.

"I also thought you would enjoy seeing your child at all of its growing stages. They are such interesting and engaging little beings. You missed out on that with Mason."

"True, but right now my stores are my babies. They are my creations and make me happy when they are profitable."

"But this will be different. You'll see. Their little smiles can melt your heart."

"Um…"

"At least he didn't say no," Gennie thought.

Mason had many playmates in their new neighborhood. Most of the families had preschool- or primary-school-aged children. Trikes, scooters, wagons, and roller skates cluttered the sidewalks.

Gennie enrolled Mason in a two-day-a-week preschool program. In the spring they had a short program at the school, and Gennie insisted that Will attend. He met her there and slipped into one of the seats she had saved. When she looked around the audience, she saw her parents standing at the back wall. She motioned for them to come down and join them in the front seats, and they shook their heads no. Will made a quick exit as soon as the program concluded, so Gennie worked her way to the back to confront her parents. "Why didn't you come up and sit with us?"

Her dad didn't answer.

After a pause, Erma said, "Will has asked us not to be present at any event when he is there."

Gennie looked at her dad, but he stayed silent.

"Yes," Erma continued. "Will came to Bob and made that request, saying it just confuses Mason."

"Dad, that's not right. Let me go pick up Mason backstage, and we'll meet at the creamery. We'll all have some ice cream and celebrate Mason's performance. This is not the time to discuss this in front of Mason, but we'll work something out later, and he will enjoy being with you."

After finding a seat at the creamery and savoring their ice cream, everyone complimented Mason on his good singing.

"I think Mason is able to have a guest for lunch at school, if either of you would like to come," Gennie said.

"What time do you eat?" Bob asked Mason.

"We have first lunch period."

"It's at eleven," Gennie replied. "And he goes to school Tuesdays and Thursdays. I'll just have to tell the teacher you are coming sometime, so she'll know who you are."

"Will you come? You can sit right next to me," Mason said, showing that sparkling little-boy enthusiasm.

"I'll come one day, and then Nana can come another. It will be fun...if we can fit into those little chairs."

When they got up to leave, Gennie called out to her folks, "I'll phone you tonight and make other plans. Okay?"

Driving home with Mason in the backseat singing all the songs from the program, Gennie thought, "My hope had been for Will to feel in command in his own home and not need to restrict any contact with Pops. The irony is that Will leaves at seven in the morning and comes home after Mason has already gone to bed at night. He hardly sees the child." Will had pleaded that this was what it took to start a business with a new radical approach. Gennie had asked him to please come home for supper a couple of nights a week. His retort had been that he was doing this all for Mason and her. "Baloney!" she thought. "It's all about his male ego fueling his ambition."

Her thoughts continued. "Will wants a loving family to be in awe of his accomplishments, but he isn't willing to put in any time or effort to build the relationships. And Mason isn't convinced yet. Denying activities with Pops isn't going to help. We'll continue to celebrate holidays and birthdays together, and Will is just going to have to adjust to that fact."

The rift between Mason and his father never did heal; even the birth of a baby girl, named Margo, did not encourage Will to be more participatory in the daily family events. Pops and Nana or Papa and Mama M took both grandchildren to the zoo, park, and playgrounds and went to Mason's ballgames. Will showed up only if Gennie insisted. Being five years older than his sister, Mason assumed the role of protector and patient big brother to Margo, and she adored him.

Life settled in to a pattern of Gennie keeping the home activities going and Will being absorbed in the making of a grocery dynasty. They moved from their small starter house into a large, rambling ranch-style house in Menlo Park, marking Will's ascent into more profitability. A nearby private country club with a golf course and tennis courts gave Will a venue for entertaining business clients on the fairways. Gennie took tennis lessons and played weekly. They epitomized the successful postwar couple.

Chapter 11

When Mason was twelve, Bob died suddenly of a massive heart attack. At the age of seventy two, he had retired from the contracting business but continued to find antique furniture to refurbish and resell. The day he died, he went to an antique auction with an old fellow carpenter who bought a couple of heavy pieces. As they loaded them into the truck, Bob grabbed his chest and groaned, falling to the ground. Because of the rural location of the auction, the ambulance response took many minutes, and by the time it arrived, Bob had succumbed. Shock reverberated through the family and the whole older community of Mayfield.

Mason went to Gennie and said, "I want to speak at the funeral. Is that okay with you?"

Gennie, aghast, replied, "Are you sure you can? It's difficult even for experienced speakers."

"Yes, I only want to say about five or six sentences. I called Miss B. from the Community Theater, who directed us last year, and asked her to help me tonight."

Gennie thought, "After living with this boy for twelve years, I still don't fathom his capabilities."

She replied, "Of course. Pops will be honored by your words, and I say that in the present tense because he will be looking down on you and smiling." They hugged. Gennie wanted to hold him forever—such a precious boy.

At the funeral Mason stood straight and tall. "My name is Mason. I am Bob's grandson. He was my 'Pops.'"

He looked at the audience and paused to take a breath, as Miss B. had told him to. Then, slowly and distinctly, he said, "There is no greater love than a grandfather has for his grandson. And the love of a grandson for his grandfather is equally as great." He continued at a measured pace. "He shows a boy the wonderful possibilities of life. Pops did that for me. He taught me to love nature and honor its natural state and to treat all people with kindness. I love you, Pops, and will miss you." As Mason stepped away from the podium, he lowered his head, and tears ran down his cheeks.

Handkerchiefs were out, dabbing at eyes, and audible sobbing filled the church. Gennie fought back a flood of tears, gulped a few times, and held her head taut.

"Daddy," Gennie thought, "you are the one who influenced this boy's life. Bless you, bless you forever."

PART III

Chapter 12

1959

Gennie stood at the kitchen sink rinsing the breakfast dishes and loading the dishwasher. Both Mason and Margo had left for school in a morning carpool—Mason to high school and Margo to eighth grade. The phone rang once, twice, as Gennie dried her hands before reaching for the receiver.

Gennie's melodious, two-tone "Hel-lo" pealed out in the quiet room.

"Hi, Gennie, am I interrupting anything?"

"No, just finishing up the dishes. I haven't heard from you in a long time, Phyllis. How's everything going with you?"

Phyllis worked for both Will and Herb as their executive secretary. Even before her employment, Gennie knew her through the school PTA. Her children were between Mason and Margo's ages, but the two mothers had worked on fund-raising projects and those recurring school carnivals. They tried to stay in touch with an easygoing relationship.

"Oh, life is hectic; it always is," Phyllis replied. "That's why I'm calling: Do you have plans for lunch? I thought I could pick up some sandwiches at the deli and meet you in the park. It looks like a lovely day."

"That's a great idea. I'll bring a thermos of coffee. What time?"

"How about one? By that time, the preschool crowd should be going home for their naps, and we'll have the picnic tables to ourselves."

"See you then."

Gennie arrived at the park first, picked out a table, laid a checkered card-table-sized cloth over one end, and placed the thermos and two ceramic cups on top to anchor it.

The natural oak grove had a few redwoods interspersed, all indigenous to the area. Gennie loved this setting and often wondered if the Ohlone Indians, who had first settled this area, from San Francisco along the coast past Monterey Bay, had realized how fortunate they were to live in such a temperate climate. She could visualize their round thatched huts grouped around the community campfire—what an ideal place to live.

On this early spring day, so sunny and clear, Gennie thought, "I surely do need to count my blessings and be thankful."

Phyllis arrived with the sandwiches and a small bag of Saratoga chips to share. They caught each other up on their children's activities and talked about the school gossip.

Phyllis said, "I have some unsettling news to report to you. That's why I chose the park instead of a restaurant. You never know who is listening in a public place."

"Uh-oh," Gennie thought. "Here it comes: the news that older, knowledgeable women had warned about—the news that one's executive husband is being unfaithful."

Phyllis continued, "It's been a difficult decision for me to tell you this, but as a friend, I think I must. The business accountant called me last week to tell me that the company is in financial difficulty. He wanted to let me have the opportunity to resign before it got ugly with bankruptcy and lawsuits."

Gennie opened her mouth to interject, but Phyllis said, "Let me finish please. He said that while working on the last quarter of last year, he finally established that Will had been defrauding the business to cover his huge gambling debts. During the middle of last year, the auditor suspected some outflow that was unaccounted for. So he has been doing some sleuthing and is certain that Will is using company money to either play the horses or the numbers game, or both. It's only a matter of days before the accountant meets with Will and Herb together, and then all hell is likely to break out."

The shock of disbelief covered Gennie's face. "I don't know what to say. I never in a hundred years would have believed Will would undermine his own business."

"I think the accountant is a credible person. He would not accuse anyone unless he had evidence. Since Herb and Alice and Will and you are scheduled to go to the annual banquet at the wholesalers' convention tomorrow night, I thought you needed to know. I am quite certain that Herb is clueless. He could have access to the bank statements but is more involved with the day-to-day relations with employees and has trusted Will with the financial end."

"When you said you had terrible news, all I could think of was that you were going to say Will was having an affair. I thought that would be the end of the world, but this is far worse. It could mean financial ruin—no business, no house, no nothing. I am devastated." At this point Gennie started trembling, and Phyllis went over to sit next to her and hold her shoulders.

"You must do whatever you have to," Phyllis counseled, "but I suggest not confronting Will. It'll only make for a horrible evening at the convention dinner with the possibility of the news of your business problems unraveling at a party—spreading like measles. You can at least observe how Will behaves in front of Herb."

"Yeah, it will be like the last meal before the electric chair."

"I didn't want to be the one to tell you. Really, I had many discussions with myself."

"You are a good friend, Phyllis, to do this. I understand the difficulty of friendship versus company confidentiality. I really appreciate it."

"I need to get back to the office. Do you want me to follow you home and make sure you're okay?"

"No, let me sit here and think about what I need to do. The beauty of this park has always been so peaceful. In a few minutes I'll head home." The two hugged. "Thanks, Phyllis; let's keep in touch, even if you resign."

There was no reason not to feel safe in this neighborhood park, which had evolved from a natural depression, where a tiny stream trickled and homes ringed the perimeter. "My, oh my. What a turn of events," Gennie thought. "What options do I have? Not many. At this point, it's kinda wait and see. If only

Momma were available to give me advice. She can always see right to the core of the problem."

Erma lived with Susan in Petaluma. She suffered from dementia, and her near-term memory seemed nonexistent. After Bob died, the two daughters had thought their mother exhibited symptoms of shock—and why wouldn't she? His death had happened so suddenly, and Bob and Erma had adored each other. Without looking sophomoric, they'd stayed close, touching hands or putting their arms around each other. But it soon became apparent that grief did not explain all the forgetfulness. Perhaps Bob had recognized it and covered for her. Regardless, the girls had to make the tough decision to move Erma out of her house and into dependent living. So Susan had volunteered to take her into her home. She and her husband, Walter, had been married for five years and lived on a small parcel of land, euphemistically called a "ranchette," in Petaluma: a sprawling one-story home surrounded by fields and a small barn. They had a few pet chickens and goats and a pond with ducks.

During Susan's second year in college, she had spent part of the summer at the new United Nations organization meeting in San Francisco. The college had then soon offered a course that required attending all the meetings and discussions. Susan had found her passion: promoting peace. She'd spent her junior year in Sweden, studying all the events that led up to World War II and how that country managed to stay neutral. Upon graduation she'd gone to the UN in New York to work. After a few years in New York, she'd followed the lyrics: "California, here I come, right back where I started from."

"Okay, I was just plain homesick," she'd told Gennie, "and tired of snow, cold, and the frantic rush of the city."

Susan had found a job with the Swedish consulate in San Francisco. There she had met Walter, ten years older, and after they'd married, he'd continued going into the city three times a week, but Susan had retired to being a "gentlewoman farmer." She offered her home to their mother, arguing that Gennie had her hands full with two children at home; plus, it seemed especially painful for the children to see their Nana so bewildered.

Susan also employed a young Mexican couple. Josefina, the wife, helped with the house a few days a week and befriended Erma, and Rafael, the husband, did the heavy maintenance work in the barn and yard. They were willing to stay overnight if Susan and Walter wanted a vacation. For the time being, this setup worked. From the sale of the Black house and acreage in Mayfield, the daughters managed the sizable estate for Erma; there were no money worries.

Gennie folded up the tablecloth, picked up the thermos and cups, and headed to her car. She needed to pick up Margo and her friend from school. Mason rode home with one of his friends, who had both a license and a car—the envy of his classmates.

As Gennie drove home, she decided she could just ignore Phyllis's warnings for thirty-six hours. After the banquet in San Francisco, she would confront Will, but not now. She often wondered how her mother stored all her early memories in a separate compartment and did not go there. Of course, Gennie would not be able to disregard these events for long, but it seemed an interesting concept that a person could pigeonhole some thoughts and overlook them.

The next evening Gennie got dressed for the banquet. She had bought a smart black Ann Fogarty dress from Joseph Magnin and looked forward to wearing it. Now it seemed insignificant. She instructed Mason to drive Margo to Mama and Papa M's house to spend the night. Mason had a driver's license but drove the family car, so when he returned Gennie planned to drive Mason to his friend's house for an overnight.

Mason came into the house after his chauffeuring chore and located his mother. They went out to the car and Gennie got behind the steering wheel. Mason sat next to her. His fingers tapped on the armrest as earnestly as a woodpecker attacks a tree.

"Mom, I have something I need to talk to you about. I know this isn't the best time. I didn't want to spoil your evening, but I don't often have time alone with you." He paused, and Gennie waited. "My girlfriend, Judith, is pregnant."

Fortunately, on these neighborhood streets there wasn't much traffic, and Gennie could digest Mason's pronouncement without careening off the road.

"I assume you are the father?" she queried. "What a cold way to react," she thought.

"Mother! If I didn't think so, we wouldn't be having this conversation."

"Is she sure? Or just guessing?"

"She had a rabbit test, and it's positive."

"What have the two of you decided?"

"Well, I offered to marry her, but she refused. She doesn't want to be a mother now and wants to go to college."

"Is she willing to go through the pregnancy and allow the baby to be adopted? You know that abortion is illegal, and it's very risky to go underground. I'm sure she knows that. Certainly her parents are aware of the danger. I assume she has told her parents." Gennie suddenly thought, "This sounds like an abstract clinical discussion. But this is Mason's baby!"

Then she asked, "What do you want me to do? Talk to Judith's parents, whom I barely know?"

"I thought you would be more compassionate."

Gennie pulled over to the curb so she could look at her son directly.

"I am in shock. I love you, Mason, and I will do whatever you want me to do to support the two of you. This is a tough decision to make at your tender age, and no one can do it for you. I guess you realize that Judith's parents can accuse you of statutory rape, since she is under eighteen."

"Yes, her father threatened me with that. But Judith defended me, saying that she was a willing and participatory partner. She would not testify against me."

"So I guess—just off the top of my head—I am thinking that the choices are to keep the baby, to adopt the baby out, or to have an abortion. I will support whatever decision you make. Can we talk about this tomorrow? Tell Judith whatever she decides, we will be agreeable."

When she stopped at Mason's friend's house, Mason reached over, and they hugged good-bye. As Gennie watched him go to his friend's front door, she felt that he had not gotten the supportive response he had hoped for. She didn't know what that answer could be.

"My mind is on bad-news overload," she thought. She remembered the old adage of bad news coming in threes. "I hope not; these two bombshells are enough."

Gennie had put Will's tux out so he could quickly shower and dress for the convention banquet. Because Herb and Alice had young children, the two couples would go in separate cars. Alice wanted the freedom to return, if necessary, for any emergencies that might come up with her preschoolers.

Her head filled with the conversations she'd had with Phyllis and Mason, the drive to the Palace Hotel seemed quiet and inconsequential. The annual banquet at this historic San Francisco hotel had always been special. Natives revered this hotel as the queen dowager of the postearthquake city; its Victorian Palm Court was the majesty's jeweled brooch. For half a century, this charming room had hosted the quintessential parties of high society. Vintage photos of the original Palace Hotel and the aftermath of the 1906 earthquake dotted the hall walls, and Gennie marveled that the "new" Palace had been built and opened in just three years.

They had reservations with Herb and Alice at a round table that seated eight. Each year they met new couples and renewed old acquaintances. The format remained the same: an open bar followed by a welcoming address by the organization's president, dinner, entertainment—usually a third-rate stand-up comedian—and then dancing at the end. The men went to the bar for highballs. The ladies were served a glass of rosé; they knew that champagne would be served during the president's speech. Herb and Will went off to schmooze with fellow grocers, while the women stayed seated and talked about family, schools, and jobs.

After dessert, Will suggested, "Let's ride the cable car out to Fisherman's Wharf for a nightcap." This was the twelfth year that they had attended the banquet, and often the entertainment proved tedious.

When the other three agreed, he said, "It's not far; we can walk to the turnstile on Market."

"I don't think so! Alice and I can't hike in these high heels," Gennie said.

"Okay, we'll go by cab. We can catch the cable at Union Square."

Even though they had ridden the cable car many times, the challenge of scrambling for a passenger seat was always the same and could be likened to the childhood game of musical chairs. A crowd gathered, awaiting the car's arrival, and then rushed on to find a good place. The men acted macho as they grabbed a place on the running board of the outdoor section of the car, titillated by the feeling of danger, since auto traffic soared right beside the tracks.

Gennie and Alice found outside seats on either side of a rotund man with a large grocery bag perched on his lap. Will stood on the running board, facing Gennie, and Herb was to Will's right, also standing. The running board was one foot below the floor of the cable car, so the standing passenger was eye to eye with the seated passenger in front of him. Two young men stood in front of grocery-bag man and Alice. They were French tourists and immediately engaged Alice in an animated conversation, asking many questions. Alice and Herb were separated, but she could lean forward and peek around the grocery sack and see Herb. They waved at each other, acknowledging the other's position.

If one chose to sit inside, the brakeman provided the entertainment, displaying extraordinary strength and stamina as he braked and released the grip on the cable. On this Saturday night, most of the riders had been wining, dining, and boozing at the many hotels in the area and were a boisterous crowd. As always, especially on the weekends, tourists crowded on, anxious to experience this distinctive San Franciscan mode of transportation. A holiday excitement always surrounded these cars.

One could not be nonchalant about holding on if standing—either inside or outside. The conductor repeatedly reminded patrons to be cautious. At one of the stops, Herb acted like he was losing his balance and made a joke of it. Gennie looked at him as he wisecracked with Will on his left and a stranger on his right. She thought, "Maybe Herb has had too much to drink. He certainly is acting more animated and less like his usual introverted self." She remembered that earlier, at the hotel, each time he had come back to their reserved table after talking with other grocer friends, he'd had a fresh drink in his hand. It had looked like his usual whiskey on the rocks, which he consumed quickly before leaving to see more friends and get another refill.

Now Gennie tried to catch Will's eye, but he and Herb continued to chatter. A tourist couple with young children on their laps sat in front of Herb and were busy looking at all the buildings. The conductor called out, "The next block, we turn a corner; everyone hold on tight." He repeated his warning again, aimed at the outside customers. Though sitting, Gennie grabbed the pole railing too.

As the cable car slowed down and swayed it went into a sharp turn, Gennie saw Will give a swift side kick to Herb's ankle. Herb faltered, flailing with his one free arm, and Will gave him a shove in his midsection. Herb fell backward onto the street below. Gennie didn't see the impact, but she looked up at Will's face, not two feet away from hers. For an instant their eyes met, and she said, "I saw that." Whether he heard her above all the traffic noise with a woman screaming and a man yelling to stop, she wasn't sure, but he certainly read her lips. She watched as he immediately scanned the faces of the other passengers, maybe looking for someone to accuse him. "In the noise and confusion, did no one else see anything?" she wondered.

Amid the screams, the yelling, and the grinding of the brakes, Gennie started to stand, wanting to run back to Herb's body. When she did Alice looked at her with a confused and questioning look. "What happened?" she shouted. Evidently, her conversation with the foreign tourists had captured all of her attention and she hadn't seen Herb fall.

"Herb lost his balance and fell off the car," Gennie answered. Alice's face blanched.

As if she didn't believe her, Alice looked past the man's grocery sack to make sure Herb wasn't there, still next to Will. Then she started screaming.

Both the brakeman and the conductor were busy applying the emergency brakes, and before the car stopped completely, some of the passengers were running back to Herb's prone body on the cobblestones. Alice and Gennie were slow getting to his side because their high heels on the uneven pavement impeded their progress. Alice appeared to be close to gagging and losing her dinner right there on the street when she saw Herb's face. A man crouched over Herb's body, trying to find a pulse at the wrist. "I can't find a beat," he said. Gennie, in an automatic medical-response mode, knelt beside Herb, pulled off her long leather glove, and tried to feel for a pulse at his neck. Seeing the pool of blood, Alice choked back her nausea, untied her silk neck scarf, and put it under Herb's head; a bystander helped lift his head. Alice's gloves became bloodied by his massive injury. She tried to talk to Herb, but his eyelids did not even flicker. She looked up at the bystanders' faces, pleading for help. Someone offered a cotton scarf to apply under the head for pressure, and Alice did, but Gennie dissuaded anyone from moving Herb.

Already an ambulance siren could be heard in the distance. Evidently a person on the sidewalk had told the man at the newspaper stand on the corner to call for emergency help.

Gennie knew from her short nursing career that all emergencies in San Francisco were handled by the police department. Ambulances were stationed all over the city at fire and police stations, and their attendants were trained police officers. Any injured person was taken to the City and County Hospital emergency room, where he or she was assessed, treated, and triaged to other private hospitals.

In addition to the ambulance, two squad cars arrived with two policemen in each one. The ambulance attendants squatted over Herb, one applying a stethoscope to his chest, another checking for a pulse and assessing the head injury. Four of the policemen started lists of the passengers on the cable car, including addresses and telephone numbers. Obviously, a stoppage of one cable car backed up the whole system, so the police knew to collect their information quickly and let the cable car continue. The medical attendants loaded Herb into the ambulance, cognizant of a possible neck injury. Alice stood watching in disbelief. The officer with the stethoscope had shaken his head, but they did not cover the victim's body as if he were DOA. As they closed the back doors to the ambulance, Gennie led the pale, shivering Alice to the side of the ambulance, where she vomited. The officers then bundled Alice with a blanket—ashen, expressionless, and perhaps in a state of shock—into the front seat of the ambulance and headed out, sirens sounding. Will also had a queasy stomach and had watched the medical personnel attend to Herb but did not interfere.

One of the police officers asked Gennie if she was a friend of the patient. She said, " Yes, both my husband and I are."

He said, "Get in our squad car, and we'll take you to the emergency room."

Inside the jostling police car, Gennie fought back a surge of nausea. Helping a vomiting person had always triggered her own gagging.

When Gennie and Will arrived at the hospital, they were ushered into a small sitting room with one couch and two chairs. Alice sat there by herself.

"They haven't told me anything," she said. "I think they were waiting for you to appear before they tell me he's died. There was little activity in the ambulance, and when we arrived here, they didn't show much urgency and spoke in hushed tones. I do expect the worst." She shuddered. Tears streamed down her cheeks. She dabbed them with a crumpled handkerchief. " How? Why? I just don't understand."

Although Alice asked the obvious questions, her eyes looked glassy and remote.

Gennie went over to sit next to Alice. She reached out her ungloved hand to hold Alice's. Both of them had cold hands. The night air had felt chilly even on the cable-car ride, and then standing on the street afterward, their short fur shrugs had not offered enough warmth.

Alice implored Will. "Tell me exactly what you saw."

"To begin with, we both had too much to drink. I was afraid that if we stayed drinking at the hotel, we would be unfit to drive home. That was the reason I suggested we go down to the wharf. We could get some cool, fresh air on the ride and get away from the bar. Then Herb started clowning around, and I just don't think he anticipated what a sharp corner the cable car was going to take. He lost his balance. I tried to grab him, but I was too late. He hit the pavement hard—really hard. There was nothing to break his fall."

A police officer came into the room, interrupting Will's explanation. A Catholic priest followed.

"This is Father O'Malley, the chaplain for the hospital," the officer announced.

Alice stood up and extended her hand. "I am the wife of the patient, and these are my two friends."

"Sit down, sit down. I'll sit with you," the chaplain said. "I have sad news, Mrs. uh..." He looked at the name on the paper in his hand. "Mrs. Jordan, your husband has succumbed to his injuries. I am so sorry. Is there a local clergyman I can call?" Alice's soft crying grew to an avalanche of body-shaking sobs.

"No, we live in Palo Alto. It's late. I will call him in the morning. May I go in and see my husband?" Her body continued to quiver.

"Yes, I'll go out and tell them you want to see him," the officer said and left the room.

"Do you want us to go with you?" Gennie asked.

"No, I think I want to go alone. Maybe you," Alice said, looking at the priest, "maybe you could stay with me." In a moment the officer motioned to Alice to follow him, and Gennie and Will remained behind in the austere room.

"I'm afraid it might take a while for all the paperwork to be done," Will said to Gennie. "I think the state law requires an autopsy unless the deceased is under direct doctor's care. They are bound to have to schedule that."

After a few moments, he continued, "We can take a cab to the Palace parking garage and get the cars. I will drive Alice home, and you can follow. Do you think you are up to that?"

Gennie nodded yes. "Or," Will added, "we can spend the night at the hotel and return home tomorrow."

"I think Alice will want to get home to her children," Gennie said. "And I doubt any of us are going to do much sleeping tonight."

While they waited Gennie mulled over her options about confronting Will. She felt uncomfortable about doing it in a public place—somehow it seemed that walls had ears. She would wait until they were alone in the car or at home.

In about thirty minutes, Alice and the officer returned to the room.

"They said we are ready to go now," Alice told the couple. "I have signed all the papers for an autopsy and the release of Herb's body to a funeral home in Palo Alto."

The officer accompanying Alice said, "We can provide a squad car to take you back to the hotel, or you can call a cab." They decided to go in the squad car; it would be quicker.

As the three followed the officer out to the hospital driveway, a man stepped up to Alice and said, "Mrs. Jordan! Many accidents aren't really accidents but are caused by negligence or mistakes. We can find out how this happened to your husband." He thrust a business card into her hand. "Call this number if you have questions. I can help."

As they scurried past the man, Will said, "Well, they certainly earn their nickname of 'ambulance chasers,' don't they?"

In the backseat of the squad car, Gennie asked Alice if she would like them to spend the night with her.

"No, the children's nanny lives in, so I won't be alone."

"Can we make any phone calls for you?" Will suggested.

"I don't see any reason to disturb anyone's sleep—a few hours won't make any difference. I have a couple of close girlfriends who will help me. I think I will call Herb's brother first and ask his advice about calling Herb's parents. So try to get some rest."

Gennie marveled at her clarity of thought. "Perhaps it's the shock, or maybe the truth hasn't sunk in yet," she thought.

As they got their cars from the garage attendant, Gennie said to Will, "I drive slower than you. Don't try to keep me in your rearview mirror. I know how to get to Alice's house, so I'll be more comfortable going at my own pace." She and Will exchanged a perfunctory kiss, and they parted.

On the drive Gennie listened to the classical music station on the radio, familiar sounds that soothed her. "I must confront Will tonight," she thought. "If I don't, he will weave and dodge me for weeks so we won't ever be alone. I'm aware of his tactics, but I must circumvent them. It's just too important this time."

Will and Alice were already in the house when Gennie arrived. She let herself in the front door and went into the foyer. The walls had wide panels of bird's-eye maple separated by oak boards, both burnished to a blond finish that her father had installed so long ago. All night she had held her emotions in check, and now, with her guard down, the tears flowed. Alice and Will came to greet her, and immediately Gennie apologized.

She looked at Alice and said, "Coming into this foyer and seeing his craftsmanship, I suddenly miss Dad and remember how proud he was of this room. I guess that's reassuring, that our loved ones are really not far from our thoughts and never leave our hearts."

"That is a comforting thought," Alice agreed.

Gennie offered, "Call us if your folks need to be picked up at the airport. I guess Herb's family will drive down, but let us know if we can help. We have one guest bedroom, and Will's folks have two guest rooms, so call when your relatives arrive. Actually, I will call you tomorrow evening and see what else you need." Alice and Gennie hugged before Will and Gennie left.

Once in their car, traveling through the familiar streets of Palo Alto, Gennie said, "I think we need to talk about tonight's events."

"We are both wrung out emotionally and so tired; let's talk tomorrow."

"No, I want to discuss this now, while it is still fresh. The next few days will be busy for both of us, and we will have little chance to be alone. I know what I saw—I saw you deliberately push Herb off that cable car. Perhaps it wasn't premeditated, but you realized Herb had had too much to drink and took advantage of his instability"

"It was an accident. I was reaching for him."

"What about that hard, swift kick you gave him before he lost his balance?"

"It was an accident. There is no reason to continue this conversation when you are obviously tired and emotional."

"No, I am thinking very clearly. I know you had a motive for killing Herb. I know the company is on the verge of bankruptcy. And I know you are responsible for that too, through your huge gambling debts."

"Who told you that?"

"Let's just say I have friends who want to help protect my interests."

"That doesn't mean that I would cause Herb's death."

"But I think the DA's office would find it interesting, perhaps a motive."

"Now you are being ridiculous, Gennie. It was a tragic accident."

"Well, I don't know if I can live with myself if I don't come forward with what I saw. Poor, innocent Herb. I wonder if he too knew of the impending bankruptcy. That might explain his excessive drinking. Maybe all of us knew and everyone gave the performance of his or her life, hoping for an Oscar, I suppose."

"Okay, you started this. Let me develop your scenario. If you tell someone of your unfounded suspicions, do you know what will happen? First of all, the insurance will hold off paying the death benefit. Without that insurance money, I cannot pay Alice for Herb's part of the company. Our company will go bankrupt while the DA investigates. We will have to hire expensive lawyers. I *will* be cleared of all wrongdoing. Meanwhile, Alice is without any funds, and so are we. She will undergo additional anguish because of your charges. We both may lose our homes, and what about the children? Even if the insurance company pays eventually, maybe months will go by. Is your hoity-toity moral righteousness worth all that?"

Gennie seldom showed rage, but now her eyes flashed with fierceness. "All I know is that you are responsible for the financial debacle the company is in and for Herb's death. If I look the other way, I suddenly become your accomplice. If I do the ethical thing, I am made out to be the bad guy destroying everyone's well-being. I'm damned if I do, and I'm damned if I don't, and you have put me in this difficult dilemma."

The car turned into their driveway and stopped. Will got out to open the garage door. When he got back into the driver's seat, Gennie continued, "This is one promise I will make, Willem Mason Mueller: however this turns out, if you ever gamble again and I find out about it, our life together is over."

They both went into the house without more conversation, each grappling with thoughts. Will followed her down the hall to their bedroom.

As she stopped to hang up her fur jacket in the hall closet, he passed her, and she added, "Also, Mason told me this afternoon that his girlfriend is pregnant." Will didn't miss a step and kept on walking toward the bedroom door.

After undressing, Gennie and Will crept into their usual sides of the king-sized bed and remained close to the edges of the mattress. A cavernous, cold space separated them. Although they were still angry, their exhausted bodies succumbed to sleep.

Chapter 13

The next morning Gennie made a pot of coffee, as usual. Will followed his normal procedure of pouring cold cereal and milk into a bowl and juice into a glass. Gennie nibbled on her toast.

"I promised Susan I would go up to Petaluma and visit with them today. I should be back by midafternoon. Mason is going up to the stables in Los Altos Hills to ride with his friend Jeff, and Mama M is taking Margo and a girlfriend to the movies after Sunday school. Since Alice and I are barely acquaintances, I doubt if my presence would be helpful."

"I'll call Phyllis and see if the two of us can find all of the managers so I can hold a meeting," Will replied. "There's no telling how fast this news of Herb's death will travel via the grapevine." They parted, cool and barely speaking.

After she'd tidied up the kitchen and made the bed, Gennie headed out to Susan's house. There were few other cars on the road this early Sunday morning. Her thoughts drifted to the previous night's events. Assuming Will had decided to kill Herb for the insurance money, he must have been waiting for the opportunity. In the frantic scramble to get seats and standing places on the cable car, Will couldn't possibly have predicted the fortuitous seating If Herb had stayed with Alice, this would not have happened. It needed luck-or bad luck-to occur,. How cold blooded. She had never seen Herb so inebriated. That also fed into the fatal equation.

"Now, if I go to the district attorney with my accusation and a trial occurs and Will is found innocent, will he hate me, want revenge, and kill me?" Instead if I divorce Will and take half of all our assets in community property, won't he feel a murderous rage, too?" By this time she had reached the Golden Gate Bridge entrance and she decided she would arrive way too early at her sister's. She pulled over into the visitor's parking lot next to the restaurant and headed up to the bridge sidewalk. Of all the times the family had driven over the bridge, they had never stopped to walk. She hoped the stroll and the ocean air would clarify her thoughts.

The morning sun shone clear, the fog having already burned off. Gennie wore a light sweater and realized that the brisk wind would challenge that. She went back to the car, opened the trunk, and found an old quilted ski jacket of Will's. Oversized, it extended past her hips. She left her purse in the trunk and took her keys. A short ramp led to the bridge's sidewalk. The parking lot had other cars in it, but she saw few people; they were either already on the bridge or in the restaurant. "I'll stop back at the coffee shop for a hot cup of coffee before I continue to Petaluma," she thought.

The slanted rays of sun skated across the small waves, turning them into golden ripples. "No one—neither painter nor photographer—can capture the magic of this light," she thought. "We seldom appreciate these aspects of nature." She stopped, put both elbows on the railing, and looked down on the slightly choppy water. A couple walked by and they exchanged greetings.

"We are so blessed to live in such a beautiful place," she thought. She gazed at the horizon with Coit Tower and the rows of whitewashed houses dotting the coast. Those pleasant thoughts were blotted out by her more troubling ones: "How can we botch up our lives this way? How could I put all my faith and love into Will, thinking he was my Rock of Gibraltar? Why did he gamble away our happiness? Why did I give him an ultimatum about gambling, when he is a murderer? Shouldn't I leave him now? The big question is, how am I going to live with myself if I keep quiet? How did Mom keep her troubled life in a sealed capsule, never to share it? Do you ever completely forget it? Or are you haunted with your decision?"

Gennie continued walking. The big bridge spire loomed ahead of her, red-orange and luminous in the bright sunlight. The occasional car whizzed by. "Why am I the only one with moral scruples? If I say nothing, what kind of hero would I be? All I am doing is covering up for Will's crimes. I'm damned either way, aren't I? What kind of life will we have, built on lies? How do I continue living with a murderer?" Tears started streaming down her cheeks. "Why am I crying? Am I feeling sorry for myself? Or is it the loss of my security?" Her tears blurred her vision and she stumbled on the concrete walk.

"If I go to the DA and divorce Will, I'll have no way to earn a living. We'll lose the stores and house if the insurance money is deferred. Mason is old enough to take care of himself but Margo isn't. I see no future with Will-- or without him." The tears had increased to sobs and Gennie gasped for breath. "My life could be reduced to one of fear, afraid to contradict him. I can't live with any of these options."

With that thought, Gennie looked at the four-foot height of the railing. Will's ski jacket was long. She pulled the jacket above her hips, climbed up on the railing, and then slid to the other side. Without much more thought, she decided that jumping would be a solution. "I cannot be true to myself and continue living with this secret," she thought.

From the moment she let go and started to free fall, Gennie realized she had made the wrong decision. "This is a long way down. I wanted to escape life, but now I'm not so sure." Her next thought was, "Dear God, take care of Mason and his baby. May the children forgive me."

The air pushed up under the big ski jacket, inflating it like a balloon, perhaps slowing her descent. She reached up to the collar of the jacket with her right hand to keep it from pushing past her chin. In just seconds she hit the water but had no recollection of the force, the temperature, or the time. She surfaced to hear someone shouting that he was coming for her. Obviously, the jump had not killed her. It was both a comforting and alarming thought. A boat came close to her. She floated on her back. A young man dove in, grabbed her, and held on to her. "Ma'am, what did you want to do that for?" he asked.

Barely conscious, her mind was fuzzy. For a moment she had a hallucination that this boy was Mason, and she wondered how he'd gotten into the water to save her. She struggled to clear her mind, but lucidity eluded her.

The teenager in the water with her, his older brother, and their father had been heading out for a morning of fishing when they'd seen the body falling from the bridge. Their pleasure yacht had a platform in the back equipped with chairs and fishing rods for deep-sea fishing. The boy secured a ski belt and a rope around her middle. The father also suggested they place her in a fishnet to bring her on board. The brother helped in the water and then got up with the father on board. It required a Herculean effort for all three to lift her onto the platform. With the bumping and pulling, the pain made Gennie aware of the seriousness of her injuries: probably multiple broken bones. She shivered with cold. She upchucked copious amounts of seawater, and each retch caused agony in her chest. They unzipped her jacket, put blankets on her body, and started looking for scissors to cut the jacket sleeves open.

Meanwhile, the father-captain had radioed the Coast Guard to say they had picked up a still-alive bridge jumper, and he asked where they should take her. The Coast Guard replied that because she had jumped on the San Francisco side, she should go to their dock in San Francisco. A Coast Guard boat would come out to escort them to that dock.

From those first moments in the water until she arrived at the hospital, Gennie had only moments of recollection. Whether because of the pain or her body's reaction to the impact of the fall, she drifted in and out of consciousness. The danger of both hypothermia and shock concerned the Guard's officers who had intercepted the fishing boat and boarded it. They cut off the rest of the coat and covered her with warm, dry blankets; elevated her legs; and tried to elicit responses from her. They gave rudimentary emergency care because IVs were administered only in a hospital setting and only by a physician or a specially trained nurse.

Gennie arrived at San Francisco City and County Hospital about twelve hours after she had left the night before with Alice and Will. Her level of consciousness allowed her to give basic information: her name and husband's name.

She told them that Will planned to have a meeting at his office. "I know that phone number is Davenport four two four four two."

The medical staff performed physical exams and x-rays and discussed the likelihood of moving her to the psych ward because she remained at suicide risk. Their tasks included stabilizing her and waiting for a next of kin to give permission to either move her to another hospital or proceed with treatment.

Phyllis answered the phone. "Super M, Palo Alto."

"We are looking for Mr. Will Mueller," a male voice from the hospital said. "This is the emergency room of San Francisco General City and County Hospital, and his wife has arrived here with multiple injuries. Do you know where he is?"

"Mr. Mueller is in a meeting, but I can interrupt him if you would like to hold on."

"That would be very helpful."

Will came out of the conference room. "Will Mueller, here. Who am I speaking with?"

"I am calling from the San Francisco General Hospital emergency room, and your wife has arrived here for care."

"Was she in an accident?"

"No, not exactly. Your wife jumped from the Golden Gate Bridge in an attempted suicide."

"No…no…*no*!" Each word got louder until the third no sounded like the bawl of a wounded animal. "Is she still alive?"

"Yes, sir. She is a very lucky lady to have survived. She is in serious but stable condition. She has multiple injuries. We suggest you come here as soon as possible. Do you know where the San Francisco General Hospital is?"

"Yes, unfortunately, I am all too familiar with your hospital. I'll be there in about an hour."

Will called his parents' house. His dad answered; his mom was with Margo and her friend. He told him only that Gennie had been admitted to the emergency room and he did not have all of the details. Will said he didn't remember who Mason was with but Margo would know.

"Keep the kids at your house until I get back."

Lem said, "Susan had called, wondering why Gennie hadn't arrived."

"Would you call and give her the information about Gennie's hospital admission? I need to get started to the hospital."

Will arrived at the emergency-room desk and gave them his name. Even though Sunday afternoons were not busy news days, the lawyer man who had approached Alice the night before stood in the hallway, recognized Will, and advanced toward him. "Weren't you here last night with that cable-car accident?" he asked. "Are you here to see the suicide jumper?"

Will brushed by him without commenting. The receptionist asked Will to follow her into a cubicle off the emergency room, where patients awaiting transfer were held. The small, plain room had white walls, a white iron bed, and a white cotton bed covering. Gennie lay on her back, an IV in her arm, eyes closed. A suicide watcher sat nearby. "Is she unconscious or just asleep?" he asked the sitter.

"She's just resting; they gave her some pain medication," she replied.

Will went over to the bed and kissed Gennie gently on the forehead. Her eyes opened, and it took a moment for her to focus and reorient herself to the surroundings. She looked up at him and said, "I'm afraid I've messed things up worse than ever."

"We'll work things out somehow. I can't imagine life without you, Gennie. Don't you know how much the kids and I rely on you and love you?"

"When I went out to the bridge for a walk, I hoped to clear my thoughts. I couldn't see any way out. I saw no future—no solution. Once I let go of the railing, I knew I had done the wrong thing."

"As I said, we'll work it out together. Meanwhile, you need to be transferred to another hospital, where they can set your bones and you can heal. I thought you might be comfortable at your old hospital. Do you think that is a good choice?"

"Yes."

"Already the newspaper reporters have gotten wind of your jump. We need to safeguard you from them—and those pesky lawyers. I'll go out and make arrangements at the desk and then be back."

When Will went out to talk with the receptionist, she assured him that the transfer could be accomplished easily. She knew the chosen hospital, All Saints Episcopal, and commented that they had a VIP floor where Gennie would be protected from the inquiring press.

"A good choice," she said with a sweet, affirming smile.

Before returning to Gennie, Will saw the annoying lawyer on the pay phone in the hall, and it seemed obvious that he was the subject of the call. As Will walked by, the man said, "I tell you there's a story here. Something fishy is going on. A cable-car accident and a suicide—sounds pretty juicy to me. I think you'd better get down here."

A private ambulance transferred Gennie to All Saints. After assessing her in their emergency room, the staff transferred her to the fifth floor, which had a reputation of housing movie stars, political figures, and industrial moguls who wanted seclusion. A private elevator and entrance for visitors and a special elevator for staff helped accomplish this. Will felt she would be shielded from unwanted questions.

Although Lem had planned to go out to the farm, he stayed at home close to the telephone, awaiting news.

When the phone rang, it wasn't Will.

"This is a reporter for the *Call-Bulletin.* Is this Mr. Willem Mueller?"

"Yes."

"Are you the husband of Geneva Mueller?"

"No, I am her father-in-law."

"What is your opinion of her attempted suicide?"

"Suicide? That's preposterous. I know nothing about it. It's impossible." Lem thought, "Who is this guy?"

"You mean you don't know that she jumped off the Golden Gate?"

"That's crazy. I don't believe it. If it is true, this is a cruel way of letting relatives learn of this tragedy." Lem thought, "Can this guy know what he is talking about?"

"Well, I meant no harm. Your daughter-in-law survived and is in serious condition—that's what I heard. Do you know Herb Jordan?"

"Yes, he's my son's partner."

"Did you know he died last night in a cable-car accident?"

"No! Where are you getting this information?" Now Lem was more than annoyed; he was pissed that this guy had no scruples about sharing these "facts." "How can I substantiate this data?" he wondered.

"They were both admitted to San Francisco City Hospital, and I cover that beat."

"I have nothing more to say to you," Lem said and hung up. He sat on the kitchen chair with a thud. His brain couldn't absorb or sort out this information. He wondered if all this could be true. Will had said that Gennie had been admitted to the emergency room but not why. The reporter really had chutzpah to call him on the phone. "What would make Gennie want to jump from the Golden Gate Bridge? Surely this was a misidentification. Should I call Susan with this news or wait until I can verify it?"

He called Susan. "Hi, Susan. Lem here. I just got a strange phone call from a newspaper reporter. He asked me questions about Gennie, who he said jumped off the Golden Gate Bridge. Then Herb, who he said died from a fall off the cable car last night."

"That sounds insane! Are you sure?"

"No, but I thought I would share what I heard. I haven't received a call from Will yet. I really thought I'd hear something more by now."

"I doubt that a phone call to the emergency room would get us much information, but I'll try pretty soon if we don't hear. No one would make up such a story without some substance, don't you think? Thanks for calling—we should get off the line, in case Will wants to call."

Later that evening, after Will had called Lem with an update, Lem called Susan. They agreed that they had never thought Gennie would try suicide. That shocked them the most. Also, a grown, healthy man falling off a cable car? Who ever heard of that?

The local television stations were filled with the details. Very few jumpers survived.

The next few days for Gennie were filled with the setting of bones, the strapping of dislocations, x-rays, and examinations. Gennie told the sitter she thought the bay waters had been kinder to her body than the doctors were. The final assessment indicated that she had a left wrist fracture, a left dislocated clavicle, a right fractured ankle, and hairline-fractured ribs. Her internal organs were bruised but not punctured. The nurses kept her sedated most of the time. Will visited daily but stayed for only twenty minutes. No conversation occurred.

Herb's funeral had been scheduled for Wednesday morning. On Tuesday night Susan received a phone call from Mason. "Are you coming to Herb's funeral?" he asked.

"Yes. Do you want me to come by and pick you up?"

"Would you consider staying a couple of days with Margo and me?"

"Okay. I'll pack some extra clothes. Walter is out of town on business, so that will work. How are you and Margo doing?"

"Neither one of us can really believe that Mom tried suicide. It's hard to imagine her being that desperate. All my thoughts begin with why and end with why. The newspapers said only two percent of jumpers survive. I guess we are lucky she did."

"Yes, I agree. I'll go to the hospital in the morning and then come to your house."

Susan went by the hospital shortly after seven o'clock to tell Gennie that Mason had asked her to stay with them for a few days. "He said they were floundering. Please be proud of him; he recognized they needed help. He said you and I are so similar that it would be wonderful if I came and stayed."

Gennie started weeping and grabbed her sore ribs as she said, "He is as intuitive as Dad. Please tell them how much I love them and that what I did had nothing to do with them."

When Susan arrived at the house, she put on the coffee, defrosted the orange juice, and set out the sweet rolls and cold cereal. When Mason and Margo came into the kitchen, they hugged their aunt and said that this breakfast was just what Mom would make. They sat down to the bar and started to eat.

The kids did not go to school, because of the eleven o'clock funeral. In fact, Mama M had kept them out of school since the incident. Neither one had learned the news until they'd awakened on Monday. Mama M had wanted to read and have her grandchildren read and understand the newspaper reports before they were confronted by their schoolmates.

The Monday-morning papers had two-inch-tall headlines saying, "Woman Survives GG Bridge Jump." The front page had many details and so did the television stations.

Almost immediately, Mason seized the blame: what he had confessed to his mother had obviously upset her. Her disappointment in him upon hearing about Judith's pregnancy must have caused her to jump.

Susan sat down in the kitchen with her cup of coffee as her nephew and niece ate breakfast. Before her sat two bewildered youths; Mason wanted to confess all his problems to someone—someone sympathetic. He told her about Judith's pregnancy, telling his mom, being banned from seeing Judith again, and coming to the conclusion that he had to be the cause of his mother's attempted suicide. Margo, age thirteen, listened. She had known none of this, and her eyes widened with surprise and dismay.

Susan said, "I cannot fathom that Judith's pregnancy upset your mother so much that she felt compelled to attempt suicide. There is something more to this story, Mason. Don't shoulder all the blame. This is new territory for all of us. None of us has any idea why your mom jumped. I am not so sure that even *she* is convinced of her motive. Nevertheless, we are family. We are here to support one another. I will stay for four or five days, and each day we'll talk about what has happened. I know some of your friends may be unkind, but I also have faith that many of your friends will be sympathetic."

She looked at both of these children, who seemed so lost. "If I know girls, Mason, one of Judith's friends will get a message to you about what is happening. Judith is even more devastated than you are. After all, she is the one who is pregnant. I hate that this is happening this way."

Mason now showed anger. "That's the whole point! I wanted to be there for her, whatever the decision." He started to sob, his pent-up emotions overpowering his desire to stay calm. Susan went over to hug him, and Margo looked on astonished; she had never seen her big brother so emotional. At this time Will came in from the garage after having gone out to check some stores. Mason appeared embarrassed that his dad would see him so vulnerable, and left the room.

"I came home to get the kids ready for the funeral," Will announced. "I didn't know you were going to be here, Susan." He went over and gave his sister-in-law a peck on the cheek.

"I thought the kids might need a ride to the funeral, since I presumed you would be a pallbearer. The children asked me to stay a couple of days. I didn't think you would mind."

"That would be great. I know the kids are having their own angst, but business is also a big challenge. I feel like a juggler trying to keep all these damn balls up in the air."

Chapter 14

Will, Susan, Mason, and Margo all went in one car to the funeral, representing a solid family front to the community.

"I will try to stay close to you both," Susan told her niece and nephew. "If I get drawn into a conversation, just linger nearby. If anyone offers their sympathy, the only answer is to say, 'Thank you for your concern.' If someone asks questions about your mother, your answer can be 'We are thankful she is recuperating.' Most friends will be considerate and friendly, but if a busybody appears, just answer questions with 'I don't know.' Try to stay pleasant. We can do this."

Alice and her parents and Herb's parents greeted all the mourners in a receiving line after the service. Susan promised she would visit after Alice returned from the burial in Herb's hometown in Oregon. Alice and Susan had a warm relationship, partly because of their similar college experiences, and it continued when they saw each other at family Christmas parties and the grocery company picnics. As they exited the funeral home and some people lingered before going to their cars, Will saw the "ambulance chaser" from the hospital waiting room. The man put his hand to the brim of his gray fedora and tipped his hat in Will's direction. He seemed to make the gesture to ensure that Will knew he was there, continuing his mission of getting to the bottom of the story.

"That man is up to no good," Will muttered.

"What did you say?" Susan asked.

"Oh, nothing. I was thinking aloud."

On the drive home from the funeral, Will said to Mason, "I understand you knocked up your girlfriend."

Because it wasn't a question, Mason did not reply.

Will continued, "Isn't that correct?"

Mason replied, "I don't think that expression reflects how my girlfriend and I think about it."

"Oh, be a man, Son. Don't pull a holier-than-thou semantic on me. What are you doing about the pregnancy?"

"I am being a man, and it has been taken care of."

"What does that mean?"

"It means that you don't need to be concerned. If I asked you what my girlfriend's name is, or who her parents are, you would have no clue. Don't pull this doting-parent act on me at this juncture." Will appeared stunned. Mason continued, "Mom's been the glue in this family, and we've tried to live up to her expectations. Evidenced by her jump, we didn't. I will try to make it up to her so she never feels that desperate again. Maybe you need to do the same."

Susan, sitting in the front seat next to Will, watched as his jaw tightened, the muscles bulging into a knot. Maybe because she witnessed this confrontation, he did not lash out again. His son had called his bluff. In the backseat, Margo sat shivering, her teeth chattering, frightened by this father-brother encounter.

At this time Mason had not heard from Judith and didn't know what had occurred. Within an hour of returning home from the funeral, Valerie, a friend of both Judith and Mason, called, saying Judith had given her a note for him and she would deliver it to the house.

When Valerie arrived, Mason invited her in. "Let's go into the den; no one is back there," he said.

As they passed the kitchen, Susan came out and extended her hand. "Hi, I'm Susan, Mason's aunt. Can I get you kids anything to drink?"

"This is Valerie, a good friend of both Judith and me," Mason said. "I don't want anything to drink right now, do you?" Valerie shook her head, so they went down the hall to the den.

"Have you read the letter?" Mason asked.

"Actually, Judith asked me to critique her first draft. She said that since I am coeditor of the school newspaper, I could help make sure she was expressing herself clearly. But she didn't need much help. It sounded good."

Mason and Valerie sat on the couch, and he opened the letter:

Dear Mason,

I am no longer pregnant. I had an abortion on Sunday morning. My dad arranged it through the clinic where all his company employees go for their preemployment physicals and where they are sent if injured. There are eight doctors at the clinic, and one of the general surgeons agreed to do the abortion as a favor. The clinic has a small emergency room with nurses and anesthesiologists on call on the weekend if there are injuries; otherwise the clinic is closed. On Sunday morning we met the surgeon, and the procedure occurred. They have two postoperative beds, and I stayed there until five o'clock on Monday morning. We left before the clinic opened at seven.

All went well. I am feeling sad, but that's partly because I miss you and know I can't see you or have any contact with you. My father is so angry; I don't dare take the risk to see you. He's threatened to send me to a convent if I misbehave again. I can't take that chance. I still care about you because you are such a great, kind person.

If we ever meet somewhere, I hope you will greet me as an old friend, not an enemy. No one at school, except Valerie, knows of this pregnancy or abortion, so any talk will be idle gossip.

Please take care of yourself—you are one special individual.

Fondly,
Judith

PS I just learned about your mother. What can I say? I am so, so sorry. I hope she is doing okay. If you need someone to talk to, Valerie is a great listener and can keep confidences. I wish I could be there for you. J.

When Mason looked at Valerie, his eyes glistened with tears, and he sniffled. He cleared his throat and said, "Well, I guess it's over."

"Is there any message I can take back to Judith? She said not to write her because her dad might see it."

"It's just as well; I don't write very well. Tell her I wish it had ended differently. I'm sorry her dad denied me an opportunity to talk with him—for both of us to talk with him. I would never consider her an enemy. She'll always be a sweetness in my heart. I hope it goes well in her new school. Both of our lives are in an upheaval. I'm also sorry that you, Valerie, and Judith will be going to separate schools. You're such good friends; I hope that continues. Sometimes growing up stinks."

Valerie smiled. "And with that profound thought, I'll leave. I have a list of errands to do for my mom."

Mason put his arm around her shoulder and said, "Thanks for bringing the letter. You're a great friend to both of us." He followed her out to her car in the driveway and watched her leave.

Back inside, he took the letter to the kitchen, where Susan had started the dinner preparations.

"Would you like to read Judith's letter?" he asked. "I think it will be better than if I try to paraphrase it."

"That is so generous." Susan sat down and read it quietly.

When she finished, she said, "What a kind and thoughtful letter. You can read between the lines that she is hurting. Neither set of parents is stepping up and being compassionate for you two. I am convinced that your mother's attempted suicide had nothing to do with this pregnancy. Please, Mason, don't take on that guilt. The old adage of 'one day at a time' is a proven method of dealing with problems. Don't become isolated; we need to talk this through together." She went over and gave Mason a big, long hug. "It's times like this that I feel that Pops is looking down on us and saying, 'You can do this.' Your mom loves you, and so do I. We'll find a solution that works."

"I'm afraid Pops would be disappointed in me too."

"Maybe disappointed but not judgmental. He never wanted to dwell on the negative but instead forged ahead to a positive outcome. He helped so many people. I don't know if you remember how many people crowded the funeral home for his service. Many of those people he had counseled and consoled. If he saw someone hurting or in trouble, he reached out with a helping hand. He often said the best thing one can do is just listen and really hear what the distressed person is saying."

"What do you think he would tell me now?" Mason asked.

"Forgive yourself. You did not intend to cause harm. Second, learn from the experience, and try not to repeat it. In your situation, Pops would be candid: be prepared with a handy condom, or wait until you can obtain one. He would assure you that boys—or young men—do not think of the consequences of their actions. That is something you must learn. Last, be benevolent to those people who find themselves in similar dilemmas—for instance, don't jump to the conclusion to label any pregnant, unmarried girl a slut. Both your mom and I heard these lectures often while we were growing up. He and Nana were so patient with us. In fact, chances are, when I visit with your mom, we will talk about these steps. The hardest one for her will be to forgive herself."

Susan paused, but Mason did not add any comments. "By the way, I will be talking on the phone with your mother tomorrow," Susan said. "Do you want me to tell her about the abortion? Or would you rather tell her yourself?"

"You can tell her. I'm not sure when I'll feel comfortable talking with her."

"Tomorrow I plan to take you both to school. You might gather up your books and do any homework. What about dirty gym clothes? Did you bring any home for the weekend laundry? Ask Margo if she has any. I'll call you for dinner in about thirty minutes."

Susan went to the stove, poured hot water out of the kettle into a cup, and added a tea bag. She sat at the kitchen table as the potatoes boiled on the stove. "How ironic," she thought. "Here we are rejoicing because Gennie is recuperating from her bridge jump, while Judith's father has cavalierly orchestrated the end of the fetus's life that Mason and Judith created. Both happened early Sunday morning. For selfish reasons, I am upset that this life has been ended. Walter and I would have gladly adopted and raised this baby. We are so frustrated because we can't seem to get pregnant. What I especially dislike is that neither Judith nor Mason had a chance to talk it out with other family members. Of course Judith had the prerogative to do what she felt was right—it's just that maybe I could have convinced her that our adopting it would have been best. But no need to fret over what is already done. Just get up and finish cooking the supper."

Will had called earlier and said he was going to visit with Gennie, so just Susan and the kids had dinner together. Susan told them that the next day she would linger around home close to the phone in case they needed to call her. If for any reason they felt overwhelmed, she could come to the school within minutes. "I don't anticipate any problems, but I will be here if you feel uncomfortable."

The next morning, after Susan had dropped Mason and Margo off at school, she called Gennie.

"Hi, Gennie. Is this a good time to talk? I just deposited both kids at their schools but told them I would be here in the house waiting if they needed any help. I think I'm safe being on the phone right now."

"Thank you, Susan, for staying with them. I sure do appreciate it, and Will does too, although he may not express it. I know I have thrown everyone into turmoil."

"How are you feeling? Do you still have a sitter with you? What are the doctors telling you?"

"The pain is tolerable—getting better. I can't use crutches, because of my dislocated shoulder, so until they put a walking cast on my ankle, I am virtually immobile. Yes, my sitter is here—she is supposed to prevent me from trying suicide again, but I'm not mobile enough to even attempt it if I wanted to." Gennie chuckled but realized that Susan didn't see the humor in her expression. "I am trying to decrease my pain medications. I don't like to be sedated. I'll have lots of time to think."

"Maybe you need to have a psychiatrist chaperone you through your thoughts. Has that been suggested?"

"Yes, one has come by, but he wasn't happy with my refusal to tell him the reason for my jumping. How are the kids doing?"

"I don't know what to tell you, since I expect that your psyche is in a fragile state. How straightforward can I be? We have never been soft-soapers with each other."

"I've had many hours to chastise myself; I don't think you can add to my distress," Gennie said. "What I need now is an insight into how I can rebuild my relationships with the family."

"Both of the children need an answer to 'Why?' Mason thinks he knows the answer: that the distressing news of Judith's pregnancy and your disappointment in him made you jump. Margo is totally confused. Suddenly she has been thrust into an adult world that makes no sense."

"I can't tell anyone why. Ever. That's the conundrum I am faced with."

"But don't you see? The children are shouldering the responsibility; they think you are disappointed in them."

"How am I going to change their perception and possibly repair our relationship?"

Susan pondered the question but could not find an answer. "One thing I do want to tell you is that Judith's parents arranged for her to have an abortion. She is transferring to an all-girls school and has been forbidden to see or talk with Mason."

"How sad. Please hug him for me. I know he's hurting."

"I'm going home for the weekend and have asked Mama and Papa M to take care of both Margo and Mason. Papa M said he wants Mason to go out to the farm and help him this weekend, which may be therapeutic. Physical labor somehow helps cleanse the mind. I'll stop by Sunday evening on my way back to your house."

"I asked Will to bring the kids here to see me, but he said the relationship between him and Mason is ice-cold—not that it ever was that great—so he's not sure they'll want to be with him. Or me."

"I think the kids are trying to sort out their feelings. I'll try to coax them, but I see no point in forcing them, since you'll be home in a few weeks."

"I want to apologize to them, and I just plain miss them."

In the afternoon, when Susan picked the kids up from school, both were quiet.

"Okay, how did it go? Did your friends treat you differently?"

Mason replied first. "Valerie came and had lunch with me. She is so kind. Otherwise, I was treated like a pariah—like damaged merchandise because my mom tried to commit suicide. No one wanted to make eye contact."

"And what about you, Margo?"

"Kinda the same. I could hear the whispering behind me and see people pointing. I think they looked at me like I was a freak. A couple of friends came up and said they were sorry. No one acted ugly, just really distant."

"Do you understand that most people view suicide as a strange solution? We all internalize the thought: 'What if one of my parents or family members attempted that? What would I do? What would I feel?' I don't think they are unkind; they just don't know how to feel or what to say."

Mason said, "But I don't know what to think. Isn't suicide rejection? Her problems were greater than her love for us."

"I don't think she loves you less. I think the problem she faced so overwhelmed her that she did not see a solution. Should she have thought about the consequences? Yes. Are we always emotionally stable and unselfish? No. There will be times when we don't have the answers. As much as she needs to forgive herself, I think you need to realize that you should forgive her too. She didn't intend to hurt you. We are all sharing the same confusion and pain. Talk to me or Mama M if you need to confide in a professional counselor, and we will seek out help."

Chapter 15

Will's visit to Gennie started with a tentative kiss. He acted as if she were a mere acquaintance or perhaps fragile. The sitter left the room.

"How are you doing?" he asked.

"I'm much better. Anxious to get out of here and go home. How are things going with you at work—and with the children?

"Work is difficult. Trying to find people to fill Herb's job is challenging. Some managers are stepping up; others aren't."

"What do you think of us—our future?"

"All I know is that I have done nothing wrong. What you imagine you saw is your problem, not mine."

"I'm still not ready to whitewash the whole incident. My gut feeling is to go to the DA and let the consequences happen."

"Find someone who will collaborate with your version of the story, and they may listen to you. No one else is raising a question."

"You have no guilt or complicity in Herb's death? You think you have gotten away with the perfect crime?"

"Damn it! You are not going to browbeat me into any type of confession. An accident happened. We move on from here." His jaw tightened and now his right eye lid twitched, He reached up to rub his eye.

Gennie knew she could not make any decisions until she became mobile. Although she did not want to be the one to ruin his career and all he had worked on for so long, she did want him to face the consequences of his actions. "Is there justice?" she thought. "And would justice be accomplished in the long run if she did nothing? Could she rely on that well-worn phrase 'The wheels of justice turn slowly but grind exceedingly fine'?" She didn't know.

Will's face reflected his tiredness. The responsibility of running five supermarkets without upper management in place weighed heavily on his shoulders. Herb had assumed the major share of supervising the stores.

"Go home and get some rest," she told him. "I'm doing okay here. Bring the kids next time."

Gennie hated that their relationship had been reduced to this barely tolerant alliance. Will could sculpt a scenario portraying him as the victim of an emotional wife and a drunken partner. Her credibility had been damaged by jumping. It could be argued that only a mentally imbalanced individual attempted suicide. So if she came forward with her story, would anyone even listen to her? Instead of trying Will, they could accuse her of mental instability and irresponsible behavior.

This time, before she took any action, she needed to consider the ramifications on their children. They were already suffering from her actions. Any definitive decisions would have to wait until her discharge, and it could be six weeks before that occurred.

Gennie's mind went back to that decision on the bridge—just an infinitesimal fraction of a second had existed between her thoughts of grappling with a solution and the tantalizing image of escaping. Remembering that moment sent a bolt of fear through her body, even now. She broke out in trembling insecurity, still questioning the why of her actions and the bigger why of her survival against such odds.

During these few weeks in the hospital when Gennie had been immobile and under pain medication, she'd had little time to ponder all the events that had happened. The first days her sitters had kept the television on from early morning until its sign-off at midnight. Now she asked that the television time be limited. She enjoyed the *Today Show* with Dave Garraway, one or two soaps in the afternoon, and perhaps an evening variety show, but otherwise, she wanted to read or write. Because she was using only aspirin for pain and was able to sit in a wheelchair, she asked a nurse if she could have some paper and a pen. The nurse brought in a tablet of blank lined progress notes the doctors used in the charts for their daily remarks. Gennie wanted to sort out her thoughts, and jotting them down helped.

In the past, she hadn't found the time or inclination to philosophize and hadn't thought about the meaning and implications of justice. Granted, every school day of her life, she had recited the "Pledge of Allegiance" with the ending stanza "with liberty and justice for all," but that had not caused her to reflect on its interpretation.

"First, how do I define justice?" she thought. "Fairness. Penalty—maybe reward." She wrote that at the top of the page. She remembered, from when she'd studied the US Constitution in the eighth grade, a photo of a statue of Lady Justice in the front of the Supreme Court building. Blindfolded, holding scales in one hand and a sword in the other, the lady was depicted as listening and making wise decisions.

Gennie remembered the saying "a rush to justice."

"Could justice be fast, sudden, and overwhelming, like rapids cascading over boulders in a mountain river?" she thought. "An immediate reflexive response with no pondering?"

"Or could it wait patiently, languishing in a deep pool or placid lake, and later surface? And perhaps let the perpetrator believe he had evaded detection and judgment?"

"Or maybe it might ebb and flow like waves on a beach, teasing and taunting for years before reaching a verdict—delayed, deferred, wavering.

"If a public trial is held, one learns of a decision. But if no trial happens, who is the arbitrator of justice? Do onlookers recognize if the suspected person receives adequate punishment or reward?" Gennie rested her head against the high woven cane back of the wheelchair. All of this thoughtful philosophizing tired her brain. Yet she had to come to some kind of conclusion if she were to find peace of mind.

When Alice returned from burying Herb in Oregon, Susan went to visit her. Although they didn't see each other often, they interacted on the same wavelength.

Without mentioning Mason's personal problem, Susan discussed the challenges the children were facing at school. Alice commiserated and was thankful that her two children were preschoolers. She said the children were accustomed to Herb working long hours and not being around. She said they missed him mostly at night—and so did Alice—because he'd tried to be home for supper with them, even if he'd gone back to work afterward.

"Something is troubling me," Alice said. "A lawyer who seems to work closely with some newspaper reporters, and whom Will called 'an ambulance chaser,' has called me a few times. He first approached me at the ER and was at Herb's funeral, hovering in the background. He asked me if I thought it a strange set of circumstances that Gennie would try to commit suicide the day after Herb's tragic death."

"And what did you say?"

"I asked him to explain his insinuation. He said that in our society, it's not unusual for extramarital affairs to occur. I told him I had never had any cause to suspect Herb of any infidelity and I didn't want his character besmirched when he wasn't here to defend himself."

"Living in Petaluma, I certainly have no inside information for you, but I would never suspect it of either Herb or Gennie," Susan replied and then paused for a reflective moment. "But I also would have never predicted a suicide attempt either."

"This fellow has put this thought in my brain, and like an itch, I seem to have to scratch it on occasion. Has Gennie said why she jumped?"

"No, she just says it is between her and Will and they will work it out."

"That's one way to get your husband's attention." Her remark sounded catty, very unlike Alice's usual attitude in conversations.

"What about your plans for the future?" Susan asked. "Have you had time to think about it yet?"

"Everyone counsels me not to make any decisions hastily. I don't feel I can concentrate on my job at the library just yet. The university has been most considerate, so maybe in another four weeks. Ultimately, my heart and home are in the Northeast. Mom is going to stay one more week, and then she's heading home. She thinks I will be happier with my family close by, but I hate to give up this gorgeous climate."

"I understand. Herb was your anchor. I don't think he would expect you to stay here."

The back door opened, and two energetic preschool-aged children burst into the room, with the nanny and grandmother trailing behind. The adult conversation ended, and soon Susan left for home.

A week went by before Alice called the corporate office and asked for Phyllis. She made a luncheon date for the following day at an outside café located in a sprawling outdoor mall. Located close to upscale boutiques, it attracted the fashionable ladies who lunched socially. After they were seated Phyllis offered her condolences. Alice told her of the lawyer's suggestion that there might be a liaison between Gennie and Herb.

"I am seeking both the truth and reassurance," Alice told Phyllis. "If you have any inclination to think there was such a relationship, I would appreciate your insight."

"I know of no incoming or outgoing telephone calls between Herb and Gennie. In fact, Gennie seldom called here, even for Will. Gennie and I had a friendship before I came to work here, and occasionally we met for lunch. Of course, I saw her and you at the Christmas party and summer picnics. In a company like this, there can be some rumors and innuendos, but neither Herb nor Will ever seemed to be straying from his wife. I can say that unequivocally. I know the circumstances of both tragedies occurring back-to-back made for a lot of gossipy tongue wagging, but I don't know of any substance to this hearsay. Herb seemed like a good ol' hardworking farm boy who felt lucky to have a career, an educated wife, and darling children. If anyone expressed how lucky and blessed he was, he did—often. I think it would be sad if you doubted Herb's faithfulness. He appeared devoted to both you and the boys."

"Thank you, Phyllis. I did want reassurance. My gut feeling toward Gennie and my husband was positive. I didn't want to accuse Gennie unless I had factual information. I will tell this lawyer guy there is no story and to get lost."

Chapter 16

Lem felt joy every time he approached the land near the airfield. He knew he had done the right thing: buying it and then reselling half of it back to the Nakamuras. Both of the families had thrived. The Nakamuras had chosen to build a rustic retail shop adjacent to the roadway in front of their home. In the rear they had built greenhouses to perpetuate small plants and get them ready for retail sale.

Lem, with Joe as his overseer, had planted most of his cultivated land in small shrubs, incubating and nourishing them until they could be sold either wholesale or retail. With minimum shipping, they could offer good prices to all the developers and homeowners. The housing boom had continued to flourish in California.

The oldest sons of Joe and the Nakamuras had sought agricultural degrees: Joe's from Cal Poly and the Nakamuras' from UC Davis. Lem hoped that Mason could visualize a future on this land too.

Lem had picked Mason up from home, and now they were driving through the gates of the farm, arriving at Joe's house, where the living room had been made into an office. Joe came out to greet them on the front porch.

"I brought some good, strong help with me this morning. You know my grandson, Mason? What's on the work schedule today?" Lem asked.

"We need to pot the foot-high Scotch pines and trim them into a cone shape. In a couple of months or so, we can fine-trim them again and sleeve the cans in red and green holiday paper and put bows on them for shipping the last week in November. It's not heavy work, so one of my younger sons and one of the Nakamura boys will join you. Can you stay and supervise, Lem?"

"Sure, just show me which plants you want done."

"I'll go out there and get you started. There are about five hundred ready for this week, and in a couple of weeks, there should be five hundred more."

They drove past rows of various sizes of evergreen shrubs. When they came upon the short pines, they saw stacked rows of pots lying on their sides nearby. Joe suggested that they make shorter stacks and randomly distribute them among the work area. While they did that, he would go back for the necessary tools and the two youngsters.

After giving gloves and instructions to all on how to extract the plants and place them in the clay pots, Joe left. Lem let the boys decide how to divide the work. He watched as Mason talked to the boys and asked questions. He liked how Mason seemed to fit in easily.

After doing a row, Mason said, "Let's stop for a minute. There must be a more efficient way to do this." Although the two boys were younger, they were more experienced, and Mason asked for their opinions. They decided Lem should be the only trimmer. Lem agreed but said the pots would have to be lifted onto the back of the flatbed truck. He couldn't stoop over all day long. So the boys got into a rhythm of potting the plants, putting them up on the truck to be trimmed, and returning them to their original holes. By noon they were more than halfway done, and Lem suggested they go to his place for lunch. He had constructed a small apartment at the back of the property, and the two younger boys were curious about it. Lem considered it his bachelor quarters. Margaret had no interest in moving to this farm property, but Lem wanted a quiet place to hide out. Only one thousand square feet, it had been planned for efficiency. He made ham sandwiches for all of them, poured milk, and served a candy bar for dessert. In thirty minutes they went back out to the fields. By four o'clock they were finished. It had been a productive day.

On the drive back to town, Lem said to Mason, "I know you may not be ready to make any major decisions about your future, but this property can be yours if you are interested. Otherwise, I think I owe it to Joe and his kids to sell it to them when I can no longer work out there."

"Papa M, I am in such a quandary right now; I'm not certain what I want to do. I'm sure I should ultimately go to college, but my current thought is to take a year off, get some work experience, and then decide what courses to take."

No more words were spoken for a few minutes, and then Mason continued, "Don't get me wrong—I am most appreciative of your offer. The events of the last few weeks have made me question everything. If I hadn't promised Pops when I was twelve that I would graduate from high school regardless of what happened, I think I may have dropped out this week. Pops foresaw a difficult time with Dad, but he could have not seen Mom's suicide attempt. No one did."

"That is precisely why I am mentioning this now. Cultivating crops and finding new ways of agrofarming can be a challenge but also a fulfilling career. It would be gratifying if you chose to farm this land, but I would be just as content to sell it to Joe's kids. It's an open offer that you can accept or reject."

"Life has been so complicated, and my grades are suffering," Mason replied. "I need to get back to studying and graduate from school."

Chapter 17

At All Saints Hospital there was a knock on the door. Gennie's sitter went to open it and welcomed the priest into the room. He walked to Gennie's bedside and extended his hand. "I am the hospital chaplain. My name is Father John Landon." A young man, his round face seemed to be puffed up by his clerical collar; his cheeks were rosy-pink. His blue eyes focused on the face of this new acquaintance.

"I visit all patients here at the hospital, but I always ask permission. Do you mind if I visit with you?"

"Not at all; I welcome it," Gennie said.

"I have been told you are progressing well. Also, I notice on your information sheet that you answered in the religious affiliation square 'None.' That is an odd answer; usually 'agnostic' or 'nonbeliever' is noted."

"My parents did not raise us with any religious affiliation. Dad's folks had been Methodists, but Mother opposed any religious training. She did not want us to go to Sunday school. When a friend would ask me to spend the night on a Saturday, we would go to her church the next morning. Mother seemed okay with that, but she didn't want us to be constant members. However, almost twenty years ago, I became a student nurse here for about eight months, so I experienced the daily Morning Prayer and weekly evening vespers."

"My dear, what caused you to leave the nursing program?"

"It happened right after Pearl Harbor; my boyfriend had enlisted and wanted to get married. I couldn't continue in nursing school and be married."

"Things have changed. I think this year they are graduating their very last class of students who will be residents. From now on, all students will live off campus, go to college, and just do token classes here at the hospital."

"The old way had its advantages. We were a cohesive group because we went to the same classes, ate together, and studied together. For the short time I lived here, I learned a lot."

"Now are you willing to talk about what brings you back to this hospital as a patient?" Father John's sweet face turned serious.

"Yes, a moral dilemma developed, and at the moment I could not see a solution. When I went to walk on the bridge, I only hoped to clear my head and straighten out my thinking. Until I jumped, I had never anticipated suicide—ever—in my life. Obviously, the damage I created, whether dead or a survivor, has overwhelmed my children. But at the time, I was thinking only of myself—my own selfish self."

"And can you share what that moral dilemma was—is?"

"No, it concerns my husband. I have done nothing wrong. I did not commit any crime. It has to remain between us. I, at the time, thought I could not live with the circumstances, but now I have decided I must."

"And can you forgive yourself for compromising your usual moral position?"

"Ah, you have the ability to see the problem, don't you?" Gennie looked at his youthful countenance with a new appreciation.

Father John continued, "I cannot imagine facing such a challenge without a religious belief system in place. Of course, being a cradle Episcopalian, it is unfathomable to me to be without God's anchor, to face such a dilemma without a faith and prospects to pray."

"I do remember praying as I jumped. I said, 'Please God, take care of my children, and save Mason's unborn baby.' But that didn't happen. His girlfriend had an abortion."

"So you faced multiple problems."

"Yes, and unfortunately our son, Mason, thinks that this pregnancy out of wedlock was the reason I jumped. That's not so. But I can't tell him the real reason, because of the moral, legal, and financial complications. And now I have told you more than I intended."

"I am not here to pass judgment on your decision. I would like to offer you solace and a way to redeem your spirit. Besides the Gideon Bible, we have an Episcopal prayer book in every room. Since you are familiar with the Morning Prayer, I suggest you read the text. I think you will find the forgiveness you are seeking. The general confession text begins, 'Almighty and most merciful Father, we have strayed from thy ways like lost sheep.' Doesn't that immediately give you a picture of losing one's way not intentionally but inadvertently? God is ready to forgive you and can offer you a sense of peace."

"I have often thought that if I'd stayed in training for the three years, I would have wanted to join the church. I found much there that I enjoyed."

"I will return tomorrow, and we can talk some more," Father John said. He then recited a closing prayer: "The grace of our Lord Jesus Christ, and the love of God, and the fellowship of the Holy Ghost, be with us evermore. Amen."

"Thank you for coming; I'll look forward to tomorrow."

For the next month, Father John stopped by to talk often—never to inquire further into Gennie's dilemma but to offer new passages to read in the Bible and prayer book. He shared questions and answers about the text, and they discussed how relevant it was to present-day living.

During one of their discussions, Gennie asked, "Do you have any insight into why I survived the bridge jump, when most people perish?"

"No, my dear, I do not presume to know how God works, nor do I know if a quirk of aerodynamics caused your salvation. Why, in a tornado or earthquake, do you survive and your neighbor is killed? I do know you can pray that you may make your life more meaningful but not dwell on why you were spared. Be thankful for each day, and ask for His guidance. I believe that God has a plan for each one of us, but there are many things none of us will ever understand. That's where faith comes in."

Early one morning, the orthopedist strutted into Gennie's room as if he were king of all the bones of the world—solid or broken. He decided that Gennie had healed sufficiently to receive a walking cast, and the fractured wrist could be wrapped with just a half cast. This represented freedom for Gennie. She could be mobile and go home. Once the casts were changed and after they dried, the physiotherapist would teach Gennie how to walk and deal with the limitations of her wrist.

When Father John returned, Gennie greeted him with the happy proclamation: "I'm going home tomorrow!"

"What joyous news! Thanks be to God." He paused and then added, "I had hoped we would have many more conversations, but I will trust that you and God will continue without me."

"I would like you to advise me on what church on the peninsula I might go to. Maybe you have a favorite rector?"

"I think St. Paul's in Redwood City might be a good fit. The pastor of the church, Father Stephen Stanley is a little older but very outgoing, especially with the youth groups, which might appeal to your children. Chances are that he has ongoing inquirer's classes, but I will be glad to call him. If you'd like him to come to your home and talk with you, I think he would; he has the energy of an athletic teenager."

"That sounds great. I have one other request: I'd like to go down to the chapel for a moment to reminisce and pray. Can my sitter wheel me down there?"

"Why don't I take you, and we can talk and pray. We can ask your sitter to come and pick you up in about twenty minutes."

The small, quiet, intimate chapel opened to the first floor of the hospital. The center aisle divided the carved mahogany benches, burnished with weekly waxing, on either side of the room. Velvet burgundy cushions matched the colors in the stained glass window of Jesus with young children that hung over the altar.

"It's just as I remembered it. I am so glad it hasn't changed."

Father John headed for the front pew. "More legroom," he explained. He placed Gennie's wheelchair facing the altar and then turned in the pew so he was facing her, his feet in the aisle.

"I have brought you a prayer book and an inquirer's pamphlet for you to take home with you. I had hoped you could read them here and I could answer questions, but Father Stanley in Redwood City can help you with any queries."

"I feel that I am a blank slate when it comes to religion and Bible studies. But I also think that the emptiness I feel is my soul searching for answers," she replied.

They continued to talk for a few minutes. When the sun shone through the stained-glass window and onto Father John's face, Gennie realized that he was older than she'd first thought. Although his face had a cherubic roundness, gray hair mingled in his sideburns, and small laugh wrinkles fanned out from his eyes. He felt her gaze, and they exchanged smiles.

"Tell me," Gennie asked. "Do you have a parish besides being a hospital chaplain?"

"Yes, my parish is a small mission church in the Castro district. Traditionally a working-family community, it has recently had an influx of homosexual males, which has presented myriad challenges. I am also a chaplain for Shriner's Hospital. All Saints has an outreach program to our community, so I try to coordinate that."

"You handle many demands. If I have questions after I return home, may I call you? If I come to the city, would it be 'kosher' for me to ask you to lunch?"

"Of course. I would be pleased if you wanted to stay in touch. One of the downsides of being a chaplain is that you often never see the patients again after they are discharged. I stapled my business card inside of that pamphlet. Feel free to call at any time. My secretary is in the office from nine in the morning until noon. So call a day in advance, and I can call you back."

Father John arose from the pew and gave Gennie a pat on the shoulder. "I'll give you a few moments to pray by yourself. I wish you well."

He faced the altar and said a short prayer, made the sign of the cross, and genuflected. Gennie heard his footsteps as he left the chapel, but she could not turn to look. Tears streamed down her cheeks as if she had lost a dear friend. Father John had brought her the hope and forgiveness she had been searching for. She knew he had opened an opportunity for her salvation—not only in a religious sense but also in the sense that she could accept her own shortcomings.

The next morning Gennie couldn't remember when she had ever felt so giddy with excitement. Going home meant that she could return to some semblance of normalcy and not be treated as a dependent patient. Granted, she couldn't resume all of her spousal, parenting, and housekeeping responsibilities, but she would be ambulatory and could participate in the real world.

Early in the afternoon, Will came to her room and said, "Your chauffer has arrived." He too seemed to be cheerful about her discharge and arrival at home.

"Come over here and give me a big kiss. I have missed being able to hug you. With this arm cast, I'm still not very cuddly, but I'm so glad you are here. I am ready to go."

On the way home Gennie said, "I've had a lot of time to think—about me, about the kids, and about us."

"That's not a luxury I have had. I seem to be hours behind all the time and never have a chance to catch my breath."

"I do think we need to evaluate how much fun we are having. The days and weeks go by, and we hardly see each other. It's been that way for quite a while. We didn't get married to just be worker bees flitting in and out of the beehive."

She looked over at Will as he turned to access the freeway entrance, and saw his jaw stiffen and his eyelid twitch. "I don't want to get into an argument with you," he said.

"Nor do I. I think we have to set some time aside to discuss our future goals. Even before Herb died and your upper management was in place, you were still looking for more stores, more acquisitions, and building a warehouse hub; the list of your ambitions is endless. Your family needs some of your time. But to switch subjects—have you had a chance to talk with either Mason or Margo?"

"No, it's not hard for them to avoid me. I know that between Susan and Mom, they've been scheduled and accounted for. The climate between us is definitely cool, and Margo especially has become sassy and foulmouthed."

"Would you be open to family counseling? All of us need to find a way to work together."

"Let's see how well things settle down, now that you'll be at home. I think your jump is no longer the topic du jour. Susan has arranged for our housekeeper or her cousin to come by each morning for a while. I think the kids will welcome things getting back to normal; I know I will."

"Have you talked with Alice? Has she made any plans?"

"I went over to her house this week with the life-insurance check. The insurance company had to wait for the autopsy and toxicology reports. They really had no questions when they read the police descriptions. The cause of death was an occipital skull fracture with internal bleeding, and the alcohol level was considered high—consistent with drunkenness." Gennie nodded, not meeting Will's eyes. "The police report stated that no one noticed any odd behavior other than Herb's boisterousness."

Will continued, "Alice said she sent in her resignation to the university. She plans to get the house ready for sale. There are always a lot of legal issues with a death, and she is slowly dealing with those. She thinks it will take her another two or three months before she moves back to the Northeast. I understand her need to return to what she considers home. It had been a long and hard decision for her to move west in the first place. She has many lifelong friends and family back there."

"Yes, I agree. Now is the time to do this while the boys are still preschool age and can more easily adjust. I'll give her a call in the next few days."

So this would be the scenario from now on: Will had committed a crime and gotten away with it. His dutiful wife chose not to squeal. Their future equaled status quo.

Chapter 18

Mason and Margo greeted Gennie when she got home. "I'm glad you're here! I've missed you so much," Mason said, hugging his mom.

Margo said, "The only reason I'm here is because Mason said he would never drive me anywhere unless I showed up."

"Margo, dear, that's an endearing way to greet your mother. Come over here and give me a hug."

Margo stood across the room from her mother and made no motion forward. Gennie resisted the urge to hobble across the room and smack her with her casted arm. "I love you, Margo, and want to make amends, but if you feel that angry, you are free to leave."

"Don't send her off," Mason said. "She has found a group of misfits who accept her, and I'm afraid she is going the hippie route."

Gennie acknowledged her son's advice. "Okay, Margo, are you willing to have a civilized conversation? Please know I have many things to tell you, much to confess. I certainly did not make good decisions. I do love you and want us to be a family again. Let us sit down and have dinner together. I trust that Mason is trying to help you."

"I have some friends waiting for me. I'm out of here. See you later."

"No, Margo, you're not going anywhere until after dinner. Are your friends parked out in front? Will, please go out and ask them to join us. Mama M sent over dinner, and I know she always makes enough for an army."

"Don't bother Dad, they won't come in."

Gennie said, "Give it a try Will. I'd like to meet them."

Margo rolled her eyes, "Whatever."

When Will returned he announced that the kids filling the auto had declined his invitation. "They said, 'Margo knows how to get in touch with us, so we'll see her later.'"

Margo murmured, "I told you so."

Gennie recognized Margo's belligerence, but she also saw the telltale signs of puberty: those nasty pustules of acne. She realized that Margo had been caught in the perfect storm: her mother going berserk and the arrival of a tsunami of adolescent hormones.

Once Gennie became situated at the dinner table, Will brought in the hot casserole from the stove, and the kids brought out the salad and set out the silverware and plates. Gennie asked Margo what activities were going on at school and what had happened to the group of friends she had known since kindergarten.

"They all abandoned me after the headlines in the newspaper. They whispered behind my back, and no one wanted to sit with me at lunch. You'll see when you go back to your bridge group and garden club; you'll get snubbed too."

"Well, I hope not. Surely adult women aren't that unkind. Girls at your age are particularly cliquey and self-righteous. You know yourself, Margo, that if the popular girl declares that Cheery Cherry is the only lipstick to wear, suddenly all the girls run out to get that color. No one wants to be different. And my suicide attempt, so well publicized, made you different. So do you miss your old friends and want to get back with them?"

"Nah, these guys are really cool kids."

"They are geeks," Mason added.

Gennie focused her gaze on Mason. "Excuse me? Geeks?"

"Yeah, there are four groups of kids in high school, and some of these kids that Margo is hooking up with are already in high school. The groups are the socials, the sport jocks and jockesses, the nerds, and the geeks.

"Okay,"said Gennie, "let me sort this out.The socials and the sports stars are self-explanatory. The nerds, I suppose, are the studious ones, and the geeks—are they the social outcasts, perhaps by choice?"

Mason answered. "They mimic the styles of the beatnik hippies. They enjoy bringing attention to their messiness. They are often sent home because they dress as if they just rolled out of bed."

Gennie turned from Mason and looked at Margo. "Margo, is that what attracts you? To prove to people that if they are going to treat you differently, then you will show them how bizarre you can be?"

"It's not like that at all. These friends stick together. We are there for each other. We choose not to be with the school snobs. And I'm tired of being questioned; I want to leave the table."

"No, stay and finish eating. I'll see if I can catch up with Mason's life. You can eat and listen."

Gennie looked across the table at Will and felt thankful that he just listened and did not interject with any smart remarks.

"Are things any better for you at school, Mason?"

"I felt lost the first week or two, but I think my head is screwed on correctly now. Papa M asked me to work on the farm on weekends, and I like that. I lunch with Valerie occasionally, and she still keeps in touch with Judith. They both are sad that they won't graduate together. Also, Judith isn't very fond of the all-girls school."

"You mentioned graduation. Have you had any discussions with your school counselors about college?"

"As I told Papa M, I don't think I'll go to college right away. I want to take a year off and work on an oil rig or maybe be a lumberjack—something physical, not mental."

"Is that some kind of self-imposed punishment?"

"No, I really don't know what career I want to follow. Maybe a year without books and studying will help me figure it out."

Gennie looked over at Will for his reaction. He shrugged his shoulders as if to say it was news to him. But he continued his silence, seeming to relish the home-cooked meal and realizing Gennie could extract more information from the kids than he could.

Gennie asked about homework. Mason said he had to study for a test. Margo said she didn't have any, but she agreed to bring her school books for her mother to see what she was studying. Mom had won round one, but many more skirmishes were to come.

The next day Gennie called Margo's school and asked for the dean of girls. Small talk about her recuperation started the conversation. Gennie then asked about her observations of Margo's new friends and her opinion of the circumstances.

"Girls at this age use ostracizing as a social tool. They bully and/or ignore. The victim is often seen as less attractive physically, or inappropriately dressed. In Margo's case, I think they sensed her vulnerability because of your suicide attempt and snubbed her. I'd have thought that Margo would fight back or at least trivialize it, like 'no big deal.' She was a lost child at that moment and didn't know what to do. Actually, Mrs. Mueller, I see a few of these hurtful incidences every year. When I first became dean, I would call the girls into my office and try to negotiate a settlement. When that didn't work, I had the mothers of the offending girls come in together. That only seemed to make matters worse; the girls blamed the ostracized one for 'getting them in trouble with the dean.' It only inflamed the issue."

"I wasn't sure if you could arbitrate a settlement or not. I don't even think Margo wants that at this point. I am concerned about the new friends she has found. Our son, Mason, describes them as the underbelly of school society and thinks they are dabbling with marijuana or other substances. Would you assess them this way?"

"I don't think our middle-school kids are into substance abuse, but they are being courted by the high-school kids, and that is glamorous to the younger ones. These kids are those on the fringe—call them misfits, maybe—whose families are often broken and struggling financially. Some of their parents are using drugs and alcohol, experimenting with LSD.

"Do you think we should seek counseling for the family? Do you have any recommendations?"

"Yes, I think this is an excellent idea. What Margo needs now is a firm and loving family. Without assuming I know your particular situation, I suspect there were problems leading up to your suicide attempt and repercussions for the whole family afterward. It is normal for you to feel guilty for causing this upheaval, and it will be difficult to be strong and decisive when dealing with Margo. Since she is in the eighth grade, graduating this year, I would not transfer her at this time. Depending on what progress you make and the counselor's recommendation, a move could be made as she enters high school. Adjacent school districts are often lenient in cases like this. I'll send you my mimeographed list of counselors for you. It is a frequent request. I wish you well, and call again if you need me."

Gennie then called the pediatrician's office and talked with the office nurse, who had known Margo since infancy.

"I am sorry to hear of your…" She paused as she tried to find the proper word and then added, "Mishap. Are you feeling better?"

Gennie said, "Yes I improve every day." She then told her about Margo's reaction and change of friends. She asked for references for counselors and wondered if the pediatrician would be open to a conference later.

"Rather than label it a 'conference,' why don't we see if Margo doesn't need some immunizations to start high school? That would be a more natural approach, and she wouldn't have her defenses up."

"That's a good idea. I'll check into the counselors on the list you send me and then see how things progress. Thanks."

Next she called Alice, who seemed most cordial and basically repeated the information Will had related to her. They agreed to get together soon for lunch.

Gennie got up to go to the sideboard for some more coffee, when the phone rang: Phyllis from Will's office. She hadn't resigned as planned, because of the tragic events that had happened so quickly.

"What are your plans for lunch?" Phyllis asked.

"I'll be right here, I'm afraid, for the next couple of weeks."

"Why don't I pick up some sandwiches or salads—whatever looks the most scrumptious—and come over?"

"That would be great, as long as you aren't bringing me bad news like last time."

Phyllis laughed and said, "Hopefully that only happens once in a lifetime. See you soon."

A little later Phyllis let herself in the side door, saying, "Yoo-hoo, I'm here."

"Come on into the den," Gennie announced. "It is so good to see a familiar friend; I felt so isolated in the hospital."

Phyllis bent over and hugged her seated hostess.

"I picked up a shrimp salad with deviled eggs and got some wheat crackers."

"Sounds good. There's an old pot of coffee still on the warmer; you might pour us each a cup."

They exchanged their news of the family, and Gennie expressed her concern about Margo.

Phyllis said, "I know you have not divulged your reasons for jumping from the bridge, but I think I have put it all together and have a theory. Would you like to hear it?"

"Okay, but however close or far away you are from the truth, I will not acknowledge it one way or another. My decision is not to reveal—period."

"Since we both know that Will had gambled the company's money and put it into jeopardy, we know he needed to find a solution. He plied Herb with drink and then suggested you all go out on the cable car. He saw an opportunity to engage Herb in a jocular exchange of muscular challenge, and Herb lost his balance. Chances are that most passengers thought that this typified the usual camaraderie of friends. I do hate to think it was premeditated.

"What I have a problem with is that if I had not told you of the financial problems, you would have never suspected that Will had an ulterior motive. So you see, I have a guilt trip going on too."

"That's an interesting aspect I hadn't thought about. If you had not told me of the financial crisis, I would have been perplexed by all the circumstances and would not have seen any connection. But I also know you are not responsible for my decision to jump from the bridge. What I saw and what I knew had nothing to do with you. Please don't try to shoulder guilt that isn't yours."

Gennie took a sip of her coffee and then continued, "You have been such a stalwart employee; I really think you are the glue that keeps the company operating."

Phyllis served them both some salad. "I miss Herb tremendously. He cared for every customer who entered a store. Will, on the other hand, only cares for expansion, wanting to compete with any other grocery conglomerate. They had huge arguments, and I'm not sure where this company will go without Herb. In fact, Herb had hired and been mentoring a young man he liked. Their backgrounds are similar—both farm boys. He came to the last Christmas party, but he seems shy in crowds. You may not have met him."

"Describe him to me. What is his name?"

"His name is Neil. He is tall with wavy hair and a crooked smile. Pretty green eyes. Herb's death devastated him. They consulted each day, as Herb was grooming him to be the personnel director: recruiting, interviewing, and hiring new employees. Herb wanted to spend more time in the stores."

"Unfortunately, the group of our employees and their spouses has grown so large that I really don't get to meet and know them all," Gennie said.

"Well, Neil is a really nice young man." Phyllis started to twist her paper napkin with her fingers. "I told you I wouldn't bring you bad news, and it isn't bad at this time. However, I see it as a possible problem in the future. Do you want me to share my concern or keep it to myself?"

"Don't treat me like a fragile flower—or worse, a psychiatric time bomb. I'm not. I would much rather be aware of what is going on, and certainly Will does not share much information."

"Okay. I don't see this exploding in our faces right now—maybe never—but I do see its potential. Neil came to me expressing his concern about Will's behavior. He said that shortly after Herb's death, Will announced at each store that he needed to downsize employees, and he dismissed all of our Japanese American staff. They were in the minority—about five per store. Then he told Neil he could interview Japanese Americans but not hire them. Without his mentor, Neil came to me confused and perplexed. After thinking about it I proposed that he write a letter for Will to sign that stated Neil was following his boss's explicit directions and it did not reflect his opinion. So I typed up the letter and tucked it in between all the others for Will to sign, and he did it without reading it."

"You can be a clever lady, can't you?"

"Devious, perhaps. I guess I am supposed to be absolutely loyal to the company, but discrimination is becoming a huge social issue, and I don't want Neil's young career to be ruined. Neil has a copy of the letter, and so do I in the company files. At least that will prevent him from becoming the scapegoat if problems arise."

"Discrimination is becoming very heated in the southeastern states with Negro marches and street violence, but do you think the Japanese Americans are that militant?"

"Generally, I think the Japanese are respected by most people. Fifteen years after the war, they shouldn't be singled out. This is an obvious and blatant case of discrimination, but Will said since he owned the business, he could do what he wanted. It may not be easy to legally prove discrimination."

"I know that Will's dad has been encouraging him to look into incorporation. Do you know how far that has gotten? Whenever I ask him about it at home, he says, 'I don't want to talk about the office.'"

"The lawyer has been contacted and is supposed to be drawing up preliminary papers," Phyllis answered. "That's all I know. Now, about you—how much longer before you are rid of these casts?"

"In about ten days or two weeks, I can go to an orthopedist here at the clinic; I have all the films with me. Then I'll have some physiotherapy and should be able to drive. Hallelujah, I can hardly wait! I'm marking the days off my calendar."

"Since you will be housebound next week, we'll do this again. I'll call first."

After Phyllis left, Gennie went through the accumulated mail that Susan had stacked. Will had taken care of the bills. Her get-well cards from friends and neighbors had been forwarded to the hospital. One handwritten envelope piqued her curiosity: the return address was C. Kessler. That didn't ring a bell. "I'll bet it's one of those bothersome chain letters asking for a recipe or a handkerchief," she thought. What a pleasant surprise when the letter turned out to be her old bridge playing buddy, Sandy (Cassandra.) They had corresponded for a year or two after their first babies were born, but Sandy's husband relocated frequently because his career as a military man demanded it. Eventually, Gennie had found she no longer had a current address, and her Christmas cards had come back. At least eight years had passed since they had been in touch.

In the letter Sandy wrote that she'd seen the newspaper write-up about Gennie's jump and thought it had to be her old friend. Subsequent follow-up stories that told more of the facts of Gennie's life and family had confirmed her inkling. Sandy's husband had recently retired after twenty years in the military. They had bought and moved in to a house in Redwood City, and he hoped to get a private-sector defense job. Their four children kept Sandy busy. She wondered if Gennie still played bridge and if she would be interested in getting a foursome together. She gave her telephone number and asked Gennie to call if she were so inclined.

Chapter 19

For most of her life, Gennie had been an avid reader of *Life* magazine and the morning and evening newspapers. The articles about the Cold War, the restlessness of the young college kids, and the blatant experimental drug use at the universities by both the students and professors troubled her. She had not realized how it had drifted to the high-school level of students, who now viewed it as an enticing lifestyle with minimum rules and the acting out of the lyrics of the popular songs: to drop out, engage in free love, and be mindless flower children. One evening, while Gennie was watching a variety show on TV, a couple of singers with guitars sang a song that said, "I belong to the beat generation; I don't let anything trouble my mind…I belong to the beat generation, and everything's goin' just fine. Some people say I'm lazy and my life's a wreck. But that stuff doesn't faze me. I get unemployment checks. I run around in sandals and never even shave, and that's the way I wanna be when someone digs my grave." She thought, "When Hollywood performers glamorize a lifestyle, the kids are anxious to emulate the stars."

The use of marijuana and LSD could lower users' moral conscience to near zero. While the older generation found the global situations troubling and felt the world less safe, thus becoming more nervous, the youngsters wanted to ignore any ominous warnings and "just be cool, man; just chill out." Even in the closed, affluent community the Muellers lived in, one could not escape the harshness of the outside world, Gennie realized.

When Gennie and Will were in high school, the rebels had chosen alcohol as the drug of choice. It too had dire consequences. The current lack of knowledge about long-term repercussions of LSD and Mexican peyote concerned many parents. No one knew their sources or how much would cause an overdose. Amphetamines could still be legally obtained by prescription, and overdosing challenged the cardiovascular system and often resulted in death.

Gennie had not considered that Margo, at her tender age, would be at risk. Just a few short months ago, Margo had hosted a sleepover with three other girls, and the silliness, giggling, and little-girl antics had filled the night. Now Margo came home with the scent of cigarette smoke lingering on her clothes. She denied smoking but appeared to inhabit a smoky world.

Gennie became more active with chores around the house, and the two weeks until the cast removal went quickly.

Gennie chose a family counselor, who sent out questionnaires to all family members before the first appointment. Margo balked and filled it out with belligerence. Mason said that because he planned on leaving the household after graduation, his input seemed irrelevant, but he did answer the questions. Will relegated it as a waste of time and would not participate. Before Gennie went to the first appointment, she knew that without Will's cooperation, the idea of family counseling could hardly be viable.

She telephoned the counselor seeking his advice because Margo appeared marginally cooperating. She explained that because of her ongoing physiotherapy, it would be difficult to get to his office for a couple of weeks but she wanted his opinion on whether just mother-daughter sessions would be helpful.

"I feel that I have been raising these children by myself for years. My husband directs all his paternal energies toward his growing grocery chain. When I attempted suicide, I think I robbed my children of any security. I had been their lifeline." She paused, but the counselor said nothing. "Without my husband's—their father's—participation, do you see any reason for therapy?"

"Yes, I think it is worthwhile. Margo is still grasping for a reason to be with her new friends versus her old home life. She is confused about why you wanted to commit suicide, although she suspects it involved your disappointment in your son's illegitimate pregnancy. Is she looking for male approval because she has lacked it at home? Perhaps, but without your husband's cooperation, I don't think we can address that. In this therapeutic community, we look for the pluses we can work on and do not attempt to solve every problem. It will be worthwhile to have a few sessions and then reevaluate.

"Are the children ever going to forget completely?" he continued. "No, you have written on their lives' blackboard with paint, not chalk. It can never be erased. Through love and their maturity, this painful image may fade, and that is the best we can hope for."

Mason drove Margo to the first few appointments.

On her own, Gennie started writing notes to Margo and pinning them on her bed pillow. It often occurred after they had argued. Gennie, feeling frustrated, jotted down her thoughts and hopes for a compromise, always ending with "I love you." Written notes are irresistible to read, and she wanted that affectionate expression to be Margo's last thought before she slept.

When Sandy came over she and Gennie talked about their families. She said her husband had been stationed in England and Germany for most of his military career. While in England, they'd attended the Anglican Church and had recently joined the congregation of St. Paul's Episcopal in Redwood City. They attended the nine o'clock morning service—the children's worship. Sandy suggested that Gennie go at that time, and they could visit afterward. She liked Father Stanley and thought Gennie's family would too.

"What a coincidence," Gennie thought. She could hear Father John's voice in her head, stating, "Maybe not a coincidence but God showing you the way."

As they talked it became evident that Will and Sandy's husband, Kenneth, had had very different experiences in the war. Nevertheless, Gennie questioned Sandy about how the war had affected her husband's personality. When Gennie related how angry Will seemed to be—still—Sandy said she expected the difference may be that Will was drafted and Ken had planned a career in the military since he was a kid, carrying on the family tradition.

Sandy said, "After going to many military and veteran meetings, I know that anger and bad memories plague many vets. Most of these guys won't talk about their experiences. So if it gives you any assurance, there are many just like Will."

After a few weeks of physical therapy, Gennie started driving again. One evening Will drove up in a shiny new lipstick-red Cadillac Coupe DeVille and presented her the keys.

"To celebrate your recovery," he announced. "Jump in, and I'll show you all the newfangled switches." No one could miss this car. Its long tailfins appeared confiscated from fighter plane silhouettes, and the white hardtop made the car look like a convertible.

"If I wanted to reenter my normal social life unnoticed, this space-age chariot wouldn't let me," Gennie thought. "What will people think? I'll just assume that they think I am a brave and somewhat brazen woman, happy to be alive. Maybe if I look the part and act the part, I will be that person. Why not? It's better than crawling around trying not to be noticed."

With her driving and walking back to normal, she called Father John's secretary to ask when he would be available for lunch. They decided on a day, and the secretary put her name on his calendar.

When the day arrived, she drove down unfamiliar streets. Although the church was located close to All Saints Hospital, Gennie had not been a student long enough to prowl around investigating the nearby neighborhoods. People in front of their tired, old apartments and flats noticed her flashy car go by. "I am conspicuous and somewhat embarrassed," she thought. She pulled into the small parking lot next to the clapboard-sided church building with a sign that said, "Mission Castro."

Once inside the narthex, Gennie saw an open doorway labeled "Office" and tentatively entered. Bright sunlight beamed through a window and illuminated the uneven floorboards. Two vintage desks stood side by side, and both the secretary and Father John looked up as she entered the room. He immediately rose and walked around the desk to clasp her hand in both of his. After introductions he suggested that she come in and see the sanctuary. The plain, whitewashed walls and simple altar reminded her of an austere colonial church, not at all like later Episcopal churches. "I'm surprised at the lack of stained glass or carvings," Gennie remarked. "I thought it would be a lot like the hospital chapel."

"All Saints had moneyed donors to finance their building; this community has traditionally been poor or middle class, and the building reflects that."

Gennie didn't want to appear disapproving and added, "There is beauty in simplicity too."

"This building and Mission Delores escaped the fire that destroyed so much of the city after the 1906 earthquake," Father John explained. "As a result, this area has more preearthquake homes. Are you ready for lunch? Do you know where we are going?"

"Well, as a matter of fact, I do have an idea," Gennie replied. "I read a review in the *Examiner* about a small Italian spot in Bernal Heights. I thought that might be far enough away so you won't run into many of your parishioners."

They walked outside into the bright sunshine, and Father John let out a whistle when he saw the red Cadillac. "No one will miss this vehicle. It'll certainly give the ladies of the altar guild fodder for conversation." He chuckled at the comical thought.

As they both got in the car, Gennie said, "Is this flashy car going to make problems for you with your congregation? Or what about your wife?"

"There is no Mrs. Landon, and this car will be noticed in this neighborhood for its rarity, not who is riding inside. Anyway, sometimes men of the cloth have to endure such extravagance." He looked around at the interior. "Is this brand-new?"

"Yes, Will gave it to me to celebrate my recovery. It's a little gaudy for me, but I couldn't hurt his feelings—and it *is* luxurious."

The small restaurant had a dozen utilitarian tables and metal chairs with a jukebox flashing lightning-bright streaks in the corner. The aromas of oregano, basil, Italian sausage, and French bread filled the room. A hot, crispy loaf of sourdough with butter arrived with water and a menu.

As they sat facing each other, Gennie realized this was their first encounter outside of the hospital setting. As usual Father John was clean shaven and had neat trimmed fingernails, but one rogue wisp of hair kept drifting downward on his forehead. Gennie wanted to reach across the table and push it back in place but realized that would be a much too familiar gesture.

After ordering, Father John asked Gennie how things were going on the home front. She related her experiences with the counselor and how Will said he didn't have time to devote to counseling.

"I'm having a harder time remaining optimistic about our marriage. We do very little together, and up until now I let the children fill the gap, but Mason plans to go off somewhere after graduation and work for a year before college. Although Margo needs love and supervision, I can't hover over her, or she will pull back even more. I'm discussing this in prayer and realize the Christian way isn't always an easy way."

"Yes. Are you familiar with the Serenity Prayer? It asks God to help you accept the things you cannot change, have courage to change the things you can, and find the wisdom to know the difference."

"It's that wisdom that can be elusive."

"Also, the Bible I gave you at the hospital was the King James translation, which is a formidable challenge to understand. If there isn't a Christian bookstore near you, ask Father Stanley to order a *Revised Standard Version Bible*. We've only had it for about a dozen years, but it has more modern language and is easier to comprehend. When you get it look up first Corinthians thirteen, verses four to thirteen. It describes what love is. It gives a good checklist, and you can see how you measure up."

When they returned to the car Gennie also told Father John about hearing from Sandy and the coincidence that she would be attending St. Paul's.

"I know you are going to tell me I am underestimating the power of prayer. I'm excited to know someone there before I start attending. I've also signed up for the inquirer's class in three weeks."

"You are in good hands at St. Paul's. But I am always available if you need me."

"Let me know how much flak your congregation gives you."

"If the pope can claim infallibility, then surely I can defend my actions as godly inspired. Actually, it is kinda fun to see who may want to make a scandal out of a luncheon engagement with a mysterious woman in a red carriage."

As Gennie let him out at the Mission Church, he said, "I enjoyed seeing you looking so well and am encouraged with your progress toward finding a faith. Please telephone just to talk. When you are in the city, stop by any time."

Gennie recognized his sincerity, and she felt warm all over.

PART IV

Chapter 20

1960

The sixties decade started on an optimistic note, with young John Kennedy being inaugurated as president and the possible sexual liberation of women due to the availability of the birth-control pill. Rumbling on the horizon—the consequences of challenging the censure laws claiming the free-speech amendment, the increasing United States involvement in Vietnam, and the mounting civil-rights violence in the South—were clouds threatening peace and tranquility.

In the spring Gennie became confirmed in the Episcopal Church, continued to counsel on Margo's progress, and investigated going back to the community college to pursue a nursing degree. Margo's grades stayed borderline satisfactory at Cs, and she lived at home as she started high school. Considering that Margo could be on the streets in defiance of any parental control, Gennie did not protest her mediocre school performance. Margo, however, spent weekends with her friends, always coming up with some excuse not to come home. Gennie had been advised to choose her skirmishes with Margo and not berate her for every infraction. Keeping Margo from running away—which the counselor said happened all too often—remained their goal.

Gennie enrolled in the local college, taking six credit hours. If the nursing school accepted her, she could go full time—summers included—and finish in eighteen months.

After his graduation Mason joined his friend Jeff and drove out to Jeff's uncle's ranch in West Texas. Jeff planned to spend the summer there and then go to Texas Tech in the fall to study farm-and-ranch management. Mason asked to work for a year, and the uncle said he would reevaluate him at the end of summer. Both the young men worked with the cowboys, and Mason found the kind of experience he had been seeking: doing hard physical work, being outdoors, and associating with men who enjoyed their simple lifestyle.

Every couple of weeks Mason telephoned Gennie, reversing the charges. The first time he called, he said, "Mom, since you're in nursing, how many muscles are in our bodies?"

"As I recall, about six hundred. Why?"

"I believe it. Every one of mine is aching. I thought I was in good shape, but I didn't know the half of it. The old hands are waiting for us to complain, but Jeff and I are stubborn cusses."

The next time he called, he told about finding some art supplies left behind by another cowboy.

"I've been sketching the horses and some of the landscape. I really find it fun. The other fellows critique the horse anatomy, and I'm learning to be a better observer."

"Your dad used to draw cartoonlike characters in high school; maybe that's where you got your talent. Certainly not from me."

When Jeff's uncle saw Mason's sketchbook, he suggested he buy some acrylic or oil paints and try his hand at that.

"There's a fledging art museum down the road a bit. Some ranch families sponsor it and have showings of Western artists. You should go there and see what others are doing."

Chapter 21

Gennie sat on the couch, her feet tucked under her, watching *The Twilight Zone* when she heard the garage door slam. Will stomped to the kitchen refrigerator and wrestled ice cubes out of the metal tray into a glass. Next she heard the liquor-cabinet door bang shut. She thought, "He's in some kind of fury. He usually doesn't drink on weeknights."

Will came in and slumped into the easy chair without coming over to kiss Gennie.

"Have you had dinner?" she asked.

"Nope."

"Do you want me to fix something?"

"What do you have?"

"I have that leftover roast beef. I could make a hot roast-beef sandwich."

"In a few minutes—not right now." He got up and muted the television sound. "I got a damned subpoena today."

"Whatever for?"

"Those detestable Japs I fired are bringing a class-action suit for racial discrimination in the workplace. A bunch of their cohorts—new Jap lawyers who just passed the bar—are eager to test the new state civil-rights bill. They call themselves the 'Nisei–Sansei for Civil Liberties,' or NSCL. One positive aspect is that since we're incorporated, I, personally, will not be financially liable."

"I guess you're going to have to hire an attorney."

"That's why I'm so late. I've been talking to a lawyer, and he thinks we can beat them because the law is not specific enough about privately held corporations."

"Didn't you realize that you might get some flak over those firings?"

"I believe an owner has a right to hire and fire whom he wants to."

"Yeah, but the mood in the country is that everyone has individual rights."

"Does that mean you aren't on my side?"

"It means I read a lot, and the current feeling is that each person has the right to be treated fairly. I just think you're bucking public opinion."

When Will didn't answer, Gennie got up. She said, "I'll fix that sandwich."

While she heated the slices of roast beef, she heard Will pouring himself another drink. He came into the kitchen and sat at the table.

"Neil suspected something was fishy a couple of weeks ago. Two guys came in to apply for the produce-manager position: one Caucasian, one a Jap. Both had exact résumés that were verifiable. Neil asked me what he should do: offer to one or offer to neither. I told him to give the job to the white guy. When Neil told that fellow he had the job, the applicant said he had already taken another position. Of course the job wasn't offered to the Jap."

"You know, even calling the Japanese 'Japs' is offensive to them. It's a very derogatory word."

"Damned if I care what they think."

Gennie served him the sandwich and some chips and poured herself a cup of coffee. She sat down opposite him and thought, "I am not feeling good vibes. His hatred is so entrenched; I don't think I can change his attitude."

In 1959 the state legislature had passed a California State civil-rights bill and named it after the author, State Senator Jesse M. Unruh. This was the law the Nisei-Sansei lawyers wanted to test.

Usually a case calls for arbitration between both parties, but the NSCL desired publicity for the trial and also wanted the state judge to rule on this law.

They did not want it to be decided out of court. Will's lawyers thought this new law may not be applicable to their case. Hearings were postponed multiple times as the lawyers on both sides jockeyed their positions. Months went by.

The law specified the monetary amount to compensate the fired employees for lost wages—up to triple their actual salaries. An appointed court monitor would ensure compliance for equal opportunity in hiring—if the defendant proved to be guilty.

When the trial actually occurred—to the amazement of all present at the proceeding, including the NSCL lawyers—the judge not only deemed Super M stores guilty and assessed fines; he also imposed a ninety-day jail sentence on the chief officer of the company, Will. He gave Will and his lawyers thirty days to either appeal to a higher court or surrender for the incarceration.

That evening after the verdict, Gennie talked to her sister by phone. "I cannot tell you how surprised we all were with the jail-time stipulation. I have never seen Will in such a state of shock. He is walking around like a zombie. I expected him to burst out crying or swearing, but he didn't."

"He's going to appeal, isn't he?

"It's too soon to make a decision, but Will's lawyers are willing. They did say that this judge is well respected, and his rulings are seldom overturned. We'll have to weigh the cost of appeal versus the merits of our case. If he does have to serve his sentence, I'm sure he will survive. It is Margo I am concerned about. Over a year ago her mother jumped off the Golden Gate, and now her father may go to prison. That's a lot for a child to accept, especially when she experienced a totally placid and uneventful childhood up until then."

"Another blow to her self-esteem, I'm sure. What about you? What are you thinking?" Susan asked.

"Will's actions were wrong. I knew it, his dad knew it, and our employees knew it. The reputation of the stores will suffer, and I am sorry for that because Lem had been so proud that his name was respected and that he was considered an honest businessman. Personally, I will weather this as before: your friends will stay with you, and all others are unimportant."

Later that evening, when Gennie answered the telephone, she heard, "Gennie, this is John." She recognized the voice, but she had never called him anything but "Father John," and it surprised her. Maybe after hours he felt more informal.

"I guess you have heard the verdict and sentence on the local news?" she asked. They talked every week or two, with Gennie always calling him during office hours; they had discussed the trial and some of its potential consequences.

"Yes, and the reporter stated that no one expected the prison time."

"A collective gasp spread across the courtroom. Will is devastated."

"How, dear, are you?"

"As I told my sister, I will cope. I've learned who my friends are and that others don't matter. I am concerned about Margo. She should be home by now, since it's a school night, but I haven't heard from her."

"I got a busy signal earlier when I tried to call. Perhaps she is trying also. Let's cut this short, and I will talk with you in the next couple of days. I just wanted to let you know I was thinking of you."

"Thanks."

"Bless you."

Gennie went back to their bedroom, which overlooked their pool and garden. A sitting area and television sat in a small alcove. Will sat slouched on the sofa with his stockinged feet on the coffee table. He didn't seem attentive to the TV, even though it was on. He had a drink in his hand. Lately this occurred more often.

Gennie had never learned to like the taste of whiskey, so she would dilute it with ginger ale.

"I think I'll join you for a nightcap," Gennie announced. "Do you want me to refresh yours?"

"No, I'm fine."

Gennie went down the hall to the dining room, where the bar ingredients were, and made herself a highball. As she replaced the cap on the whiskey bottle, she thought, "It's interesting that the judge stipulated jail time—so unexpected according to court watchers. Could that judgment be a small wave of justice washing up on shore and covering Will's ankles?" She smiled to herself as she walked back to the bedroom.

She sat next to Will on the sofa. The black-and-white images flickered on the screen, but the volume was muted.

"It's been quite a day," she said. She reached out for his hand and held it. "Any thoughts?"

"Even harder than looking at jail time is being forced to hire Japs. I don't want to look at their slant-eyed faces and have to accept them as employees. Where is the freedom to conduct one's private business without government interference?"

"But you had them as employees before."

"That's because Herb owned half of the business and wanted to hire and agreed to deal with them. I didn't have to."

"Chances are that Neil is capable of the same sort of arrangement. He knows your feelings and would take on that responsibility."

"His testimony didn't help me any."

"I think he told the truth: he personally has no prejudice against Japanese and just followed your directive."

Will replied, "Um…" which to Gennie meant "No comment."

Trying to be more cheerful, Gennie said, "We'll get through this—jail time or not."

"Yeah, it comes down to how much money I'm worth out of jail. The price of filing an appeal may not be cost-effective, especially since our liability insurance has a clause saying that it pays only a percentage of appeal costs."

Gennie put her glass on the coffee table, reached for Will's chin, and turned his face to hers so she could kiss him on the lips. He tabled his drink, reaching for her, pulling her closer. The alcohol had relaxed them, and intimacy beckoned.

The doorbell rang. Gennie looked at the clock: eleven thirty. Margo hadn't come home yet, but she had a key. Who could that be? She jumped up, walking quickly to the door with Will right behind her. She opened the door, and there stood Margo and a police officer.

"Mrs. Mueller, Mr. Mueller, your daughter has violated the school-night curfew law."

"Yes, we have been worried about her. She's well aware of the curfew."

"This first offense is a warning. I could write her up because it appears she has been drinking alcohol and smells of marijuana. She is a minor, but I still have issued only a warning. I hope this will be a wake-up call."

"Thank you, Officer. We appreciate your understanding."

With the door closed, Gennie faced Margo and asked for an explanation.

"I tried to call you, but the line was busy. We went to a movie."

"You know the curfew isn't only our rule but the city's too. And you've no business drinking and smoking pot."

"We just passed the bottle between us, and the others smoked; I didn't."

Will interjected, "You are lucky the policeman didn't arrest you."

"Yeah, otherwise you and I could share a jail cell." With that said, Margo turned, head tilted back, nose in the air, and sashayed down the hall. Gennie grabbed Will's arm when he started to follow her.

"Let's talk about this in the morning. Maybe we will all have clearer heads."

Will met with his lawyers and asked for the projected costs and ramifications of an appeal. They said a favorable appeal had minimum chances because the judge had followed the letter of the law, as far as they could analyze. However, an appeal could be dragged out timewise for months, even years. They could also argue that this state law impinged on Will's constitutional right to conduct his private business. On the other hand, if he surrendered in one month, the whole thing could be over within four months.

"Done and behind us," Will said. He sat in his chair, tilted and pushed back from the conference table, balancing on the two rear legs. He rocked to and fro. A few moments of silence passed, with Will gazing into infinity. Finally, he said, "Tell the judge I will surrender in thirty days. I want this total event to be history."

Over the next few weeks, Will met with the management team of each store and reviewed procedures with Neil, Phyllis, Gennie, and Lem—the latter two were officers of the corporation. Lem would be the ultimate go-to man for decisions because he had years of experience in the grocery business.

There is no good time to go to jail, but Will had to report on October 15, which meant he would miss the holidays and be released on January 15. November and December were the busiest months of the year for the grocery business, and Will relished them. Yet he would miss the one task he disliked: inventory on January 1. He asked Lem and Gennie to bring the daily totals for him to examine when they visited him, but he would not know where he was assigned until the day he surrendered.

Chapter 22

Gennie continued her classes at the community college and was also assigned hours to work at the Santa Clara County Hospital. Nurses' training had changed in many ways since Gennie had been a student before. Although some practical courses were taught, hospital experiences contained more observation and written reports. She wore a lab coat over her street clothes. Gennie's usual assignments entailed observing all the patients' symptoms—mostly on the chart—interpreting the doctor's orders, and interviewing the patients. Instead of being limited to bathing patients and changing the bedsheets, the RN student-nurses' education prepared her to be a head nurse or administrator. Years before, there were no LVNs (licensed vocational nurses) or nurses' aides, and RNs performed all chores. Now the RNs started IVs and blood transfusions, which had been done by interns in the 1940s.

Gennie felt the challenge associated with taking on so much responsibility. "It's no wonder that kids do so well learning to drive a car," she thought. "There is less fear when you're young. Now, at my age, I am more cautious and apprehensive."

On the fifteenth of October, Will surrendered to the judge. Gennie and Lem accompanied him to court. Lem wanted to take his son to the facility the judge had chosen. Grovesville State Men's Prison, a minimum-security prison in Southern California, would be Will's home for the next three months. The judge allowed Will to arrive by six o'clock in the evening at the facility. Whether they drove or flew, Lem had been instructed to stay with Will until he was booked into the correctional institute. Gennie had classes, and she had already used up her quota of excuses, so she left for school.

She had told Will, "We have had to say good-bye before, and we got through it, and you were gone a lot longer. We can do it again. I love you."

She also thanked Lem, saying, "I know this is a tough trip for you. No one wants to see his child incarcerated, even for a short time." She hugged his neck. "Thanks for taking him; it's so much more dignified than being transported as a prisoner."

She also said a silent prayer: "Please, God, help me guide Margo so that I don't have to see her in prison too."

At the San Jose Airport, Will and Lem caught a commuter-type plane to Los Angeles. They took a cab from the airport to the admission gates, and it waited as Lem checked Will in. An old prison, austere on the inside, it had a hint of art deco architecture on the exterior. The fence around a rear and adjacent pasture with cows had the only barbed wire visible. On the side were a couple of baseball fields and outdoor basketball courts. Well-tended lawns bordered the driveway and parking area.

"It could be worse," Lem thought. Being confined would chap Will's ego, but Lem felt that his son's arrogant behavior in the courtroom had invited the jail time. They bear-hugged, and Lem left, promising to be back in ten days.

On Thanksgiving Day, Gennie and Margo flew down. It was Margo's first plane trip, and she seemed enthusiastic. They spent about four hours visiting Will before returning to the airport for a quick snack and the flight home.

Chapter 23

Mason wrote that he planned to come home for Christmas. He had been gone for six months and hoped to talk with Bob's son who attended UC Davis, and the Nakamura son who had graduated from Cal Poly, about their college and horticultural experiences. Jeff also planned to be home from Texas Tech, so Mason had a full calendar. Besides going down to see his father, he also wanted to talk to Lem about the farm.

Mason called to get plane reservations from Amon Carter Airfield in Fort Worth to San Francisco. He learned from his coworkers that he could telephone the Greyhound bus station in Big Spring and arrange for them to stop and pick him up at the ranch's front gate. The bus would deliver him right to the entrance of the American Airlines terminal at Amon Carter. The ultra-modern airport surprised the first-time air traveler. Looking the part of a tall Texan, Mason arrived in San Francisco wearing a cowboy hat, suede leather jacket, worn Levis, and cowboy boots. Gennie ran to grab him and hold him tight.

"You look like you just stepped out of the movie *Giant*," she said.

With a twangy accent, he replied, "At your service, ma'am." They laughed and hugged again.

When he noticed Margo standing back, watching, he went over to her and said, "Hey, little sister, give me a hug." Gennie saw her smile. "How seldom she smiles," Gennie thought. "I didn't realize how much she missed her brother. They were good friends growing up."

After getting Mason's luggage, Gennie drove them to Mama M's for dinner. "She wanted to cook for you and hear all your tales firsthand. I know you'll want to talk with Papa M too."

"That's perfect. You have no idea how many nights I've dreamed of Mama M's pot roast, mashed potatoes, cake, and everything else."

When they arrived home after dinner, Gennie followed Mason down to his bedroom to see if he needed anything she hadn't thought of. She took this private time to tell Mason that he should keep his belongings either locked in his suitcase or in her bedroom, which now had a lock on the door.

"At first Margo squirreled away food out of the cupboards. Then it escalated to the contents of the bar, some of my costume jewelry, and her doll collection."

"Did you confront her?"

"Yes, and she replied it was stuff we didn't use or need anyway. When I told the counselor, he said not to make a big issue out of it. No doubt her peer group pressured her for this stuff, and these were her dues to stay with them. Her other alternatives would be breaking and entering, stealing, or prostitution. So a showdown would drive her further away."

"Twisted logic is my opinion."

"Mine too. But they are supposed to have the educated answers."

Because Christmas fell on the weekend, Gennie suggested that Lem and Margaret go down to visit Will on Christmas Day. She thought the children deserved to enjoy their traditions at home and then, the next day, drive down to visit Will. On the way they could stop at Cal Poly and visit both campuses—San Luis Obispo and Pomona. The school would be open the week between holidays for graduating high-school seniors to tour the grounds and talk with advisors. They would continue on to Los Angeles to see Will, and Mason would fly back to the ranch two days later.

When Gennie talked with Father John by telephone, she mentioned that she would like to go up to the mission for the midnight Christmas Eve service and bring both Mason and Margo.

"Splendid," he said.

"Could you join us for Christmas Day dinner at about two p.m.?"

"That's a wonderful idea. Thanks for the invitation."

On the drive up to the city on Christmas Eve, Gennie told Mason and Margo what to expect during the service, that they had a choice to go to the altar railing with her and receive a blessing when she received communion or stay in the pew.

The church, lit with candles and filled with red poinsettias, bright against the plain white wooden walls, brought to mind the simplicity of the manger scene. The young choir with piano accompaniment had clear, innocent voices. Being in unfamiliar surroundings, Mason recognized Margo's uneasiness and reached for her hand. It was a gesture that said, "We can do this for Mom."

After the service Father John greeted the congregation in the narthex: a mixed group of elderly Caucasians, Hispanics, Asians, and homosexuals. Gennie stayed back so they could be the last to talk with Father John. He put his arm around her shoulder, shook Mason's and Margo's hands, and thanked them for coming with their mom. "I'll see you tomorrow. Have a safe trip home," he said. He then hugged Gennie.

During the few days he'd been home, Mason had driven the Cadillac around and become very fond of it. "I'll drive us, and you can tell me where to turn," he suggested.

They talked about the old neighborhood and the congregation, passed the All Saints Hospital, and headed out on the Bayshore Highway.

"You know, Mom, Father John has the hots for you," Mason ventured, not taking his eyes off the road.

"Mason, I think you have been in a cow pasture too long to make a remark like that."

"Okay, would you rather I say he has an ardent passion for you?"

"No, I would rather you didn't make an observation like that at all."

"Are you unaware of his attraction to you?"

"We are good friends. He helped me when I was floundering after my bridge jump. I will always be indebted to him for his support. He is a priest, and I am a married woman."

"Whatever you say, but I remember studying Greek mythology, where unrequited love was a universal theme."

"With unhappy consequences."

"I guess if you don't recognize it."

"Now you are going to make me feel very uncomfortable tomorrow when he comes to dinner."

"Why? He cares for you deeply. You are a wonderful woman. You can be loved by more than one man. In fact, including me, there are three of us."

"And I love all three of you."

After Mason and Margo had gone to their rooms, Gennie took a warm, soothing bath. Wrapped in her bathrobe, she returned to the living room, curled up on the sofa, and gazed at the lighted Christmas tree. She mixed herself a grasshopper—a bright-green Christmas color and an extravagance she seldom indulged in—and sat back enjoying the moment.

"Of course Mason's observation is correct," she thought. "I have been aware of John's growing fondness for me. I am flattered, and I also realize how quickly I could fall in love with him. Thank goodness he is a priest. Otherwise I might entertain a more intimate relationship. I could never succumb to my desires when it might jeopardize his career. This may be a test of my faith. I need to constrain myself because it is the right thing to do."

On Christmas morning Will called to wish them a merry Christmas. It helped soothe the emptiness the family felt without him. They opened their presents. Mason's gift to Margo was a painting of a small picture he'd copied from a photo of Margo and him. Instead of copying the background of the photo, he'd painted from memory the Black homestead with its palm trees in the driveway. (It had been demolished to make way for new larger homes.) Although he gave it to Margo, Gennie became emotional about it. She knew Mason had loved that old house as much as she had. He gave Gennie a painting of a Texas scene with horses grazing. Gennie in turn gave him a 35 mm camera he had requested so he could photograph exceptional scenes and paint them later. He had remarked that the sunrises in West Texas filled the early mornings with a rosy glow—seldom seen with such intensity on the West Coast—and he wanted to capture the beauty, if possible.

After sausages in a blanket and fresh citrus fruit, their traditional holiday breakfast, Gennie put Christmas music on the 33 rpm phonograph player and started preparing dinner. Mason left for Jeff's because he had painted a small picture of his uncle's ranch as a gift for him. Margo went to the hall phone to talk with her friends but came to help set the table when called.

The good father arrived on time and carried a bottle of Mateus rosé and a box of See's chocolates. He also showed his knowledge of photography by helping Mason figure out all the stops and settings on the new camera. Margo seemed shy but politely answered questions and went to her room to retrieve the painting Mason had given her to show Father John.

After a dinner of roasted beef tenderloin with a horseradish cream sauce, mashed potatoes, vegetables, and a molded cranberry salad, Father John offered to help Gennie in the kitchen.

"No," she said, "you are a guest; just relax in the living room."

"I am so satisfied that I would promptly take a nap. I don't want to miss a moment of this visit. Mason, I saw a basketball hoop out in the driveway. I'll challenge you to a game of HORSE."

"You're on." Predictably, the next sentence was, "Mom, do you know where the ball is?"

Once they'd located the ball and pumped it up with a bike-tire pump, the game began.

Christmas days in California are often filled with sunshine, so every new bike, trike, or outdoor activity can be tried out that same day.

Gennie could see the action out of her kitchen window over the sink. Soon the laughter and noisy challenges caused Margo, who was helping scrape dishes, to say, "I want to go watch."

A boy on his bike came by and asked to join. Another friend of Mason's from his high-school days stopped his car to talk and joined in too.

"Thank you, Lord, for allowing my children to see what a nice man Father John is," Gennie murmured as she loaded the last dishes into the dishwasher. She went out to the driveway to watch.

"I was wondering when you were going to rescue me," Father John said. "They are skunking me. Margo, can you take my place?"

“Do you want to walk around the block?” Gennie offered. “Most of the houses are decorated and will have their lights on today.”

They talked about Gennie’s plans to go with the children down to visit Will, and about term papers she had due when school resumed. She didn’t think she would get up to the city for at least two weeks, and in twenty-one days Will would return home.

As early dusk started to cool the air, Father John reluctantly said good-bye. They each thanked the other for a very special day. He took Gennie’s hand and assured her that this was one of his best Christmases ever.

“For me too. You made what could have been a difficult day for us all a very pleasant one.”

When Mason had talked with Papa M about his future, he’d related that he thought ag school would help direct him. Right now he had no concrete plans but would love to raise horses and have a riding stable. Whether that could be cost-effective, he would have to learn. People who raised Arabian horses usually had deep pockets and did it as a hobby; their livelihoods funded their hobby. He hoped somehow that a horse or horses would be in his future, but he didn’t know how. Because of its strong fine-arts school, Mason was leaning toward going to Cal Poly. Its neighboring campus also had equestrian classes. He had a lot of questions ready to ask school officials when he visited.

He also gave his grandparents a West Texas painting. Aware that he had a lot of techniques to learn, he had been encouraged by the Sweetwater group of artists and collectors, who’d bought two of his paintings.

On Thursday Mason phoned Valerie’s home. As expected, she’d also come home for the holidays. He learned that she attended UCLA and loved it. When he said he might go to Cal Poly, she said they needed to get together. Without being asked, she related that Judith still lived at home and went to Stanford.

“She’s really feeling oppressed by her domineering father. I hope she can live on campus next year,” Valerie said. Mason promised to call Valerie in the summer if he enrolled at Poly.

Visiting Will at the prison, Gennie shared the daily business totals of the grocery stores. They equaled last year's gross. Lem had been in charge of giving each employee a ham or turkey as a Christmas gift. This tradition dated back to the years when he'd owned the grocery stores. Gennie said Lem suggested that all the managers receive extra in their paychecks for meeting their holiday quota in sales and, in some cases, exceeding it. For tax purposes, the checks needed to be cut before the end of the year, but Lem wanted to wait until Will had returned to work to distribute them. This seemed to touch Will—that his Dad would be so considerate.

They pored over the expected profits and came up with figures for those bonuses. They had very little personal conversation. Gennie shared news about her school activities, but Will seemed distant. "Perhaps he is depressed," she thought. "Maybe the fact that the stores did well without him challenged his ego." Mason and Margo visited for a short time, and then Gennie let them take the car and explore the nearby area. The kids had found a brochure about abandoned movie sets that were close and wanted to check them out. They returned by late afternoon and picked up Gennie. They all went to dinner and back to the motel. Gennie felt disconnected from Will. Of course he was tired of being locked up, but wasn't that the whole point of the sentence? Did he yet realize that he couldn't be so cocky and make his own laws? In eighteen days he would be released; surely he could find some positivity in that.

The following Monday Mason flew back to Texas. He hoped to return in July to get ready to go to college. Because car prices were cheaper in Texas, he thought he would buy one there and then drive home because he wanted a car at school. Both Gennie and Margo returned to their studies. Gennie read some pamphlets about Marijuana side effects and started watching Margo closely. The symptoms were there: the red eyes, the constant use of breath mints and the lessened ability to follow a conversation, Gennie became convinced that Margo was smoking pot on the weekends.

Gennie asked the counselor if it wouldn't be wise to send Margo to a drug-treatment center. The counselor said that most treatment facilities existed because the courts sent offenders there for treatment, and the environment would be worse than what Margo experienced now. Surely Margo wasn't the only teenager whose wayward activity dismayed her parents; yet Gennie could not find other solutions.

Will returned home, and their separate but parallel lives continued.

PART V

Chapter 24

SUMMER 1962

With her classes completed, Gennie studied daily for the state boards. After two long days of tests in San Francisco, she then had to wait six weeks until the results came in. Meanwhile, she had a job as a graduate nurse at the county hospital, working three evenings a week. Margo attended individual tutoring classes during the summer in an effort to pass her classes. Gennie deemed them a necessary expense.

Mason had finished his first year at Cal Poly and stayed down there during the summer to take some extra art classes.

In July Susan called to say she had an opportunity to go to Sweden and stay with some old friends for ten days. Her husband, Walter, couldn't get away, but she wondered if Margo would be tantalized with such an experience. They would have to leave in a week, but she thought Walter could get an expedited passport for Margo through the Swedish consulate.

"Can I call Margo and see if she would like to go with me?" Susan asked.

"Sure, that might brighten her outlook on life," Gennie replied.

Margo acted enthusiastic, especially when she learned they were going the polar route from San Francisco to Stockholm. She and Gennie went shopping for clothes; although it would be daylight most of the time they were there, it could still be cool. Margo consented to a professional haircut that erased her scruffy and unkempt look. Gennie asked her to promise not to take any drugs with her.

"I don't want you to get Susan in trouble with authorities. Customs agents will search your luggage. You could be jailed or sent back on the next plane."

"Aunt Susan already talked to me about that."

Susan also obtained forms from the travel agent for Gennie and Will to sign: one form to allow Susan to take Margo out of the country and a consent form allowing Susan to make any medical decisions if Margo became ill.

Gennie again saw glimpses of the younger Margo: sweet and cooperative. It gave her hope that the most difficult of these teenage years were behind them. Travel often opened up possibilities never seen before, and hopefully, Margo could see a brighter future.

Will and Gennie both drove her to the airport, meeting Susan there. Lem and Margaret surprised them by being there too—Lem with his ever-present camera to document the departure.

The freedom of not having any children at home gave Gennie the idea of a short getaway with Will, but he claimed he had too much work. So instead she went up to San Francisco to visit with Father John; they went to a play at the Curran Theater.

She also went to Petaluma for two days to relieve Josefina, who cared for Erma in Susan's absence.

When Gennie drove up the long driveway to Susan's house, she saw the clothes line filled with neatly pinned towels and bed sheets. They hung limp in the inert air. A yellow dog greeted her without barking but sniffed and responded to his name Rex when Gennie patted his head. Another dog barking from his lounging place under the shade tree came over for a head pat and neck scratch also. Josephina and Erma emerged from the chicken coop with Erma holding a basket of fresh eggs. Josephina offered to help with Gennie's suitcase.

"Come in and we'll have a cup of coffee," Josefina said. They went through the screen door and into the kitchen. She instructed Erma to come to the sink and wash her hands, then asked her to get out cups and saucers. "Three cups and three saucers."

They sat at the round kitchen table and chatted. Josefina's English was adequate for simple conversation. If she wanted to describe an event she faltered trying to find the right word but could express herself eventually.

Erma stood and started searching for something. "Are you looking for your cards?" Josefina asked. "They're in the desk drawer where we keep them." Erma returned to the table and started to play Solitaire.

"Are things going okay?" Gennie asked.

"Yes, as long as we stay on a simple schedule. I've written it out for you and today, she can help you bring in the clothes and fold them. She likes to help."

Josephina offered Gennie a refill on her coffee.

"Momma is blessed to have you as a friend. She's really perked up. You are so kind to play games with her. It's good to see her smile."

"I enjoy the games as much as she does. I was the oldest of twelve children and seldom could play as a child. Miss Erna taught me to play jacks. I had never played them as a girl."

"I want you to know Susan and I appreciate all you do."

"Gracias. Let me tell you what happen the other day. Miss Erma asked questions—the same ones over and over. "She said, 'Did you have brothers and sisters?' When I said yes, she did not say anything. The next time she asked me, she added, 'Did you live with them?' I said yes and then she said, 'Lucky dog. I had to live with an old man.'"

Gennie said, "Isn't that strange? Did she say anything else?"

"No, Miss Erma doesn't like to be questioned." Erma sat at the table while they talked but did not indicate that she was understanding the conversation.

"If Momma tells you more, let us know."

On her drive home Gennie wondered about that story. "Was it a true recollection, or was her mother confusing it with the first couple of years of her marriage to Dad?"

Upon arriving at her house, she called Will to see if he would be home for dinner, before starting to cook. He said he would, so she was in the kitchen when the phone rang. An operator told her she had a telegram to read: "Dear Gennie," *Stop.* "I have tragic news." *Stop.* "Please sit down." *Stop.* "Margo needed emergency surgery." *Stop.* "She had an allergic reaction to anesthesia." *Stop.* "She did not survive." *Stop.* "I will bring her home ASAP." *Stop.* "Love, Susan." *Stop.*

The operator said, "Do you want us to send you a copy through the mail?"

"What did you ask?"

The operator repeated the question.

"Yes," Gennie said, "please." Her mind melted. Margo dead? Is that what the telegram said? What could have gone wrong?

Suddenly, Gennie had difficulty breathing. A thunder-and-lightning storm waged in her brain. The tears started and developed into sobs. She put her head down on her arms, which were crossed on the table. Her breaths sounded like hiccoughs. "Dear God, help us! Poor Susan, help her. Bring them both home safely—and soon," she thought.

That is how Will found Gennie as he entered the kitchen. "What's wrong?" Obviously something had occurred in the last thirty minutes since he had talked to Gennie on the phone.

"I got a telegram…on the phone…from Susan." Her breaths still came in gasps. "Margo is dead…She had emergency surgery…Something went wrong."

"Oh my God, no!" He crouched next to her and put his arm around her shoulder. "Have you talked with Walter?"

"No, I just heard five minutes ago."

"My poor baby. Can I get you something? I'm going to try to reach Walter." He stayed in the kitchen, looking the phone number up on their plastic index next to the phone.

"Hello, Walter? Will here. Gennie just received a telegram from Susan. Have you talked with her?" Then Will listened, saying, "oh" and "uh-huh," and finally said, "Call us as soon as you hear what flight they can come in on. We will want to be there. Oh, wait a minute. Gennie has something to say…She wants you to tell Susan she loves her. Okay, thanks a lot; we'll wait for your call."

Will reached for Gennie's hand. "It's a long, convoluted story. You look so pale; can I get you a drink? I think I need one."

When he came back into the room with the two drinks—his a Manhattan and hers a lowball with ginger ale—he turned off the burners on the range. "I don't think either of us wants dinner right now." He went to the cupboard and poured some Ritz crackers into a bowl and cut up some cheddar cheese slices. "It might be best to have a snack with your drink." Will could be kind and understanding when he saw Gennie so distressed.

"Walter said Susan sent the telegram because it took three phone calls for her to tell him what happened. They either got disconnected or couldn't hear because of the noisy static.

"The story is that Margo approached Susan to take her to Sweden to get an abortion." Gennie gasped and teetered on her chair. "Susan tried to talk her out of it, saying Margo could have the baby and Susan would happily adopt it. Then Susan learned that Margo had been raped by a couple of her 'friends' after taking drugs and Margo thought the baby would be damaged by all the drugs she had been using. Susan said that legal abortions could be performed in the United States in case of rape. Margo was adamant that you were never to know of her pregnancy. She said you tried to commit suicide because of Mason and his girlfriend's pregnancy. Margo threatened Susan that if no one helped her, she would commit suicide. Susan believed Margo and realized that parental consent would be needed anywhere in the United States and you would have to know.

"So there you have it: Margo was scheduled for an abortion after being interviewed by the Swedish physician. They give her an anesthesia that she was evidently allergic to—causing extreme high blood pressure. They tried to reverse it, but her muscles became rigid, her organs stopped functioning, and she died without regaining consciousness."

Gennie sat there trying to absorb all that Will had recited. It seemed so bizarre. Finally she said, "Susan attempted to help Margo out of love, I know. But why did this have to happen?" A tidal wave of tears again overwhelmed her. After a few moments Gennie asked, "Did Walter know how soon they could come home?"

"He said it might take a day, but he has contacted the Swedish consulate here, and Susan notified the American embassy in Stockholm."

Suddenly, Gennie had a surge of clear thinking, knowing that people needed to be notified.

"Are you willing to call your mom and dad? I think I need to call Mason. I also want to call Father John."

"Of course, the dear reverend needs to be called."

"Please don't be so sarcastic. Father John has been a stalwart friend."

"I think I should go over to Mom and Dad's in person to deliver the news. This will be quite a shock at their age, and I want to be there to help them understand. Do you want to go with me?"

"No, I am so emotional. It would only make it worse for your mom. I will be okay. Don't be gone long; I'm not feeling like superwoman at this point."

After Will left Gennie dialed Mason's telephone number and retold the whole story. He had only a week left in the first summer session. He would need to talk with his instructors in the morning to see if could turn in his art project late. There would be a week of no classes between the summer sessions, so he could be home for about ten days if necessary.

Gennie knew that because Mason had been away from home for a couple of years, he heard the news with a sense of detachment. He hardly knew this teenage sister but would grieve for the younger child who had idolized him. The tragedy of the situation might remind him of the sadness after Judith's pregnancy. Gennie thought, "Do we ever finish paying for our mistakes? Although God forgives us, our memories aren't erased. Margo made a decision based on my secret, and Susan didn't have any facts to contradict her assumption. Mom was right; secrets are insidious, like an undiagnosed cancer."

The phone call to Father John would also be difficult because he had been a patient listener to all the tribulations that rebellious Margo had presented. His sensitivity and caring had often brought tears to Gennie's eyes. "I need to 'gird my loins' and just dial his number," she thought. She swallowed hard as she heard his phone ring and admonished herself not to sob and blubber her way through the conversation.

After they'd exchanged hellos, Gennie said, "I received a telegram from Susan." She paused to swallow again, and it gave Father John a moment to reply.

"Are they having a good time?"

"No, it was very sad news." Gennie then related the whole story, sniffing from time to time but not succumbing to sobs.

"Is Will with you now?"

"No, he went to tell his parents in person. He suggested it, which I thought was perceptive and kind. He said he would come home shortly."

"Can I do anything for you tonight?"

"No, I will call you as soon as Susan and Margo return. I want you to help with the funeral arrangements. Other than for my dad's, I have little experience in planning one."

"I will do whatever you request. You must know I admire your strength, and I pray that God gives you the ability to deal with this too."

"Thank you, John. You are a dear friend."

Gennie went to the den, where she sat at the writing desk. She yearned to be able to talk with her sister and tell her that together they would get through this. How all alone she must feel, to be without Walter or family.

Gennie opened the desk drawer, pulled out a sheet of stationery, and wrote the following:

Dear Susan,

It has only been about an hour since we received your telegram. I know I am in shock and only feel a tenth of the grief I will experience for my baby. Yet I want to write you now, before all the busyness of funeral activities starts.

First, thank you for taking care of Margo. You responded to her with a big heart. She reached out to you because you have always been dependable, ready with help and good answers. Your choice to assist her was magnanimous and the correct one. You did the right and loving thing.

The physician who chose the anesthesia made the error. You could have had no input in that decision. I will never blame you or harbor any bitterness toward you. I love you and am lucky to have you as my sister.

However, Margo's decision to ask for help goes back to my suicide attempt and my refusal to give the reason for my jump. I know that. Therefore, I plan to tell the family and a few close friends my secret after the funeral. I want no more sad consequences to occur because of my silence.

I hope you will keep this letter and reread it any time you second-guess your actions about this trip. I had a joyous week with Margo before she left. She seemed clean of drugs and happily looked forward to this adventure. You helped her give me a final happy image.

All my love,
Gennie

Gennie tucked the letter into an envelope and put it in her handbag. She wanted to give it to Susan at the airport. She took out another piece of stationery and started to make a list. She had been taught recently in school to prioritize lists of care, so she started with "Call the hospital and take a leave of absence." Well, that could be done right now. She called the nursing office and asked for a leave of absence of undetermined length, telling them her daughter had emergency surgery overseas and died because of a reaction to the anesthesia. She put a checkmark next to that: done. Mortuary? Ask Will. Cemetery? Old Settlers Mayfield Cemetery. Which family plot? Both the Blacks and the Muellers were buried there. Chapel? Use the one at the cemetery? It was small, but she anticipated just family attending. Ask Father John to do the service.

Her mind drifted to Margo's friends. She didn't even know who they were—a moving mass of people whom she saw from a distance wearing dark clothing, unkempt. Margo always met them outside of the house and down the street. If they drove her home, they never came in; it was always a car filled with other bodies. Gennie knew some of them were in high school, yet others had dropped out. Anger boiled into rage as she thought of these kids plying Margo with drugs and raping her. Margo had always had a feisty streak—did the use of drugs diminish her determined spirit? The counselor had attributed it to the lure of the drug itself: the promise of friendship and a place to belong.

Gennie had seen other families use toughness and throw children out of the house and onto the streets to "learn their lesson." When she went to the counselors, they advised compromise and kindness. And when paying for professional advice, it would seem foolish not to follow it. Yet she'd never gotten the desired results either. “One plus is that Margo came to the family for help; she knew she was loved. I’ve got to hang on to that thought,” Gennie told herself.

Her drink was lukewarm and flat; she added ice cubes and took another sip. Will came in through the back door.

“Whew, Mother is a basket case. Dad is calling her doctor for a sedative.”

“Do you think I should go over there? Would it help?”

“No, I think that would start her on another emotional roller coaster. Maybe I shouldn’t have told her the facts. She focused on the attack by Margo’s so-called friends. She was so proud and protective of her granddaughter.”

“This past year, your mom didn’t want to see the changes in Margo. She still hoped that Margo would want to come over and bake cookies. I’ll call your dad in the morning and see how she is doing.”

“Do you want another drink?” When Gennie shook her head, Will went to replenish his.

When he returned she said, “I guess the first decision is what mortuary to use: the one here in Menlo Park or the one in South Palo Alto, closer to the cemetery? As soon as we know when the plane will arrive, a hearse should meet it.”

“Let’s use the one in South Palo Alto—or Mayfield. It will be more convenient for everyone.”

The next morning, close to noon, Walter called Gennie and told her the plane was due at about seven o’clock in the evening. Susan would deplane with the rest of the passengers, and then the plane would taxi to a far hangar, where the coffin could be retrieved and loaded into the hearse. Gennie had called the mortuary earlier to forewarn them of their need and only had to confirm the time and flight number with them. “We are meeting a passenger also, so please don’t leave the tarmac until we get down there.”

After Walter’s call Gennie went to Mama M’s to tell her the time of the flight and also see how she was. As always, a pot of coffee sat on the stove, and a German type of coffee cake resided under a glass dome. The cheery kitchen remained the same. “How can it seem unchanged when our world has been overturned?” Gennie wondered. Mama M had aged overnight. Her usual erect posture drooped like a wilted tulip in a vase. She started to tear up, lamenting the circumstances of Margo's death. When Papa M came in, Gennie hugged his neck and asked if he had developed the photos he had taken at Susan and Margo's departure. He said they were at the drugstore and should be ready to pick up.

Gennie said, "I want to see if there are any good head shots of Margo that we can use in a frame on the closed coffin. Also, I thought the mortuary could use a good recent photo to look at while touching up her face. She didn't wear much makeup, so I don't want her to be painted up like a tart."

He asked, "Are you having an open coffin?"

"Yes, I thought it would be open before the service and then closed during the service. That's when I would like to put a photo on top of the coffin. The only recent photo I have is a school photo that isn't very flattering."

"I'll go right now." He got up from his chair, leaving the newly poured coffee behind.

"No, finish your coffee and talk. Bring them to the airport tonight, and we can see if any of them will work."

Once home Gennie went out to their backyard and sat on the patio near the pool under an umbrella. She heard the telephone ringing and rushed inside to answer it.

"Hello."

"Mrs. Mueller. This is Hope Clinic. Margo missed her appointment yesterday. She knows the policy of our clinic that all patients are to notify us of a cancellation twenty four hours in advance. I hope you will reprimand her because she inconvenienced the counselor and other patients."

Gennie screeched, "Margo is dead. The dead cannot cancel their appointments." She slammed down the receiver and picked up a glass paper weight off the desk and threw it against the wall where it shattered. She dragged herself to the couch and she collapsed in a spasm of sobs.

Hours later Phyllis called and offered to notify any of Gennie's friends. Now more composed, Gennie said,"When I started back to school, I took a leave of absence from my bridge club and garden club, I just didn't have time for all that socializing and classes too. I had little contact with parents at the high school. I made acquaintances at college, but most of us had families or jobs—or both—and had little time to socialize. In this upscale neighborhood I'm a maverick to be working outside my home. So thanks, but we're putting an obituary in the *Palo Alto Times*, so most of our old friends will see it there. By the way, I would like to ask you to join our family after the burial in the parlor of the chapel. Privately, I plan to tell everyone close to me the real reason I jumped from the bridge. My secret has only caused havoc in our lives. It's time to remedy that."

"I'll be glad to come and lend my support. Call me if you can think of anything I can do," Phyllis said.

At the airport Susan hugged her husband and then went to Gennie, apologizing—"I'm sorry; I'm so sorry"—over and over again.

Gennie countered with, "It's going to be okay. You did the right thing. Thank you for being there for Margo." Maybe neither one heard the other's apology; each was so engrossed in getting her message across. Gennie slipped the envelope into Susan's handbag. "For you to read later," she said.

Lem arrived without Margaret. A neighbor had volunteered to stay with her. It had been a difficult twenty-four hours. He showed Gennie the photos he had taken, and two were exceptional. He had stopped by to ask a photographer friend if enlargements could be made in a day. Gennie picked out the one she liked best, and Lem said he would take care of it. Will, Gennie, Walter, Susan, and Lem walked to the far end of the terminal, where they were directed to the stairs to the tarmac. A flight attendant accompanied them to the plane, where the hearse slowly backed up to the cargo door. Gennie attributed her sudden shudder and chattering teeth to nerves, not the cool breeze. When an electric hoist lifted the pine box and lowered it onto the hearse's cart, the full impact of Margo's death engulfed her. Will held on to her to prevent her from crumpling. Lem stepped to her other side, and a wave of tears swept over all three of them. Once the box sat securely in place, the driver walked over to the family to extend his condolences. Gennie thanked him for his services and cautioned him to drive safely. "We will be in tomorrow to talk with you about the arrangements." They watched the hearse drive off and returned to the terminal's waiting room.

"Do you want to sit and talk?" Gennie asked Susan.

Susan shook her head. “I am so tired. I’ve been up for twenty-four hours and didn’t sleep on the plane.”

“Father John is coming tomorrow to help make arrangements. Mason should be home by the time we get there. I’ll call you when I know what the exact plans are. Do get some rest. You brought her home to us. I love you.”

“You are so understanding. I’ll talk with you tomorrow.” The sisters hugged again and parted.

Chapter 25

The next morning Gennie sat across from Will at the breakfast table. He dove into his cold cereal and milk while she sipped her hot coffee.

"We plan to meet at ten o'clock this morning at the cemetery chapel. Your dad, Mason, Father John, and I will be there, so I hope you can help make decisions about the funeral." Gennie tried to make eye contact, but the cereal evidently consumed all of Will's attention.

"I'll do my best."

"After the burial I am asking your mom and dad, Mason, Susan, Walter, my mom, you, Phyllis, and Father John to meet in the parlor of the chapel.. I intend to tell them the reason I jumped from the bridge and why I felt I had to keep it a secret."

Will looked up from his cereal bowl. "Why, for God's sake, are you doing this now? Aren't we under enough stress as it is?"

"I am doing it because I don't want anyone else to make a decision based on false beliefs. If Margo had known the truth, she may have considered staying in the United States for the abortion. If Susan had known, the outcome might have been different. I want Mason to know everything."

"Then why not just tell him? The more people you tell, the bigger chance there will be that someone will go to authorities with the story."

"I don't want Mason to feel that he has to keep this secret and talk to no one. You were pretty cocksure, when it happened, that you would beat any accusation. Where is all that confidence now?"

"I *should* beat any charge if there is justice. After my last trial I'm not sure if justice exists. I will never be incarcerated again."

"It's not anything one aspires to, but it didn't seem like you thought your prison experience was that bad."

"You don't understand how insidious it is to lose your freedom, to be at the mercy of guards who lord it over you. Most of them aren't very smart, but they have the power, and you don't. I'm surprised my head didn't explode from the pressure I felt. If you go through with this little confession of yours, I will leave you. You cannot love me if you do this."

"You don't know the burden I have carried by keeping this a secret. I trust these people to do the right thing. Actually, I could be accused as an accessory to the crime for keeping quiet, so I am taking a risk too. I must protect Mason."

"The threat to leave you isn't an empty one. I will do it."

"Then I guess you need to pack."

Will left the table without finishing his coffee. He went out to his truck, started the motor, and gunned the engine, causing the tires to spin on the loose pea gravel.

Gennie said a silent prayer: "Dear God, you've guided me this far; please stay with me. Amen."

She looked at the kitchen walls that had heard so much contentious rhetoric and said, "It's over. It really is over."

At ten o'clock the group trickled into the chapel, with the funeral director and cemetery representative at the front, ready to conduct the meeting. Mason and Gennie had arrived first. When Father John came in, Will followed directly behind. Mason jumped up, grabbed Father John's hand, and thanked him for his help. Then they hugged, and Father John told Mason he was practicing his basketball shots and Mason had better be ready for a competitive game. As they laughed quietly, Will witnessed the friendly exchange. Gennie directed her gaze at Will, who glared at Father John. "I've seen that look before," she thought. "Is it envy, dislike? Whatever it is, it is dark. Yes, it is the same way he looked at Dad—at Mason's pops."

The men at the front of the chapel had a checklist, and when Gennie had no suggestions for music, Father John suggested a simple child's hymn, with words echoing a youngster's innocence. The funeral director stepped out and asked his secretary to call their vocalist to make sure she knew it.

Lem said that Margaret requested a gospel hymn be included in the service. She'd always sung it to Margo—and Mason too—when she'd put them, as toddlers, down for a nap. "The name of it is—or at least the first sentence is—'I come to the garden alone while the dew is still on the roses.'"

Mason started humming the tune and then sang, "And the voice I hear falling on my ear."

"That's it," Lem said. "Maybe the congregation could sing it, since most people are familiar with it."

The funeral director continued down his list of assignments: next was floral arrangements for the casket. And Father John offered to go over the prayerbook burial of a child with the secretary so programs could be printed. The director said he would take the obituary and photo to the newspaper. When all the questions had been answered and everyone seemed satisfied, they dispersed. Mason had come with Gennie, so he went with her into the cemetery office to reserve the adjacent parlor for after the burial. She needed coffee, cups, and plates to be provided, and the baker would deliver sandwiches and cookies. She also requested privacy and assured them that no employee would be needed to serve them.

When she and Mason left the office, Lem came out right behind them, so they waited to walk together.

"Thanks for fulfilling Margaret's request," Lem said. "That will make it special for her. Although I expect that the floodgates of tears will open up."

"Is she doing okay?" Gennie asked. Lem nodded. "After the burial I am planning to have the family join together in the parlor so I can reveal why I jumped from the bridge. I do not want to hurt you and Mama M, but what I say will put Will in a very bad light. You and she have the right to decline my invitation, but I think Margo's death is the direct result of my secret, and Mason needs to know. The rest of you should have that information too. Will is not happy with my decision to share my secret, and you may side with him and be angry with me too. But I have to do it, Papa M. I will not lose another child to this secret."

"I've always thought you were shielding someone, and I suspected it was Will. I will be there, and I'll let Margaret decide for herself. Margo's death has pulled the rug out from under her. I don't want the floor to cave in too. The doctor wants her to take these antistress pills for a couple of weeks; perhaps that will help."

Mason and Gennie continued on to the florist, where she ordered roses: various hues of pink, coral, crimson, and yellow for the two bouquets on either end of the casket. Father John had offered his church's pall to cover the closed coffin. The large white cloth had been embroidered by parishioners nearly fifty years earlier, and on the underside, as a record, each person's name and date of death had been embroidered. On the front side the large cross had intricate embroidery stitches in many bright thread colors, so the multicolored roses would look coordinated.

When Gennie explained her reasoning for her choice of flowers, Mason said, "Don't you hear Margo saying, 'Mother, it all doesn't have to match perfectly'?"

"Yes, she always fidgeted when I tried different colored bows for her hair so they complimented her outfits." Their eyes met, and they shared a smile.

They went on to the bakery and ordered sandwiches and cookies.

Late in the afternoon the funeral home called to say that Margo was ready for the family to view her and approve of their work. Gennie called Will's office, but the receptionist said he wasn't in and she would try to find him and give him the message. Gennie asked Mason to take her and told him Will could meet them there. As they started for the door, Gennie said, "Just a minute." She walked down the hall to Margo's room and came out with a scruffy stuffed bear under her arm. "I want to tuck ReeSee in with Margo. When I went in to awaken her each morning—even recently—ReeSee usually shared the bed with her. He's seen many suds in the washer and tumbling in the dryer over the years, but he's always been her favorite. He deserves to go to a better place with her."

On the drive over, Mason said, "I don't know if I can go in and view Margo."

"If it makes you too uncomfortable, just sit in the waiting room. Some people would rather remember their loved ones as when they were alive, and that's okay. I'll ask one of the employees to go in with me. I hope to be in control, but who knows?"

Gennie gave the receptionist ReeSee and asked if he could be snuggled in beside Margo so that just his head peeked out. When the funeral director came out to get them, Mason decided to go in with his mother. Margo wore the dress that they had just bought ten days before on their mother-daughter shopping trip. The memory of that excursion, which had been fun and made Gennie so hopeful, crashed into the reality of the moment, and the tears came.

"Margo, my sweet baby, I wanted it all to turn out so differently," Gennie said, weeping. "I thought I had a chance of grabbing your hand and bringing you back to a good life, but you slipped away. I can't dwell on what might have been, but I'll miss you so."

Seeing his mother so upset, Mason started crying too. He did not find words to soothe her, and they just held on to each other.

The next day the funeral exuded simplicity in a country setting. The old cemetery dated back to one hundred years prior, and the Gothic-designed tombstones and family mausoleums dotted the landscape under a canopy of oak trees. The chapel, built of native stone, reflected the pure spirit of pioneer people. Mourners filled the one hundred or so seats. Many of Lem and Margaret's friends attended. Gennie also recognized some of the store managers and the members of the Nakamura family. She saw some mothers and daughters who were Margo's previous childhood friends and wondered why.

In the front pew Gennie's mom, Erma, sat on one side of her and Mason on the other. Will sat next to Mason. The parents' schism could be seen by the discerning eye. During the reciting of the Lord's Prayer, Gennie heard her mother's voice loud and clear. She looked at the paper program in her mother's hand; it wasn't open. "She is saying that from memory," Gennie thought. "How odd."

After the service most of the congregation walked to the nearby Mueller-family plot, only a few hundred feet away. The hearse drove the short distance on the narrow driveway. Father John and the family walked behind the hearse. After Father John had repeated prayers at the gravesite, the family greeted their friends. Will drifted away with the rest of the visitors.

When just the invited family remained, Gennie said, "Let's go into the parlor."

Both Susan and Gennie thought Erma would benefit from being part of this family gathering. Josefina could soothe Erma easily, and the sisters thought their mother might recognize what was currently happening.

As the family and friends entered the room, Gennie offered them the food. She stood before them and announced, "I have a bit of good news. Yesterday I received in the mail my notification that I have passed my state boards; I am officially a registered nurse in the state of California. Dad always encouraged me to be a nurse. He said, 'If you are an RN, you can always take care of yourself.'

"As you see, Will is not in attendance. He threatened to leave me if I revealed the reason I jumped. So God is taking care of me: I now have my license, even though I have no husband. Actually, our marriage has not been happy, but I vowed to stay in it until Margo graduated from high school and became established in college or a career. But enough of that. I am here to tell you why I tried to commit suicide.

"Let's go back to 1959. Phyllis told me in confidence that the company faced bankruptcy due to Will's excessive gambling. The next night, Herb, Alice, Will, and I had reservations at the annual grocers' banquet. Before the dinner, I drove Mason to a friend's house, and he revealed that his girlfriend was pregnant with his child. This shocked me, but I assured him we would work it out."

Gennie continued with the scenario of what had gone on that night, ending with Herb's death on the trolley. The group responded with a collective gasp at that news.

"Will then said that if I went to the authorities, the partnership insurance would not pay promptly, the business would fail, we would lose our home, and Alice would not get her insurance money. Unknown to me at the time, Will had recently increased the insurance amount, so it paid Alice, the whole business became Will's, *and* the additional money paid his gambling debts.

"If I had gone to authorities, it would have boiled down to my word against Will's. A trial—whatever the outcome—would devastate so many lives, but could I live with a murderer? Or myself?"

Gennie walked across the room and picked up her glass of water to take a sip. She told of her walk on the bridge and her ultimate decision to jump.

Suddenly, Erma stood up, looked straight at Gennie with clear eyes, and said, "I always knew you didn't jump because Mason got that girl pregnant."

Gennie gave her mother a questioning look and said, "I didn't know you understood those events." Erma's clear thought lasted only seconds. She again retreated into a cloud of dementia. Gennie went over to hug her mom, but the recognition had faded. That brief moment of lucidity astounded the group.

Gennie went to the front of the room again and said, "Thank you, Mother, for your vote of confidence. This leads us to the ultimate reason I am now telling you my story. Both Mason and Margo were convinced that my suicide jump was due to his girlfriend's pregnancy. I had given them no other justification. This is the reason that Margo, upon learning *she* was pregnant, asked Susan to take her to Sweden for an abortion. She believed I would attempt suicide if, again, one of my children became pregnant out of wedlock.

"Yes, instead of telling all of you, I could have told only Mason, but then he would have to be a secret-keeper. My friends, secrets are sneaky thieves; they rob us of peace of mind and happiness. What you do with this information is up to you. I will leave it in God's hands."

Looking over at Father John, she asked, "Would you dismiss us with a prayer?"

"Yes, yes, I would be glad to." He stood up in front next to Gennie. "Let's bow our heads. Almighty God, we entrust all who are dear to us to thy never-failing care and love, for this life and the life to come. The Lord bless us and keep us. The Lord make his face to shine upon us and be gracious to us. The Lord lift up his countenance upon us and give us peace, this day and evermore. Amen."

Gennie went over to Margaret and said, "I had to do this. Please forgive me."

"Darling, Gennie, you will always be our daughter. You have been a gift to our family. As I have told you before, until you started dating Will, he was an angry and vengeful kid. Lem and I were worried about where he would end up. I know he loves you."

"Remember: he is leaving me. It is his decision."

"Mason and you will continue to be our family," Margaret said, dabbing her eyes with her handkerchief.

Lem stepped forward and gave Gennie a big hug. "We are saddened by these new facts, but we truly understand," he said. "I think Will is going to reconsider and want to come back."

"I doubt it; he's very angry. I don't know whether I could take him back."

Susan came up to the three and told Gennie, "You blindsided me. I never dreamed that you were holding on to such a secret."

Phyllis waited for Susan to leave and said, "I wasn't so far off with my theory. I just wasn't sure if it had been premeditated or just a fortunate accident. In the next few days, let's get together. Call me when it's convenient."

Soon only Mason, Gennie, and Father John remained in the room.

Father John asked, "Did you come together?" Mason and Gennie nodded. "Mason, why don't you drive your car home, and I will take your mother."

"Smooth move, Father," Mason retorted. The two men smiled.

Father John hugged the lad and said, "Thank goodness you are going back to school. It would be a challenge to visit with your mother with you around."

In the car Father John said to Gennie, "Congratulations on passing the state boards. Now you can be an independent woman. One thing I've learned about you is that you are a planner. I think you have already thought about the future without Will. I am quickly going to offer my hope that your plans will include me."

"I am just divorcing Will. I'm not eliminating my friends too."

"I am hoping to be more than just a friend. I guess my impatience is showing. Let me pursue a more immediate query—do you fear for your safety?"

"No, I haven't in the past, but I haven't openly defied Will before. I feel safe with Mason at the house, and he is staying for the next few days. I plan to have all the locks changed, not only because of Will but because Margo had a house key that her friends may have confiscated."

A moment of silence ensued, and Gennie said, "I don't think our relationship should show any obvious change at this time. Your car doesn't need to be in my driveway frequently. I don't want to antagonize Will. Let's see how he reacts to divorce inquiries. I don't want Will to view you as presumptuous. Even though he threatened to leave, I think he expected me to plead with him not to."

As they approached the house, they could see Mason hadn't arrived yet, so Father John offered to go in with Gennie to make sure Will wasn't there ready for a confrontation. They walked through the house and found that Will had cleaned out his clothes closet and taken a TV. Father John left after taking Gennie's hand and kissing it.

"If you don't call me tomorrow evening, I will call you," he offered. .

Chapter 26

Father John correctly assessed Gennie's propensity for planning. Many of her classmates in nursing were divorced, and she had questioned them about their lawyers and what they thought of their abilities. When two names kept coming up, she'd gone to their offices only to get their free predivorce booklets that outlined the general procedures for divorce in California. She knew that after she filed for divorce, a six-month waiting period was required. Because all of the commercial properties and the house had been acquired during their marriage, all of their assets would be considered community property. A lot of records needed to be collected. She also recognized that beyond grieving for Margo, she would also feel sadness that her marriage had ended. She could not entertain the idea of a romance with John. In the past she had shut out any thoughts beyond a deep friendship with him, and her circumstances hadn't changed. Whether she was a married or divorced woman, the church discouraged a priest from marrying her. What John had in mind, she didn't know, and she wasn't even going to discuss it with him for fear that he would feel encouragement. She recognized that she could love him but that it would only lead to huge frustration for both of them. What would that accomplish?

When Mason came home he sat at the kitchen table as she put together some soup. As it simmered on the stove, she asked Mason if he wanted a beer or glass of wine. Beer was the answer, so she poured herself a glass of wine and handed him a beer.

"Were you surprised with my revelation today?"

"Yes and no. I drove around and stopped by the old home-place property. Of course the house isn't there, but some of the trees still are. I thought about all the changes there and in our lives. In a way, it doesn't surprise me that Dad would do anything to protect his business—to prevent bankruptcy and failure. But to kill his best friend and partner? The one he enlisted with and later spent time with on a ship? At what point does the alarm in his moral compass sound? It is beyond my understanding and basic reasoning. I have to wonder if being forced to relinquish half of the company to you in a divorce is going to trigger that kind of animosity toward you. Should I think of dropping out of school to stay here for a few months?"

"That's sweet of you to offer, but that would give him two targets instead of one if he is that vengeful."

"I think he has a Wizard of Oz complex: 'I am the great and powerful. No one defies me.'"

Gennie said, "Perhaps, but anger seems to be his motivator. It didn't seem that my revelation surprised Mama or Papa M, yet he is their son. In the light of what I said today, you might check with Papa M to see if he's changed his mind about deeding the farm to you. I wouldn't want you to go on expecting it if today's news altered his decision."

She pulled out the telephone book and looked in the yellow pages for a locksmith. She remembered the company that had put the lock on their bedroom door, and called the manager. He said he could be out in the morning.

The doorbell rang, and Gennie flinched.

"Who could that be?" she asked. Mason went to the door, and a deliveryman stood there holding a long florist box tied with a deep-red ribbon. Mason handed the box to his mother. Inside were a dozen crimson roses. The note said, "I don't want you to forget me. Fondly, John."

"Looks like I need to stay home to protect you from this ardent Romeo," Mason said.

"He's making sure he'll get a phone call tonight. Aren't they beautiful? Why don't you get the soup bowls out, and I'll get a vase. The soup is ready."

"Talking about phone calls, is it okay if I call a girlfriend tonight?"

"Sure, is she down at school?"

"Yes, but she has been living at home this year in Paso Robles—about a forty-minute drive. We took a drawing class together, and she saw my sketches of horses, so we share that interest. Her folks have a couple of horses, so I've gone there to ride occasionally."

"What's her name?"

"Lisa." His smile wrapped around those four letters, and the sound of her name oozed with a warm softness.

"She sounds important. Is she?"

"We're both thinking of transferring to the Pomona campus because of their emphasis on equestrian management. Right now our advisors say to stay next year at the current campus because the art department is better. We plan to go look at Pomona when I get back. She's also been in dressage classes since her childhood and hopes to eventually try out for nationals. So yes, I'm very interested, but we both have lots of school left."

"Let me know when you plan to call her so I don't pick up one of the receivers trying to make a call."

After Father John had left the florist shop, he drove his old Ford coupe back towards his apartment in the city. He parked in a rented garage one half block from his place. An old refrigerator sat in the corner of the garage and he pulled out a frozen dinner, put it into a briefcase, walked up the hill to the remodeled post Victorian house and then climbed the outside metal stairs to his attic apartment. His one room studio had a small sink, an under the counter oven, a miniscule refrigerator and a hot plate, He turned on the oven to heat and poured a jigger of Jack Daniels sour mash over some ice in a glass. He seldom drank but this bottle had been given to him by an All Saints Hospital board member and on days like this he was happy to have it available. Taking off his white collar and loosening the neck of his shirt, he sat in the only stuffed chair and looked out the screened door at the roofs of houses that squatted on the rolling hills of the city.

Presiding at a child's funeral had always wrenched his emotions but today was even worse. Beyond the sadness he had felt, he wanted to console the child's mother by holding her in his arms and making her feel safe. He sipped the whiskey and felt the burn as it slithered down his throat.

Shortly after he'd met Gennie in the hospital he had felt attracted to her but once she was discharged, he'd realized he could not try to contact her. Two long months went by before she invited him to lunch and this was the first time she lamented about her failing marriage He wanted to feel encouraged. He prayed. God's answer was "Be patient." Today he had momentarily forgotten God's advice and in his eagerness to express his feelings he had frightened her. He saw it on her face. Now that he knew Will was capable of murder, it was no wonder that she might be scared. He hoped the flowers would be a peace offering for over stepping his bounds.

God had never said, "Forget her," so he needed to march in step and not advance.

John also recognized that Gennie had only expressed admiration for his efforts to teach her about God; she had never tried to go beyond the mentor-student relationship.

He thought, "I've had many flirtations in my lifetime but none compares to what I feel about Gennie. Right now her life is chaotic and I don't need to muddle it up with my romantic needs. I will wait and watch and hope and pray."

Chapter 27

After the locksmith left the next morning, Gennie went to her divorce lawyer's office. She picked up a sheath of papers to be filled out before the first interview with the lawyer, which could lead up to separation papers being served to Will. While Will had been incarcerated, Gennie had asked both Phyllis and the accountant for a history of all the properties bought and sold. The value and debts might have changed, but she basically had what could be considered community property.

Because the Super M corporate offices were nearby, she stopped to say hi to Phyllis. Gennie told her she planned to file for a divorce, and Phyllis did not seem surprised at the suddenness of the decision.

Phyllis said, "Well, there are changes in the air: I have decided to give my four-week notice of resignation. My husband and I talked long into the night. I know this company inside and out. Will pays me well. To hear your story, even though I suspected it, shook me to my core. It sounds dramatic to say, 'I feel a sense of evil here,' but I am no longer comfortable. Did you know that Neil resigned about six weeks ago? One of our competitors offered him a great deal. He's wise to have taken it." Phyllis paused for a moment. "Do you fear for your safety?"

"You know, Father John asked me that last night. I haven't in the past, but I have never defied Will like I'm doing now, by divorcing him and reducing his assets. I can't placate him just to feel safe. I'll see what the lawyer says.

"I'll miss having you as an ally here in the office," Gennie continued. "You have been a splendid friend and confidante. I have one last request: Could you gather the information about the partnership payment to Alice and also the name of the insurance company? I was in the hospital during that time and never did know the specifics of the transaction. Just mail it to me so I can have it in my financial folder.

"Please let me know where you are going to work. As vice president of the board of directors, I can give you a letter of recommendation if Will won't."

As Gennie walked to her car, she mused that Will may feel abandoned. Neil, his head human-relations employee; Phyllis, the only secretary he'd ever had; Gennie, the only wife he'd ever had; the death of a daughter; and the loss of his residence. Where would his breaking point be?

That afternoon Mason telephoned Papa M to see when it would be convenient to see him.

"How about coming over in the morning? Since Mama M suffers from arthritis in her knees, the climb up the stairs to our bedroom has become painful. We've decided to move downstairs into the guest room. That's where Margo had her sleepovers, but now it makes more sense to use it as our bedroom. I've called Joe to borrow a laborer, and we can go out there to pick him up. If you can stay and help, it will go a lot faster."

When Gennie heard of the plans, she offered to go with Mason to the house and help Mama M bring down all the toiletries, linens, clothes, and other smaller items. It would be an opportunity to help the elder Muellers and do something besides sit around a table and weep.

It took about four hours of effort. By the time Mason and Gennie left, the bedroom had been configured downstairs on the other end of the house and stood ready for a good night's sleep.

On the drive home Gennie asked Mason if he'd been able to come to some conclusion about the property and if Papa M still felt he would deed it to him. Mason responded that Papa M remained determined to give him the land if he wanted it.

Mason said, "Joe's son has studied the ever-increasing globalization of food sources and wants to get out of growing crops. He has been enamored with rose culture and wants to eventually make the best and largest rose center in California. The climate is right, and we seldom have long spells of fog, and the roses he's planted have done well. He would like a combination wholesale-retail endeavor.

"I told Papa M I want to do something with horses: stables, boarding, Western-style lessons, riding trails, and an arena to practice for rodeo events. Or if Lisa stays in my life, the emphasis could be on dressage and the European type of riding. I asked him if he knew how many acres he thought Joe's son would need for his venture. I also wondered what the Nakamuras' long-range proposals were. He said he would be glad to talk with everyone and go to City Hall to check on zoning restrictions and the requirements for a master plan."

Mason added a last-moment thought: "By the way, Dad has moved into Papa M's hideaway apartment out there."

The following day Gennie called the lawyer's office and made an appointment. After looking at all of Gennie's paperwork, he quizzed her about her thoughts on alimony. She said she planned to work but may need some transitional alimony while she sold the house and the car and downsized considerably.

"You don't have to anticipate or endure a lower standard of living when you divorce," the lawyer assured her. "It's my job to see that you won't. I don't see any reason not to serve these papers tomorrow and get this six-month waiting period started. I will be in touch."

As Gennie rose to leave, the attorney stood and gave her a business card. "This has my home number on it, and you may call it twenty-four hours a day for any emergencies."

"My friends have expressed concerns for my safety, but Will has never given me cause to fear him before. I will keep in touch."

With the weekend coming up, Mason proposed that he return to school on Sunday night. That would give him time to finish his art project and have a day to prowl Pomona with Lisa before the next summer session started.

Mason left after dinner. Gennie read in bed until she felt sleepy. It was close to midnight when she turned off the light. Moments later the phone rang. How fast and loud a frightened heart can beat—especially a mother's—when her offspring is driving late at night. Gennie's first emotion was fear: Did Mason have an auto accident? She answered the phone on the bedside table.

"Gennie? Is Will there?" a male voice asked.

"No, who is this?"

"I'm Floyd, Lem and Margaret's neighbor. Their house is on fire." She sat up in the bed and fumbled for the light.

"Are they safe?"

"Yes, they got out okay. I don't know how; the kitchen and their upstairs bedroom are engulfed in flames."

"Has the fire department arrived?"

"Yes."

"I'll be right over. It will take me about twenty minutes. Tell Margaret or Lem to stay there, and they can come home with me. Take them to your house now if it's too chilly out there."

"Okay, I'll tell them."

Gennie quickly dressed and grabbed a couple of woolen throws from the back of the sofa and foot of the bed. With the light traffic at this late hour, she could drive fast, and she arrived in fifteen minutes. Turning off the old Mayfield Main Street toward the Muellers' house, she smelled the smoke and saw the glow from the fire and the emergency vehicles' lights in the sky. A large group of cars was parked on either side of the street, so Gennie drove up into the neighbor's driveway. Lem stood with his friend in the yard, dressed in a heavy coat, maybe his or his neighbor's. His pajama trousers covered his legs, and he had slippers on his feet.

She ran up to him and asked, "Are you okay, Papa M? What about Mama M? Is she inside?"

"Yes, we're okay. But all of my photos are gone." He started to tear up.

"Where were they?"

"In the upstairs hall closet," he said, wiping his nose with the back of his hand. "The firemen are suspicious that it was set deliberately."

The shock of that statement left Gennie without words. Questions started forming in her mind.

The fire chief came over to Lem. Recognizing Gennie, he asked if she planned to take them home with her. When she said yes, he said, "Since their clothes are at the end of the house where they were sleeping last night, they can follow one of my men in and pick enough clothes and toiletries for tomorrow. We'll have a couple of firemen and a policeman here all night, so their things will be safe until morning. I think they need to go now, get a warm bath and warm clothes, and try to sleep." The chief had known Lem for years and showed his concern for his old friend, who now looked so downtrodden.

Gennie went into the neighbor's house to fetch Margaret, told her to get clothes for the next day and any medications—including her stress pills—if she could find them.

Lem and Margaret came out of their home, each with a big paper grocery bag filled with their belongings. "Like two war orphans," Gennie thought. "What a shock to their systems—their elderly systems."

Lem got into the front seat next to Gennie after helping Margaret into the back. As they drove down Main Street past his old grocery store, now a gift boutique, he said, "At least that store is untouched."

The car radio, tuned to the classical station, played soft piano music and filled the silence. All were too stunned to talk.

After some thought Lem said, "Will telephoned me today. He'd received your divorce papers. He asked me to give him his inheritance now so he would have enough money to settle with you without jeopardizing any stores. I asked him what he anticipated. He said the farm. I told him Mason would inherit that land. He said, 'Sons always inherit their fathers' properties. You don't skip over them to the next generation.' I said that, knowing how he felt about the Japanese, I didn't think he would be a good neighbor to the Nakamuras. Then I told him I had promised the land to Mason ever since he was twelve—if he wanted it. 'And he wants it,' I said. Will slammed down the receiver so hard it almost broke my eardrum." Lem cleared his throat. "I don't know what to make of it."

Gennie said, "I don't either." Thoughts swirled in her head: "I'm going to call the lawyer at home. Won't he be thrilled to get a call from a brand-new client this late at night? I'll ask him to get a watchman out to our house tonight. Because Mason doesn't have the property yet, I don't think he is in any danger, and Will doesn't know he has returned to school. Actually, I don't know where Mason is—whether he went to his dorm or Lisa's home. No need to alarm him now."

When they got to Gennie's house, she sent Margaret to the master bathroom and Lem to the guest shower, and after calling the lawyer, she went in and made up the guest bed. Because that bedroom had a seating area, she took in cups of warm milk for the two to drink.

After Lem and Margaret had showered and settled in the guest sitting room, Gennie explained, "We learned in nursing school that warm milk induces sleep better than anything else so I brought you each a cup. Let's not discuss the events tonight, because once we start, we'll be up all night. Let's say our prayers and thank God you are safe."

Margaret said, "We wouldn't be here if we'd slept in our old bedroom."

"Mama M, we'll talk about this tomorrow. No more tonight."

Like a defiant child who had to get the last word, Margaret mumbled, "And Will didn't know we had moved downstairs."

"Margaret, enough. Come to bed," Lem admonished.

"I do have one thing to tell you," Gennie added. "I called the divorce lawyer, and he is sending out a watchman to come here tonight. I think we can all sleep better knowing someone is out there. Good night."

Gennie went to the kitchen with the empty cups and looked out the window at the driveway, where a truck already sat parked with a man inside. She opened the garage door and went out to talk with him. He assured her that he would stay in the truck and occasionally walk around the perimeter of the property. She felt safe.

The next morning the lawyer called Gennie to ask her what had happened. She related the fire—possible arson—and the telephone call Will had with his dad.

"Does your father-in-law have a will? Where does the property go if your son dies?"

Gennie gasped and said, "I know he has a will, but I don't know the other answer. You don't think Will would kill his own son for that property, do you?"

"You answer that, Mrs. Mueller. What son tries to torch his parents' home? I am not accusing him, because I don't know all the facts, but we have to act defensibly. If a crime has occurred, we need to get into possible motives of the perpetrator.

"I would like to talk to your father-in-law's attorney—whoever drew up the will. I'd like to make sure that if your son dies, Will isn't the beneficiary. Then I want to call Will's divorce lawyer so that Will is made aware of that. I assume Will is after the money, not just the demise of family members."

"I'll talk to my father-in-law when he wakes up and get that information." After hanging up, she thought, "I hope it's the money he's after and not the secret-holders...if he did it. There is always the possibility that the firemen will find another cause of the fire other than arson."

The next day, Gennie had plans to go up to San Francisco to have lunch with Father John. She called the church office and talked with the secretary.

"Hi, this is Mrs. Mueller. Father John and I had a lunch date."

"Yes, ma'am."

"I am going to cancel because my in-laws had a house fire last night, and they are staying with me. I will be busy helping them today."

"Yes, ma'am. Is that all you want me to convey to Father?"

"Yes, he knows how to reach me. I'll be in and out."

"You know, Mrs. Mueller, that isn't going to be enough information for Father John. He is going to be infuriated with that paltry amount of facts and be very angry at me."

"Okay, my in-laws escaped the fire uninjured. I am fine, and Mason is back in school and fine. Do you think that will satisfy him?"

"No, I doubt it, but at least that amount of explanation might save my job."

"Well, then, just tell him to have faith."

"Oh, ma'am, I don't think I can say that."

Lem remembered that his will had been in a locked box in the hall closet and had burned, but he did have another copy in the bank's safety deposit box. The bank key stayed in the top dresser drawer at the house. As he recalled, Margo was to receive the land if Mason died. The old city judge who had drawn up the will had died a few years ago.

The divorce lawyer belonged to a large group of specialty attorneys, so the expert in family law met with Lem to add a codicil. While he did that, Gennie and Margaret went looking for temporary housing. The insurance adjuster had viewed the damage and said that their insurance covered the cost of living elsewhere during their home's reconstruction. He suggested some long-stay cottages built behind regular overnight motels on El Camino between Palo Alto and Mountain View. They looked at three locations and picked the one closest to their home. It had a living area, bedroom, and kitchenette, with shared laundry facilities in a central location. Margaret wanted to continue attending her clubs and bridge groups. The entire area also had a night watchman.

When they went back to the burned house, Lem stood out front talking to the adjuster. The house could be declared 100 percent damaged and bulldozed, or Lem could decide to keep the front façade and basically build on the old foundation. They decided to bulldoze, save some light fixtures and the mantel, and then build a one-story house to better suit their present needs. The insurance company would supply workers to pack their dishes and salvageable kitchen objects, put clothes in cardboard closets, and deliver them to their temporary rooms.

Gennie called Father John, told him the basic scenario, and arranged to meet him for lunch the following day. Then she called Mason and told him the same story. She didn't want to alarm him but felt he needed the bare gist of the events. He said his father could have the farm if he wanted it that badly; it wasn't worth harming anyone. Gennie explained that the will had been rewritten so Will couldn't receive it in any circumstance. She appreciated his benevolence, but rewarding such alleged outrageous behavior wouldn't be right.

She also called Susan and recited this bizarre saga. Gennie told her she planned to visit Erma and Josefina in a few days.

The thought that Will may have set this fire had shaken her core of confidence. Gennie didn't want to live in fear, but she also couldn't act naïve.

Amid all this activity, the grayness of grief swirled around her like a ground-hugging fog. Many thought processes could be active above it, yet swells of sadness arose spontaneously. Unpredictably, her throat would tighten, she would start salivating, and then the tears would flow. She couldn't explain or control it. The dichotomy of mourning the tragic loss of one family member while another member appeared to be trying to eliminate two others defied logic.

Chapter 28

Gennie drove up to the city to see Father John. The exciting strains of one of Rachmaninoff's piano concertos on the car radio engulfed her.

Although he looked glad to see her, John's face also reflected his concern for her safety. He suggested that she move, but Gennie said she had employed the neighborhood watchman, who made rounds hourly and randomly, so she felt fairly safe.

They sat in a small café in the Ferry Building overlooking the bay and were serenaded by seagulls.

"I talked with my bishop this week and asked permission to be entered into a call list for a change in parishes," he said.

"Are you not happy at the mission?" Gennie asked.

"I'm still happy at the mission," he replied. When Gennie said nothing, John said, "Aren't you going to ask me why I'm asking for a change?"

"I feel a trap. I think I'm being set up. Okay, John, why?"

"I was assigned to this mission when I became a priest. It did not pay well, but because I was unmarried and fairly young, the bishop thought this would be a good assignment. Now that I am planning on marrying, I will need a greater salary and a larger parsonage. Do you know where we should live?"

"John Landon, you cannot marry me. You know that, and I know that. You are following pipe dreams. Nothing has changed; I am unavailable to you, whether married or divorced."

"Mrs. Mueller, I also talked with the bishop about a possible marriage, and he sees no reason it wouldn't be acceptable in the eyes of the church. In this diocese, a number of priests are married to divorcées, and also some have remarried after a divorce."

"You went into the priesthood with higher standards than that. Don't you see that you would be compromising your moral code if you married? It's wrong to go against the inner fiber of your ethical principles."

"Even if God and the church say it's okay?"

"Far be it from me to put my judgment before God's, but the God I'm listening to says it's wrong."

"Whoa, Gennie, you are a tough one." His endearing grin showed his dimples. "Okay, let's go hypothetical. If you could pick a community where we could be together, where would it be?"

"I'm not even going there. I could so easily visualize a cute parsonage with a white picket fence next to the church, and there you are on the steps greeting all the parishioners—but what good is an impossible dream?"

"Well, I'm not giving up."

"I think that is a foregone conclusion." Their eyes met, her gaze betraying her fondness for him. "You are making this very difficult for me," Gennie said.

"How so?"

"I don't see any future for us in this relationship but heartache. I think we need to stop seeing each other. You deserve to find someone to love who is unfettered and able to marry you. I never meant to be a romantic interest. I have always been so appreciative of your kindness and understanding that I wanted to continue our friendship. But now I feel it is going beyond that. I realize how unfair that is to you. I have prayed about this, and all I see is how selfish I am to continue seeing you. The scriptures say one should not lust after his neighbor's wife. But I would add to that, 'The neighbor's wife should not encourage it.'"

"Gennie, are you serious?"

"Yes, as painful as it is, I think it's the right thing."

John appeared stunned—shell-shocked.

Gennie changed the conversation topic to Mason: his new girlfriend, Lisa, and his plans for the farm property.

After being together for three hours, it was time for them to part. John grabbed Gennie, hugged her tight, and then kissed her on the forehead.

On her drive home Gennie had to admit that her suggestion to become estranged wasn't totally altruistic. Lately, it had been harder for her to hide her growing passionate feelings for John.

The next day Gennie drove up to Petaluma using the Golden Gate Bridge. She said a simple "thank you for saving me" prayer as she passed the spot where she had jumped nearly three years before.

She and Susan walked the back roads of rural Petaluma under great rows of eucalyptus trees that guarded the sides of the lanes. The gentle breeze moved the leaves, and their pungent aroma permeated the air.

They talked about Margo. Gennie related that in the very early-morning hours, she would lie awake and ponder all the events leading up to Margo's abortion.

"I'm trying to second-guess my decisions and actions, which isn't productive. Yet there must be a lesson to be learned—besides don't jump from bridges."

"Yes, I have wondered why all the love we bestowed on her as a family wasn't enough to save her," Susan said.

"When I asked the counselor if we shouldn't send her to another environment, away from those wayward friends, he said she might consider it a rejection and only be more rebellious. If I hadn't jumped from such a headline-grabbing place, or if I hadn't tried to self-destruct at all, would Margo have been content in her childhood coterie of friends?"

Susan stopped and gave her sister a hug. "It's those kinds of questions that are self-defeating yet linger on. By the way, have you ever considered whether you should tell Alice your secret?"

"Up until recently, I didn't plan to tell anyone, least of all Alice. I'm not so sure it would be beneficial at this point to stir up old emotions—especially now that you just told me she's moved on and is dating a nice young man. Wouldn't I be unburdening my guilty complicity in the crime and upsetting her life?"

"Yes, that's one way to look at it. Another is that Alice may harbor anger at Herb for overimbibing and abdicating his responsibility to his family. I've read that it's not unusual for a widow to feel abandoned because her husband left her through death, and if there was reckless behavior involved, it might compound the feelings."

"I'll have to think about it. I don't need to deal with it immediately. I have so much stress as it is. But if you and Walter come up with a definitive answer, let me know."

Susan said, "To change the subject, Walter wanted me to talk to you about finances. Since you are in negotiations with Will, he thought you needed to know what your inheritance from Mom will be. Both he and I—and Josefina too—are noticing a slowing down of her daily activities. She sleeps longer, sits more often, and is generally more sluggish. When I talked to the doctor at the last visit, he said this is normal aging and we should accept it as inevitable. He did not think any medication would be helpful.

"Walter has been handling her account, investing it in a broad base of stocks and bonds, and it has consistently increased. We have only withdrawn money for the extra hours Josefina works, medical visits, and personal items for Mom."

"You mean you haven't paid yourselves for her room and board the seven years she's lived with you?"

"No, she and Dad housed you and Mason for over three years without charge, and we felt this was a privilege to pay her back."

"It doesn't surprise me that you thought that way. You are both generous."

"Walter said you and I will each inherit close to one million dollars, which came from the sale of the house and those thirty acres of prime land. The stock market has been good, and the investments have doubled in value in these eight years. He wanted you to know so that your lawyers don't push you to nickel-and-dime Will. Walter isn't suggesting that you accept less than your share, but he doesn't want you to shove Will beyond his limit. He also thinks you should keep this out of the conversation with your lawyers; otherwise, their fees may go up accordingly. As you know, personal inheritance is not included in community property."

"I knew it had increased, but I had no idea how much," Gennie said. "I trusted Walter and knew he had a keen understanding of investing. I hope he will consider managing my account after I inherit it. Perhaps he can also help me navigate the tax implications of the divorce and the inheritance. I also think you and Walter need to plan a huge vacation and use the money before we divide it. You've made Mom's life so pleasant."

They continued to talk about their childhood and other topics, but Gennie could not mention her decision to be estranged from John; it was too raw. As the sun started to move to the west, they headed home.

Chapter 29

The weeks went by, and Will did not respond to the lawyer's requests. They cautioned him that the expense increased as the negotiations became more contentious. Ultimately, laws existed that dealt with an uncooperative respondent, but those didn't apply until after the six months. Meanwhile, Gennie had minor repairs done to the house, knowing it would be sold whether she retained ownership or not. She also put her application in at several outpatient clinics and school districts for a daytime nursing position.

Walter had been investigating all the circumstances surrounding Margo's surgery in Sweden and the concluding diagnosis of the Swedish doctors, which read, "Irreversible hyperthermia due to anesthesia." The report named Halothane, an inhalant anesthetic, as the culprit.

Gennie decided to take this information to the medical library at Stanford. Years earlier, when Alice first worked there, she'd said part of the library's mission statement included helping educate the public with up-to-date publications on medical issues. They invited laypeople to come in and research their questions. Gennie had only read about the large, newly constructed campus and found the information desk at the hospital entrance. She received a map and, after driving to the appropriate building, started walking through the outdoor corridors with decorative concrete grillwork. This large medical complex had been hailed as an architectural innovation, and she marveled at its aesthetic as well as practical design. She walked past a large water fountain, its center cone of water erupting into bubbling splashes.

She entered the library and approached the librarian at the desk, told her story, and noted what information she hoped to obtain.

"I just filed an issue of *International Magazine on Anesthesiology* the other day, and it highlights an article about malignant hyperthermia in children," the librarian said. "That might be a good place to start. As I recall, the research is out of Australia and is brand-new." She walked over to some shelves, came back, and handed Gennie the magazine.

Gennie sat and read the article. When the report delved into the chemistry and microanalysis of muscle fibers, she felt lost, but the researchers concluded that in the patients they'd studied, a defect in the chemistry of the muscle fibers caused the severe reaction to this specific anesthesia. The trait appeared to be inherited and had no known antidote. The symptoms of this phenomenon included a sudden increase in body temperature, a rapid and uncontrollable heart rate, soaring hypertension, and rigidity of all skeletal muscle, which so far had been irreversible. Not all types of anesthesia caused this reaction in these susceptible patients, but a full list of safe and unsafe types had not been identified. They were working on a diagnostic test, but it had not proven successful. The article said the probability of inheriting the defect appeared low, but all relatives of a known casualty should tell their medical doctors before surgery. Gennie felt satisfied with the explanation and left, thanking the librarian. She would notify the other family members.

John and Gennie had not talked for the last three weeks since she'd suggested they stop seeing each other. It had been difficult for both of them. John called her and offered a compromise: see each other every two weeks, and he would cool his ardor. They would return to their original friendly relationship. What could Gennie say but "Okay, let's try that."

Chapter 30

About three months later, during one of their weekly conversations, Susan told Gennie that Erma had developed a persistent cough. No fever, but she stayed in bed most of the time. Unless she had difficulty breathing or ran a fever, the doctor suggested tender loving care. Josefina felt obligated to stay with Erma and became the epitome of a bedside nurse. A few weeks later Susan called to say Erma had been admitted to the hospital. The doctor thought she would be more comfortable with oxygen and minimal pain medication. Even though it appeared she had pneumonia, he didn't want to treat it aggressively. Susan agreed, but the doctor wanted to talk with Gennie to get her approval of their passive-care plan.

Gennie asked John to go with her to Susan's home in Petaluma. On the way John said, "You have often wondered about your mom's early life, but you've never asked me about mine."

"You expect to learn about your parents' history because it's partly yours too," Gennie replied. "You don't pry into acquaintances' backgrounds, especially when they are persons of authority or teachers. You wait until they want to share, or so I was taught."

"I think you might have some false assumptions about me," John continued. "I am not an inexperienced puppy. You might have speculated that I went from high school to seminary to priesthood, but that is incorrect. Like every other boy, I enlisted after Pearl Harbor. My two brothers and I signed up on the same day. Our action devastated Mother, but we kids were all caught up in the excitement of patriotism and fighting for our country. My oldest brother died in 1943 in Sicily. My middle brother and I both participated in the D-day invasion, but he and hundreds of other Americans died on those beaches. I came back home to finish college, since I'd left in my junior year. I'd seen far too much killing, and the senselessness of it overwhelmed me. I'd drifted away from attending church in high school and college, but in my search for some meaning, I decided to go to the seminary. I found the call to help give hope to others. I thought someday I would have all the answers, but instead I found that the more I learn, the less I know—the mystery only deepens. Faith is the key."

"You never talked about family, so I guessed you didn't have any."

"My sister and mother both live in Arizona. They are next-door neighbors; my sister is married and has two children. My dad died a few years ago. Mom still mourns her sons, especially when I go home. My presence seems to trigger those thoughts of what might have been. My sister said Mom is sadder when I am there and after I leave, so I go only about once a year."

Gennie looked over at John when he said this and saw that his hands were clenched. She reached over and put her hand on one of his. Obviously, this was a painful memory for him to share.

With sympathetic thoughts, Gennie said, "Cherishing those memories without becoming sad is difficult. 'Remember the happy times' is good advice, but accomplishing that can be a challenge.I always wondered how old you were. You look so young. Now I know you are about two years older than me."

"You could have just asked."

"It was more fun being the detective—like if you remembered a certain song or movie, I would be assured you were close to my age. So you see, you've been on my mind more than you know."

"And I'm flattered."

When they arrived at the house, Walter suggested that he drive all of them to the hospital to meet the doctor. Sitting in the front seat next to Walter, Susan questioned him about his chosen route. He replied that he was checking something out.

In a few minutes he said, "We have a tail."

"A what?"

"Someone is following us. I've taken him on a wild goose chase, and he continues to be in the rearview mirror. I expect your home phone is tapped too."

Walter had been in the SS in Sweden and worked with the underground during the war. His work with the Swedish consulate now involved some undercover work.

"I guess that is Will's doing, but why?"

"I'm not sure, since this is a no-fault divorce state. Maybe he's hoping to learn more about your financial position or strategy. My advice is not to talk with your lawyers from your home phone."

When they reached the hospital, they all went to Erma's room. An oxygen cannula was in her nose, and she seemed to be asleep. Josefina sat beside the bed, holding Erma's hand.

"The doctor asked that you page him when you arrive, and said he would come back," Josefina said.

When the doctor arrived, he took Gennie into the hall.

"I understand you are a nurse, so our plan is to keep your mother comfortable, give her oxygen, help keep the fever down, and feed her ice chips for fluids. She has an indwelling catheter. As you know, we could pump her full of antibiotics, but what's the point? She's had a good life. Do you agree that nonaggressive care is best? Do you want us to do anything differently?"

"I agree. Without memories, quality of life is negligible."

"You understand. I wanted to hear your consent for myself."

Gennie stayed to visit awhile, and then they returned home. About thirty-six hours later, Susan called Gennie to tell her that their mother had died in the early-morning hours. They had already decided on a graveside ceremony. A couple of days later, Mason drove up for the service.

"The school is starting to think this excuse of another funeral is a little fishy," he told Gennie.

Besides Susan, Walter, Mason, Gennie, and John, the Muellers would join them. The simple service featured readings of Khalil Gibran that Susan and Gennie remembered their folks reading to each other, and the singing of two of

Erma's favorite songs: "Over the Rainbow" and "Playmates." Walter strummed his guitar as accompaniment. John read a prayer from the liturgy of the prayer book, and Mason talked about a few of his early memories.

Margaret and Lem invited them all over to their newly completed house for a late lunch. Mason said he needed to head back to school. Susan said, "I found some interesting things among Mother's belongings. We'll look at those first, Mason, and then you can be on your way. You'll only be delayed an hour."

When they had all arrived at the Mueller house, Susan brought out a cloth shopping bag from I. Magnin and opened it up to reveal a jewelry box, a couple of small ring boxes, and a Bible.

The jewelry box had an inscription of Tiffany & Company on its lid. Inside was an elaborate diamond brooch in a ribbon motif.

"I don't remember Mother ever wearing that. Do you think it belonged to Dad's mother—our grandmother?" Gennie asked.

"Yes, I think it's an early-nineteen-hundreds piece. So many people dismantle these old pieces and remount the diamonds in a more modern setting, but with the Tiffany mark, it is more valuable as it is."

Next, Susan showed a beautiful diamond ring with a large, old-fashioned-cut center stone surrounded by smaller ones.

"This is Mother's engagement ring. She seldom wore it. Once, she told me that she certainly couldn't garden with it on, so she just put it away. Mason, I wanted you to know that it is available when you need it."

"What about Mom?" Mason asked. "She may need it before me."

Gennie blushed, a true teenager-type blush. She just looked at Mason and shook her head. The motion could be interpreted as "What am I going to do with you?" No one—especially not Mason—knew about John's and Gennie's semiestrangement.

Susan proceeded: "There are also two other beautiful rings. One has rubies and diamonds, the other sapphires and diamonds. Again, I had never seen these before. Now to the biggest surprise for me: the Holy Bible and its contents.

"Inside this old Bible is a yellowed newspaper clipping. It is crispy and about to fall apart, so rather than pass it around, I will read it to you:

Grass Valley Union-Gazette
July 15, 1899
Abducted Girl Found; Perpetrator Jailed

Yesterday, two hunters on horseback brought in a young girl to the sheriff's office believed to be Erma Hart, missing since 1893, when she was assumed abducted. She was eight years old when last seen and is now fourteen. They reported that she had been living in a shack in the mountains virtually hidden by brush and trees with the man who had kidnapped her. They brought her in after assuring her that her abductor would be jailed. He has been identified as Jimmy Bullock, a latecomer to the Gold Rush. Described as a ne'er-do-well, he had been suspected of petty crimes when he came into town but was never arrested. (See firsthand account by rescuers.)

U/G Exclusive Interview with One of the Hunters

My friend and I had been out all morning looking for small game, and our horses were thirsty. We were following the sound of a small brook, looking for a place where we could reach it easily. There was a lot of tangled underbrush. We heard a girl singing. Both the brook and the voice seemed to be coming from the same direction, so we went deeper into the underbrush. There, in a small clearing in a sudden patch of sunlight, stood a young girl hanging up wash—mostly faded rags. She was startled to see us. She started for the shack and then stopped, like she wanted to talk. We told her we were looking for access to the water so our horses could drink, and she pointed to a trail and said that's how they got to it. We asked permission to take our horses on the path down there, and she said yes. My friend guided his horse on the narrow walkway, and I stayed back and talked with the girl. I asked if anyone else lived there, maybe her father. "No, he's not my father."

I asked, "Is a woman here?"

She said no.

"Is the man here now?"

"No, he went down to the river to pan for gold."

I asked if he was successful, and the girl said, "No, some pebbles now and then, but no nuggets."

I continued questioning. I asked her name, and she said Erma. Suddenly, the light came on in my head. I had been on one of the searching parties when Erma Hart had disappeared.

"Erma Hart?" I asked her.

"Yes," she said.

I told her that after she had been abducted, people had looked for her for weeks and I was in one of the search parties. I told her, "Every year on the anniversary of your disappearance, the newspaper prints a story asking if anyone knows of your whereabouts. They do this because your mother asks them to. Can I take you home?"

She said the man threatened to kill her family if she ever ran away. He also told her she would get lost and starve to death if she struck out on her own. So I told her, "If you go with us right now, the sheriff can be out here waiting for him when he returns home, and he will be arrested. We'll keep you safe."

While we had been talking, my friend had come up with his horse and exchanged it for mine. Now he was back from getting both of the horses watered. I briefly told him what I had learned and that we were taking her back home. She is now home with her family, and Mr. Bullock is in jail.

During the last paragraph, Susan kept dabbing at her tears, making it hard for her to read.

Gennie said, "Poor child. Even though she was free, with the Victorian morals still prevailing, she must have been singled out as a tainted female."

Susan said, "There's more. Walter, will you read it for me?" She handed the paper to him, and he cleared his throat.

Editorial:

This editor had the opportunity to interview both Mr. and Mrs. Luke Hart, parents of Erma, the recently found abducted child of our community. Mrs. Hart exuded her happiness that her child had been found.

"Whatever she's been through, I will help her find a normal life again, of going to school and having friends," she said.

Mr. Hart, who likes to be called Reverend Hart, is a self-proclaimed pastor of a small church group that meets in a barn and has five to ten families who attend regularly. He claims his church is a fundamentalist offshoot of the Nazarene sect.

When asked to comment on his daughter's return, he said, "God was testing my daughter, and if she has not returned chaste and pure, then she has failed his test. She will be punished for the rest of her life."

As a newspaper editor, it is not my place to argue religion with an interviewee, but I mentioned the scripture: "Suffer little children to come unto me." I asked him, "Do you not think God regards the innocence of children differently than that of adults?"

He replied, "I raised her in a good and godly manner. If she strayed from those teachings, she is a sinner and deserves to be penalized."

The editor would like to suggest that our community embrace this child and help her return to a normal childhood. It is not for us to judge, and chances are that she has suffered enough.

When he finished Walter looked around at a group of teary-eyed folks.

Gennie spoke first. "What an indomitable spirit Mama had! As sweet and kind as she always was, who would have guessed that she suffered so much? That explains why she could recite the Lord's Prayer from memory at Margo's funeral."

Susan said, "I can also understand why she didn't want to talk about it, especially to us young girls. She kept the clippings, though, because she knew we would find them and finally know."

Mason rose, saying, "I wish I could stay and continue to talk with you all, but I really need to get back to campus." He hugged each adult's neck and told Mama and Papa M how great their house looked. As he headed out the door, Mama M thrust a sandwich wrapped in waxed paper into his hand. Gennie followed him out to his car and said, "Susan and I are thinking of driving down next week to see you, meet Lisa, and take you out to dinner. We plan to stay at Pismo Beach for a few days, just walking along the beach and watching the tide come in. We'll call you before we start."

When Gennie returned to the house, Margaret had gone to the kitchen to finish the final prep for lunch, and Susan was helping her. Gennie took this opportunity to talk with Lem.

"I don't want to hurt you. I've been married to and loved Will for half of my life, but I'm concerned. When we were in Petaluma to visit Mom at the hospital, Walter pointed out that we were being followed. He suspects my home phone is being tapped also. Have you had any conversations with Will since the fire? I will tell you that he's not being cooperative at all in this divorce proceeding."

"Will has come by to see the progress of the house construction. I've not confronted him about the fire. Margaret and I also feel intimidated by his alleged aggression. Our question is whether it's all for the money or in retaliation for your telling us the reason you jumped."

"Did the fire department make a final decision about whether the fire was arson?"

"They kinda prevaricated; they labeled it as 'probable.' That's less than a declarative statement but more than 'possible' arson."

"So do you think that means that neither the fire department nor the insurance company will pursue it as arson?"

"Well, let me tell you what I think. If the insurance company suspects that it was possibly Will, they may not be inclined to press charges. Why? All my insurance—house, store, and farm—are with the same agent as Will's. The family has used that company for years. So our stores, trucks, houses, and cars are all with them too. Even if they thought they had an ironclad case, wouldn't they be killing the goose that lays the golden egg—so to speak?"

"That makes it sound like it all boils down to a business decision—regardless of morals," Gennie said. She paused, realizing that Walter and John were listening intently. "Also, now, with Mom's death, he knows Susan and I will inherit a nice amount of money. I have already changed my will so he no longer gets anything. Both Mason and I would have to be eliminated before he could attempt to get any of this money in a special judgment. Do you think he is desperate enough to pursue that? Are his grocery stores that precious?"

Gennie turned to Walter and said, "With your expertise, do you think I should move to a hotel? Should I notify Cal Poly about the possible danger to Mason? Or is this overreacting?"

Walter replied, "Let's figure out the time frame. Erma's will won't be probated for four to six weeks. There isn't any reason for him to harm you before it's probated. We could also ask for a delay in the process."

Mama M came into the living room, wiping her hands on her apron, and announced that lunch was ready. This ended the discussion because Gennie did not want to trouble her more. The death of her granddaughter and the house fire had taken their toll on her. She carried all those disappointments in her hunchback posture.

After lunch John and Gennie returned to her house, where John had left his car. She said, "I feel like a prisoner in my house. If the telephone is tapped and I'm being followed, where's my privacy?"

"You've changed your locks, and all your valuables are in a safe. I would tell your security company to double their surveillance while you're gone. I think getting away with Susan is a great idea. You both need a break."

Chapter 31

Susan and Gennie met Lisa, who had wholesome good looks and the straight carriage of a horsewoman. Even if Gennie had not known Lisa's surname was Riley, she would have suspected she had Irish ancestry. She had long red hair—not brassy—but softened with blonde strands. She wore it in the popular flip style, parted down the middle with the ends flipped up instead of turned under. Intense blue eyes and a sprinkling of freckles over the bridge of her nose complimented her leprechaun-like mischievous smile.

The sisters discussed afterward that Lisa had a quick sense of humor and wit that matched Mason's facetiousness. Their repartee of tease and taunt was like watching a tennis volley as they lobbed loving and clever remarks back and forth.

Susan said, "I'm glad to see Mason has found someone he cares for. After all his losses, he needs a special person to be fond of."

"I agree, I think he is attracted to her. Maybe besotted would be a better word. Or as Mason would say, 'I've got the hots for her.'"

"Oh my. Did he actually say that?'

"No, not about Lisa but that's how he described John's interest in me when Mason first met John." She laughed at the memory.

A week at the beach investigating adjacent seaside resorts rested both Gennie and Susan. The change of scenery fulfilled its refreshing promise.

Susan drove Gennie home, went into the house with her to make sure everything remained untouched and secured, and then went home to Petaluma.

When she arrived, Walter, who enjoyed puttering in the kitchen, fixed a chicken Caesar salad with sourdough bread and a cool glass of Chablis. Susan had much to talk about. The sisters had discussed giving a significant gift to Josefina and her husband, Rafael. Their suggestions were a trip, a new car, or possibly paying off their house mortgage. Walter said he knew the couple made payments on a small home in the Mexican American neighborhood of Petaluma. He would talk to Rafael about his future plans. He thought they were regarded as the senior statesmen of the neighborhood and would not want to leave their community.

After dinner Susan said all she wanted was a warm bath and to go to bed in her own home. They retired by eleven o'clock. A couple of hours later, Walter woke up when he heard the repeated low grumbling of the chickens. He nudged Susan. She did not awaken easily.

He whispered, "I hear someone trying to scale our patio wall. Go to the kitchen. Telephone the police, and then hide in the pantry. Be sure to close the door. Stay there until I come for you. Especially if there is more than one intruder, I don't want to shoot you by mistake."

His tone stripped the sleepy gauze wrapped around her brain. She ran to the kitchen.

In the country, moonlight provides the only source of light; on this night, clouds obscured the faint quarter moon. Beyond the city's street lights, the dark landscape could challenge the unfamiliar eye.

Their bedroom had a glass door that opened to a small patio area surrounded by an eight-foot-tall brick wall. Greenery in numerous pots climbed the walls, decorating the space, and at night the sliding door usually stood ajar a few inches to allow the evening air in.

Walter always slept with a pistol nearby. He went to the darkest corner of the room, adjacent to the patio door. The open drapes gathered against the wall, gave him further cover. The intruder slid the patio door open just a bit wider and then stopped after he stepped into the room. Walter saw the shiny gun in the man's hand. He watched.

The trespasser raised his gun and shot into the mound of bedding where Walter and Susan had been just moments before. At this point Walter shot the prowler in the back of his head and then the left side of his back, aiming for the heart. After the person fell Walter waited for a second accomplice. He didn't want to expose his position until he was certain no one else would appear. When he felt confident that no one else was there, he went to the light switch and turned it on. He turned over the body and looked at the victim.

"Oh my God!" he exclaimed out loud. "I just killed Will. I never thought he would try to do this himself."

He walked to the kitchen, flipping on every light switch as he went along. He wanted the police to realize the crisis had passed and not attempt a military assault of the house.

"Susan, all clear. It's over."

"I heard three shots! Are you hurt? How many intruders were there?"

"I'm fine. Just one, but brace yourself. It was Will, and I killed him."

"Walter, no! What was he here for?"

"He shot first, and the bullet went into the bed. I think he planned to kill us."

"Why? What have we ever done to him?"

"I guess we'll never know, but if we were both dead, all of Erma's estate would go to Gennie." Walter went to the front door, turned on the porch light and also the one at the end of their driveway. He saw two sets of headlights down the road and expected they were the police cars coming.

The officers swarmed the house and property when they arrived. They questioned Walter and wrote down all of the information. One officer remarked that he didn't like to see anyone shot in the back. Walter showed him the bullet hole in the sheets and mattress. When they retrieved the bullet, the officer withdrew his criticism. As the police measured and photographed the crime scene, Susan asked Walter if she should call Gennie.

"Wouldn't it be better for me to call her than for her to get a cold police call?" she asked.

"I hate for you to do that. We have been the bearer of bad news about Margo, your mother, and now Will, but I guess it's the kinder thing to do."

Susan went to the kitchen phone, looked up at the clock—three in the morning—and dialed Gennie's number. Her groggy sister answered but became alert as Susan relayed the details.

Finally, Gennie said, "Poor Will. I don't know what drove this rage and revenge. I feel badly for Walter being responsible, but I'm glad he's such a good marksman. I can't imagine Will succeeding with his wild scheme. Makes me realize Mason and I could've also been targets." Gennie stopped for a moment and then said, "How am I going to tell Lem and Margaret?"

"Maybe you should let the police call them."

"No, I think I'd better get dressed, call Lem to tell him I'm coming, and deliver the news in person. Since I'm still officially Will's wife, tell the police there in Petaluma that we'll use the same funeral home in Mayfield, so the police can call them when the body can be released."

"Do you think you feel up to doing all that?"

"It's the right thing to do. I won't regret it this way. Suddenly, that insidious fear that has pervaded my every thought is gone. Part of me feels relief; I had no idea how this would all end. I felt anxiety for us all. As soon as I tell Lem and Margaret, do you want me to come there?"

"No, Walter is telling me we need to go down to the police station as a formality. So I need to get dressed. They said they would release him on his own recognizance until the judge convenes the court later this morning. I'll call you afterward."

Gennie hung up and called her in-laws' house, waking them up. She told Lem that she had very sad news to tell them in person.

"Please put a pot of coffee on. I'll just throw on some clothes and be there shortly."

When Gennie arrived at their house, they were anxious and tense. She started to tell them the story from the beginning but couldn't delay the ultimate news.

"Susan called me to say that Will is dead."

"Susan? Why Susan?" Lem asked.

Then Gennie told all the details to their shocked and unbelieving faces. Margaret cried—no big sobs. It was as if the recent sadness had depleted her tear production.

"I guess I'm having second thoughts about whether I should've revealed the real reason I jumped from the bridge. That seems to have triggered Will's anger." Gennie continued, "Yet it seemed unfair to let Mason continue to carry the guilt. Did the potential money Will would lose in the divorce fuel his rage? I've been frightened ever since your house fire."

Gennie reached for Margaret's hand. "This isn't the boy I married. At some point he became very irrational. Although we aren't divorced, I want us to make the funeral plans together. I will defer to your preferences."

Gennie asked if she could use their phone to call Mason. She wanted to catch him before his morning classes. She called and told him the news. After listening to all the details, he said, "What was Dad thinking? It's difficult to understand what his reasoning was." Then he paused and said, "The school for sure isn't going to believe me when I say I need *more* bereavement time. Sometimes I think I'm living in an episode of one of those old-timey radio soaps like *Ma Perkins* or *Pepper Young's Family*."

"I don't know when the funeral will be," Gennie said. "It depends on when the police release the body. Come as soon as you want. If you think you can concentrate and accomplish your studies, stay there until the funeral. It seems like we are swimming in sadness. If being with the family helps, come now. I love you."

After hanging up, Gennie told her in-laws that Susan was going to telephone her after the arraignment. She wanted to be home for that call.

"Are you going to be all right? Should I phone one of your neighbors to come stay with you?" Both Margaret and Lem assured Gennie they would rather be alone for a while.

She drove home with a queasy stomach from too little sleep, too much coffee, and emotional angst. There Gennie fixed herself a piece of toast before calling John. It was now seven o'clock, and he should be up. The call surprised him.

"John, I know I'm violating my own rule of contacting you only every two weeks, but I wanted you to know that Will is dead."

"How? When?"

"He was shot early this morning."

"Hopefully not by you."

"No, but by Walter." She told him the whole scenario.

"What can I do? I will gladly come to you."

"I think I'm going to try to nap. I only had three hours of sleep last night. I'll wait to hear if all went well with Walter's arraignment and then call the divorce attorney and our corporate lawyer. Lem is going to call each of the store managers. If you are free this evening, would you like to come by for supper? I can at least put together a soup and sandwich."

"Does seven work?"

"Yes. It already feels good not to be fearful. I have such a hodgepodge of emotions, and relief is one of them."

"Let's also remember that he was a good and faithful husband for years. May his soul rest in peace."

"Amen to that. I'll see you this evening."

When Gennie hung up, the phone rang, and the Petaluma medical examiner requested that she, as the next of kin, go identify the body and provide information for the death certificate. She told them she could be there in about two hours.

As she went to take a shower, Phyllis called. After talking for a moment, Gennie explained that she needed to go to Petaluma, and Phyllis offered to drive her.

"Bless you, Phyllis. I dreaded making that trip by myself."

On the ride over they talked like the old friends they were. When they arrived at the morgue, Phyllis went in with Gennie for the identification. Strangely enough, Gennie felt detached from this proceeding. There were no tears. When the ever-present fear had left, the void had been filled with outrage and questions. Tender emotions were nonexistent.

After giving all the information, Gennie asked about the protocol for receiving a copy of the autopsy and a few copies of the death certificate. She paid the fees for those, reaffirmed the name of the mortuary that would pick up the body, signed for all of Will's personal effects, and left.

In the car, as Phyllis drove, Gennie went through Will's wallet. She found a doctor's appointment card.

"I didn't know he was seeing this doctor," Gennie said. She read the name and address aloud.

"Will's been going to him for years," Phyllis said. "He also saw someone else occasionally."

"I've never seen any bills at the house."

"No, everything came to the office. Most of the time he paid at the time of the visit, but occasionally when a bill arrived, I put it on his desk."

Gennie extracted a folded paper with names on it, torn from a memo pad. "This is a sheet from the cemetery. Its name is on the top of the page. I remember them being in the racks on the backs of the pews with the hymnals. The names—definitely in Will's handwriting—are the people I asked to come to the parlor after Margo's funeral. Only Erma's name is crossed out. There are checks next to Lem's and Margaret's names. This is scary, Phyllis. Do you think he planned to systematically kill us all?"

"If that's the case, then Walter is our hero."

When they reached Gennie's house, she invited Phyllis in for a late sandwich, but Phyllis declined.

Opening the car door, Gennie said, "I'll check with Lem and see if he wants to write the obit. Whether he writes it or I do, we may need to verify some dates about the corporation history with you. We'll talk soon, and thanks again for driving me."

That evening Gennie warmed bowls of split-pea soup. She opened the kitchen cabinet and put a small can wrapped in white paper on the counter. "Do you like deviled ham? I thought I'd mix some with mayonnaise and sweet relish for our crackers."

'Gosh I haven't eaten any in years. I remember that white paper wrapper with the red devil on the label. My mother used to pack our school lunch boxes with deviled ham on white bread. It was quite a treat."

Gennie told John she recognized that being a widow would make their situation different. Nevertheless, she could not entertain a romance at this time.

"I have too much to sort out in my head and heart right now. I know you're going to see this as a green light, and I've been flattered by your affection, but I *will* grieve the loss of Will. How can I not? He was my husband for twenty years. I did not want this to end in his death. It may take a year for me to sort out all my feelings and my sense of loss. Hopefully, then I can give you all my unfettered attention and love."

"I will continue to honor our estrangement agreement until you tell me otherwise," John said, looking into her eyes.

Gennie said, "Don't get me wrong; I have missed you terribly these last several weeks. How many times I wanted to lift that receiver and call you. Hopefully, the time will come quickly when I have faced my emotions and dealt with them."

"You're a caring and sensitive woman, which is part of what I love about you. I will pray for patience. I have waited all my life for someone like you. I can surely wait longer." He kissed her lips, and she responded, not spurning him. This time she allowed herself to show her fondness for him.

Chapter 32

The funeral transpired four days after Will's death. The newspapers had attempted to find out more of the story. The police report contained facts but didn't reveal details about motives and background. Reporters called the house and camped outside, trying to find out more, but Gennie continued to say, "No comment." They retreated but not without dredging up the old news of Gennie's attempted suicide.

As Lem and Margaret desired, the funeral was at their German Lutheran Church, followed by the burial in the family plot. Family and friends went to the parents' house afterward, where the church women provided food. The same community members who had been at Margo's funeral offered their sympathy to Gennie as the widow, unaware that divorce proceedings had been initiated.

Two weeks later Gennie received the death certificate and autopsy report. Number one cause of death: bullet to the head. Number two: bullet to the heart. Number three: amphetamine toxicity, high levels of testosterone.

The third diagnosis surprised Gennie yet explained so much. The anger, the aggressiveness, the short temper—all could be explained by excessive amphetamines and high testosterone doses. Gennie knew the pills he'd taken were legal and used mostly to curb appetite. She also knew that during WWII, the government had issued amphetamines to the troops to give them extra energy and require less sleep. She'd confronted Will when he'd returned after the war about the continued use of the drug. He'd promised to cut down and take them only occasionally. Because Gennie never saw any prescriptions or doctor bills, she'd assumed that he'd curtailed his usage. Could he have been taking them all these years?

Recent newspapers and magazines had featured articles cautioning about the addictiveness of "uppers," or amphetamines. Pressure to monitor the prescriptions had recently grown, but they were still easy to obtain. She knew from her studies that amphetamine psychosis had been a recognized condition but wasn't a true psychosis, because if the drug was withdrawn, the patient could function normally again. Why he'd wanted to take testosterone injections, she wasn't sure. The ads touted them as a fountain of youth. Had he questioned his manliness? He had never confided in her.

With her medical training, she should have recognized the symptoms, but his anger and resentment had become pervasive and a constant facet of his personality. Gennie had always been thankful that Will had not turned to alcohol, which so many veterans chose as their numbing drug. Yet these uppers had destroyed their family as efficiently as alcoholism would have.

When Gennie reported the autopsy results to John, he related having had similar experiences during the war.

"We called them 'feel-good pills.' We were given them by the handful. They had two specific effects: energy and aggressiveness. Perfect attributes for a soldier. They also caused lack of appetite. The K-rations weren't appetizing, so it didn't matter how it tasted. I never liked the jittery feeling that accompanied frequent doses. I had no problem stopping taking them."

Gennie couldn't help but wonder about the motivations of the doctor who'd supplied Will with the amphetamines. Did he think that placating Will with pills represented an ethical prescription for a good life? Or was he just pleasing a patient and collecting the office-visit fees? After two weeks she decided to make an appointment and confront him. The medical community did not welcome challenge. If employed by a group of doctors, one might hear the scuttlebutt about a physician, but it was considered privileged information. An outsider could not easily figure out if a physician seemed esteemed or bordered on unethical practices. When she telephoned the office, Gennie explained that she wanted to have a conference with the doctor, and she obtained a late-afternoon appointment.

A medical tower that had seen better days housed the doctor's general-practice office. Built near a hospital that had been abandoned when another bigger, more modern hospital had been constructed, the interior halls had linoleum floors and ceiling tiles, both stained with old water damage. The waiting room also seemed tired, with pots of mother-in-law plants with spindly leaves, and withered cacti "decorating" the magazine tables. None of the furnishings appeared younger than twenty years.

After Gennie checked in with the receptionist, she sat down with her book. Three other patients sat on the plastic-covered chairs. When everyone else had left the waiting room, the receptionist ushered Gennie into the doctor's office. While Gennie waited she looked at his license on the wall. The doctor had finished his internship in 1939. She figured his age in her head and thought he must be about fifty years old.

When the doctor opened the door and came into the office, Gennie stood. Standing when a doctor entered a room had been ingrained in her since her early nurses' training days, almost a Pavlovian automatic reflex.

"Sit down, sit down, Mrs. Mueller. I am Dr. Cole," he said, extending his hand. "What can I do for you?" He placed a thick patient chart on the desk in front of him as he sat. Gennie assumed that the chart held Will's records.

"I have an autopsy report that surprised and troubled me." Gennie brought out a copy from her handbag and gave it to Dr. Cole. He tilted his head back, looking through his lower bifocal lenses.

After reading the paper he said, "Yes, that troubles me too."

"I found numerous prescription bottles for Dexedrine Spansule with your name on them in his office desk drawer. I know it's legal to prescribe amphetamines, but I do question your ethics in prescribing enough to have caused him to test toxic. Also, the excess testosterone in his system concerns me."

"Our office did not give Mr. Mueller any testosterone injections. As for the Dexedrine prescriptions, they were refilled on a legitimate schedule. Oh, occasionally we might refill a request early, but usually it can be justified by a patient's planned vacation or business trip. He would have had to stockpile many months' of pills and take them a few days before his death for my prescriptions to have been responsible."

"Will's secretary said there were two doctors who he went to—you and another. I checked with the county and state registries for MDs and also osteopaths, and they had no record of the other doctor. Unfortunately, I don't have any prescriptions with that doctor's name on the labels."

"It's conceivable that Will went doctor shopping or hopping. If you want to pay more, you can buy drugs on the black market. That's hearsay for me of course; I haven't any direct dealings with them."

"This autopsy report blindsided me, Doctor. Although I'm an RN, I had no inkling that Will still took amphetamines. When he came home from World War II, he promised me he would taper off the pills. The navy introduced them to him while he was serving. He came home an angry and belligerent young man and plunged all his energy into building his supermarket 'empire.' I attributed his extra vigor to his Type A personality and a drive to make up for those lost war years. Will never had any medical bills come to the house, and I didn't see any prescription bottles. At times he seemed nervous and jumpy, but he excused it by saying the business was going through tough times."

"As you can see by the thickness of his chart, Will has been a longtime patient," Dr. Cole replied. "Although he was healthy I had him return every four months for a blood-pressure and heart check in order for me to continue writing him prescriptions. I set up practice after the war—because I too was drafted—and he started coming here. His story about getting hooked on amphetamines while in the service mirrored so many returning veterans'. I tried to dissuade him from continuing with the drugs, and that's when he told me his story. I think I can find it here in the early pages," he said, rifling through the papers.

"Will told me he stayed on the same ship all three years. The first time out, they were mainly new recruits. The atmosphere replicated their high-school days: bullying, minor fights, and frayed nerves due to the close quarters. Each time they came into port, there might be a change in personnel. On the second tour Will was attacked and sodomized anally by three guys he didn't know. He thought they were thugs from the Northeast because of their accents." He looked up at Gennie, whose face had lost color. She seemed to be hyperventilating.

"Are you okay?" he asked.

"Yes, I need to take a few deep breaths." Dr. Cole pressed the intercom button and asked the receptionist to bring in a glass of water.

"The attack occurred in the boiler room, a noisy place. The workers were required to wear earplugs to protect their hearing. Will didn't hear them approach from behind. He hadn't anticipated that any of his coworkers would ambush him. And they weren't his coworkers.

"After the first guy penetrated him, the trio planned to change places, but as they did, Will got one arm loose and grabbed his assailant, sending a fist to his head. The guy fell, hitting his head on a boiler, and lost consciousness. At this point the other two fled. But the psychological damage had been done. Men, just like women, never understand why they were assaulted. The why can overwhelm a person's life."

The receptionist brought in the glass of water.

Gennie said, "I guess I've been ignorant of different—aberrant--sexual practices. I thought male-on-male encounters occurred only between homosexuals."

"That's part of why Will was so distressed. Had he sent a homosexual signal to these thugs? Or had they seen him as vulnerable and weak? As I explained to him, rape is not usually sexual. It's a crime of violence, conquest, anger, destruction, and terror. Chances are that they realized what easy prey someone was in the boiler room, where no victim could hear them approaching and no one else could hear his yells for help. But his manhood was challenged to the core. It changed who he was—how he looked at himself, his self-esteem. If he sought testosterone, he may have been looking for additional assurance that he appeared manly."

Gennie felt drained. She had spent so many years trying to understand Will's anger and nondisclosure. How futile their lives had been because of a lack of communication.

"Will went to his commanding officer with his account. The officer told him, 'We're in the middle of the South Seas in a war; I can't do anything about these men. Stay vigilant. You are not the only victim on this ship.'

"But Will saw his assailants often—in the cafeteria, in the laundry room, and on deck. They leered at him, and he found it difficult to be brave.

"Fortunately, on his third tour, these men were transferred, and his friend Herb came on the ship. Yet I cannot tell you what devastation this event and the subsequent fear had wreaked on him. When he came to me as a patient, I realized that he stood on the precipice of a deep depression. He said he'd thought of going AWOL and disappearing into another identity after his second tour, but he could not abandon you. He loved you and wanted a life with you. We physicians did not—and still don't—have any good antidepressant drugs. The ones we do have zap the patient's ability to function; the patient appears and feels like a drone. Too often people abandon those drugs because of the side effects. I chose to keep Will on an even keel with amphetamines."

"I didn't know what to expect when I made this appointment. Now I realize that every time I pleaded with him to confide in me, I opened that festering memory." Both the doctor and Gennie sat quietly a moment as she tried to assimilate all the information.

Gennie stood and reached out to shake the doctor's hand. "Thank you for sharing this information. I know you and your receptionist are ready to go home. I won't keep you any longer."

"Feel free to come back if you have more questions. My files are open to you for your perusal. I have nothing to hide."

Gennie turned to go and then turned back to the doctor. "I have a son, now twenty-one years old, who never had a good relationship with his father after they were apart for the first three years of his life. Would it be useful for me to share this information with him? Do you have an opinion on that?"

"Since I don't know your son, I hesitate to counsel you. It could put some more pieces in the puzzle for him. On the other hand, it might make him question his own manhood—or mental health. If you know a pastor or former teacher or anyone who knows your son, you might ask that person. Usually, I don't encourage family secrets."

"Thanks again, Doctor Cole. You told me a story I never expected to hear."

She drove home with many conflicting thoughts that she could not sort through. Once the door to her house was shut behind her, the sobbing overwhelmed her. She cried with nothing but tangled reflections for more than an hour. Before this, she hadn't felt grief about Will's death. Instead, anger and fear had dominated her emotions. Now she felt sadness for Will's plight. She remembered the high-school football hero who had been so full of himself, confident, going off to war to be the patriotic hero. She remembered how she'd adored him—heads over heels in love. "If he'd confided in me, would I have understood the repercussions on his psyche? Do I even understand all of this now?" she wondered.

She went in and heated up a can of chicken-noodle soup, a comforting food from her childhood. Her mom had served it as a treat when Gennie had stayed home sick with the measles and chicken pox. Sick children, in those days, would be relegated to bed all day with only a radio for company. Her mother would come into her room with a serving tray and sing the commercial song: "Mmm, mmm good, that's what chicken noodle is..." Gennie smiled at the warm glow of the recollection.

The next morning she called Lem and asked him to come to lunch. He said, "Margaret is playing bridge, so she can't come." Gennie replied that she really wanted to talk with him alone anyway. But she did have trepidations. To talk to a physician in a clinical climate about a patient's untoward sexual experience is one thing; to talk to her father-in-law about his son and her husband posed another challenge.

Over sandwiches and coffee, Gennie told him the story of going to Dr. Cole and what she'd learned.

"Papa M, if we had known back then, do you think we could have helped him? He obviously didn't want to reveal his vulnerability, his self-doubt about his sexual prowess."

"Each generation seems to become more knowledgeable and sophisticated about sexual matters," Lem said. "I can't imagine how naïve and country I was. As young stallions, we kids got into fist fights defending our claimed knowledge. If one of the group sent off for a package wrapped in plain brown paper—from a magazine that advertised fifty ways to have sex—and shared it with us, we spent a couple of afternoons poring over its contents. Such macho posturing we displayed. Now the books and movies are showing things that would have singed our young country-bumpkin eyebrows." He paused for a moment to take a sip of coffee. "I would like to think we could have helped him, loved him enough, accepted what he had endured—but I'm not sure."

"We knew so little about homosexuals and their behaviors then—and even now," Gennie said. "They were—and in some cases, still are—called 'queers' and 'faggots,' and even comedians make jokes about them. People thought they were all sexual predators and dangerous around children. That opinion still persists. I think Will felt it necessary to keep up a fearless and virile façade. By telling us, he would have had to admit his misgivings to himself. Instead he tried to bury them."

"Yes, it's not hard to understand why he didn't want to talk about it."

"My next question is, do you think it serves any purpose to tell Mason? Part of me says it would help him understand his father; the other side of me is protective—why tell him all the details?"

"I'm going to have to ponder this. I think a man should tell him, and I'll volunteer."

"If you'd like to visit with Doctor Cole, I think he would be open to offer any information he has. Also, I don't know if you're aware that John spent three years in the infantry and ended up on the Normandy beaches on D-day. I think he's very knowledgeable about the psyche of the soldier or sailor. I know he's open to talking with you. He's fond of Mason too."

"Okay, I'll educate myself and then ask your permission to tell Mason, if that seems best. I think we've learned that secrets do a disservice to all of us."

Gennie also asked Lem to research all the possibilities of selling the grocery chain.

She knew that Lem's hope of continuing the family grocery legacy represented a huge loss of a dream. She just trusted that the plans for the farm property would ignite some excitement for him.

Gennie had given up any hope that the résumés she'd sent to a private clinic and to county, city, and public health departments a few months earlier would bear any leads. However, she received a telephone call from the director of a coalition of organizations in Palo Alto who was trying to address the need to improve schoolchildren's health. Gennie went in to interview for a job.

When Gennie was growing up, a school nurse assigned to each school had handled all the health needs of the students. Because each school had had a small population, the nurse had conducted height and weight assessments twice a year, plus vision and hearing tests on each child. This close monitoring had quickly pointed out any child's possible problem. However, after the Second World War, when the West Coast population had expanded rapidly, school nurses had been stretched among many campuses, and their efficiency had been compromised. Now people in the community realized they were not assessing their schoolchildren adequately.

This group wanted to form a cohesive body to canvas every school campus. They were meeting to form a plan. They needed RNs to make assessments and wanted to recruit Gennie. Other professionals, such as audiologists, dental hygienists, and nutritionists, would join in the effort. This was exactly the type of work Gennie relished, so she eagerly said yes to the job offer. She hadn't earned her RN designation just to have a certificate to hang on the wall.

She scooted off to work in her new car: a BMW beetle. Gone was that ostentatious Cadillac.

Chapter 33

Lem went to the Mountain View city-planning department and inquired about the requirements for making his property into an equine stable and training facility. He also talked with Ben Nakamura and Joe about their sons' plans.

Ben's oldest son wanted to continue the nursery business, both wholesale and retail. His younger daughter, Yoshi, planned to marry Joe's son, who wanted to develop a rose center. Yoshi loved dahlias. She had done some hybridizing of them and hoped to have a dahlia center next to the rose garden. Ben's second-oldest boy, Warren, had become an outdoor space planner, architect, and landscape developer. He had done some city-center planning for smaller towns and wanted to draw up the plans for the whole property. When Lem said he'd have to consult with Mason to see if that expense was in the budget, Ben said, "I have a story to tell you. In Issei households, from when they first immigrated to America, a picture of George Washington always hung in their living rooms. Raised in a patriarchal tradition in Japan, the new residents learned that George Washington was called the father of the country. Since honoring their fathers was important, the Issei hung a picture of President Washington and often named their firstborn son 'George.' After the war, when we came home here again, our kids teased that we should hang a photo of Mister Lem on the wall because my father always said, 'If any of us can ever repay Mister Mueller for his kindness, it is our family's honor to do so.'"

Ben cleared his throat and continued, "On behalf of the family, Warren would like to draw up the plans as a gift to you and Mason. It will be our privilege."

Now Lem cleared his throat and wiped at his eyes. Taking a step forward, he hugged the shorter man and said, "Thank you, my brother, thank you."

When Mason and Lisa came up for a weekend, Lem related to them the conversation about Warren Nakamura. Gennie offered a quick dinner invitation to the architect so that they could all discuss their plans. Because Warren had no previous design experience with horse facilities, Gennie suggested that he join Mason and Lisa on a tour of successful stables and dressage farms in the East and Midwest. She would fund the trip after the two students researched at the school to find the best facilities.

Although the kids' graduation was a year and a half away, Lem could oversee the construction of roads and water and necessary sewage. With a master plan that all three families could agree on, any construction would be permanent progress. Warren also proposed that they approach the city for money to fund the infrastructure. What he envisioned was a park-like pavilion that would attract families and customers. Any private land that would be accessible to the public could be eligible for tax relief or funds.

Meanwhile, Lem reconfigured his hideaway on the farm to accommodate a drafting table and office for Warren in the living room. On a nearby table he kept a pot of coffee ready for any visitors—especially city dignitaries—curious to see the property and look at the plans. He knew personal contact would be invaluable in persuading the planning board and councilmen to approve their vision. The preliminary plans included a central plaza featuring a large fountain and reflecting pool. Bench seating would separate the stable area from the flower business of Yoshi, Joe's son, and the Nakamura Nursery. Behind this would be a picnic area, preschool play equipment, and permanent bathroom facilities. Landscaped, paved parking would be adjacent to the pastures.

Between going to council and planning-commission meetings and getting bids for land moving, Lem knew he would need every bit of the eighteen months to get everything done before Lisa and Mason graduated.

Chapter 34

After the probation of Erma's will, Gennie completed her plan of action. She wrote a letter to the insurance company that had records of the policy on the partnership agreement made in 1959. She called the company in San Francisco to find out the president's name and pulled out her portable typewriter, which had been her faithful companion all through school, to compose a letter.

Dear Mr. Armstrong,

In 1959, my husband and his partner had a business-partnership insurance policy with your company. When Herbert Jordan fell from a cable car and suffered a fatal injury, your company paid the claim to my husband, Will Mueller. I witnessed my husband push Mr. Jordan off the trolley. It was no accident.

Recently my husband died, and I feel obligated to come forward with this information and offer to pay back the amount of money you paid on the insurance policy.

Please advise me of the amount I should send your company and to whom it should be sent.

Yours sincerely,
Geneva Mueller

Gennie felt better even as she mailed the letter. She hoped to systematically cleanse her mind of all its clutter and enter her new relationship without dragging any emotional tow sacks.

The reply from Mr. Armstrong arrived in a couple of weeks.

Dear Mrs. Mueller,

I am sorry to hear of your husband's death and wish to extend my condolences to you and your family.

I pulled the file on the 1959 accident and read the account thoroughly. The investigators interviewed twenty passengers on the cable car. Not one saw any aggressive action by your husband or any other passenger. They did comment on the assumed inebriation of Mr. Jordan. Two even stated that they had commented to their companions that he should have been taken inside the cable-car cabin.

I showed the file to our legal department and asked for their opinion. They do not see any grounds for our company to reverse its original decision; therefore, we will not accept any repayment.

I appreciate your candor and concern and respectfully suggest that you donate any amount of money you feel appropriate to a charity of your choice.

If I can ever be of any service to you in the future, please do not hesitate to contact me.

Sincerely,
William Armstrong

Gennie chuckled. How many gray hairs and wrinkles had all this caused? And for what purpose? "Okay, Lord. I still don't understand it, but it's done—D-U-N, done. It can no longer color my life."

Settling an estate could take months, and the complicated evaluations of the properties, finding buyers for all five stores, and selling the house did involve a lot of time and effort. Lem mourned the loss of the Mueller grocery dream. The evolution of the grocery business could not be denied. The single-proprietor store, when it had jumped to being a large supermarket, had lost its personal contact—could no longer please each individual customer. Lem recognized that and could not blame Mason for not wanting to continue the family business. The days of greeting customers by name and letting them know when one of their favorite products had arrived in the store were gone.

Gennie leased a garden apartment in Palo Alto for a year. She started her part-time job, medically evaluating all first- and second-graders in the school district. They documented all their findings and hoped to construct a syllabus showing all the criteria of care so it could be a nonprofit model for state funding.

Every week Gennie visited with Lem and Margaret—either at their home, her apartment, or a restaurant. Lem enthusiastically related all the events about the farm property. Gennie recounted incidents from her work, which she found challenging. Margaret languished for a few months, mostly just listening to the other two. Then one evening she announced, "I've found me a new career too."

Lem seemed surprised, and Gennie prodded, "Tell us. What is it?"

"I am developing a new lunch menu for my friend who owns Mary's Tea Room on Main Street. She wants me to supply the recipes for some authentic German foods: soups, salads, and hot sandwiches. They will be featured as 'Margaret's German Special.'"

"What fun! When do you start?"

"I've already given Mary some suggestions, and once she chooses from those, I'll teach the cooks, and we'll taste test them. If this is met with enthusiasm, Mary wants to open in the evening once a month for German night."

"I'm excited!" Gennie said. "Keep me posted. Some of my medical colleagues and I will want to stop by."

Chapter 35

Susan sat in the canopied porch swing next to the fish pond at the side of their house. She watched the swirling dance-like movements of the goldfish as they nibbled at the food she had just sprinkled on the water. The warm afternoon sun and the to-and-fro movement of the swing reminded her of Erma and how many hours she had spent sitting there. Nowadays, when Susan thought of her mother, the desire to know about those years of her mother's life after she was found—following the kidnapping—had become overwhelming. She had called the information line in Grass Valley, asking for any phone listings for 'Hart,' but the operator had said there were none. She'd also asked for a telephone number for the newspaper, the *Union-Gazette*, but no listing for it existed either. Now she didn't know where to look; Erma's siblings could live anywhere or be dead.

Walter came around the corner of the house and said, "Well, there you are. I looked all through the house."

"You're early." She tilted her head to receive his kiss and moved over so he could sit next to her.

"I thought we might look for that new restaurant on the Bodega Bay Highway. It's in an old farmhouse, an old fruit orchard. Young chef. His specialty is seafood—imagine that."

"Do you have an address? Or is this one of your adventures?"

"The name of the place is the Orchard. It's on the north side of the road. How can we miss it?"

"Yeah, maybe I'd better make us a snack—just in case."

"Ye of little faith."

"I've been down this great adventure trail before, you know."

Once they were in the car and on the two-lane road, Walter said, "There's not much going on at the office right now, so I thought we might get away for a few days."

"Did you have a destination in mind?"

"I've found this great interest in the Gold Rush of 1849 and the mines. I'd like to explore some small communities and learn the history."

"Perhaps Grass Valley would be on your list?" She took her eyes off the side of the road to look at him.

"How intuitive you are. How did you ever guess?"

"It's you who is intuitive. You know how curious I've been about Mom."

"I'm curious too. She was fourteen years old when she came home after the abduction and thirty-eight years old when she met your dad in San Francisco. At that time, she worked as a legal secretary and was single. That's all we know."

"Oops, I think we just passed it. The sign is small, and I hardly saw it."

"I didn't think the restaurant would be this close. I'll turn around."

The unpaved driveway and adjacent front yard had no designated parking spots, so cars were positioned haphazardly. A screen door covered the entrance to the two-story farmhouse. Inside, whitewashed walls and light-blue and white checked tablecloths created a Scandinavian vibe.

Once seated, they each ordered a drink: a martini for her, an old-fashioned for him. Walter pulled out a package of Pall Malls, tapped the end of a cigarette onto the table, and lit it. He liked to smoke with a cocktail. The smoke of his cigarette joined the haze of other dining clients' and hovered near the ceiling.

After perusing the menu, they chose the newest craze in salads: a wedge of iceberg lettuce with a blue-cheese dressing. For their entrée they picked the catch of the day and felt adventuresome, ready to see what the chef would produce.

The next day the couple headed northward from home and by midafternoon stopped at a motel between Nevada City and Grass Valley. It appeared clean and had a small kitchenette, so they went out to get breakfast groceries for the next day and stopped at a small roadside café for dinner. Walter obtained a map of the area and drove around to try to become oriented.

The following morning, after breakfast, Walter dropped Susan off at the Grass Valley Library and then began to look for better lodging and generally canvass the territory. The library held a prominent place in the community. Its bold, brick rectangular façade featured large white vertical columns framing the windows. Susan stepped inside an enormous room; in the center sat an older lady at a desk. Her gray hair, with tight marcelled waves, framed her face, which had no makeup. On the desk the sign said "Harriet Durham."

"Miss Durham? My name is Susan Cornell, and I'm interested in the archives of the *Union-Gazette.* Are they housed here?"

"Yes, we have a large collection—but not complete by any means. Fires, floods, and landslides have damaged copies over the years. What time period are you wanting?"

"It would be 1897, perhaps 1898. I want to learn more about the kidnapping of a young girl named Erma Hart."

"Are you a reporter? You wouldn't be the first, you know. It's been a popular case for reporters and law students."

"No, I'm her daughter."

That remark shot a shudder through Miss Durham's body, and she jerked her gaze immediately to Susan's face. "My stars! No one has ever known what happened to Erma. That's been a mystery. Often, over the years, residents claimed they'd seen her wandering in these parts."

"I doubt that she did that. My sister and I just learned about Mother's past—we found a newspaper clipping in her possessions after her death. While she was alive, she didn't share any of her childhood history with us. We knew nothing."

"I'm sorry to hear of Erma's death. Her younger sister, Fern, would have loved to see her again."

"Is her sister still alive and living around here?"

"Yes, she's unmarried and lives in Nevada City."

"But when I asked long-distance information for phone numbers of any Harts, they said there weren't any."

"Fern lives in a boardinghouse and has access to the house phone. She doesn't have her own listing."

"Do you think she would be willing to meet with me? I never dreamed I had an aunt still living." She sounded like an excited schoolgirl.

"Fern and I have kept in touch over the years. She sometimes comes to the library, but mostly I've seen her at the school reunions and such. I have her telephone number at home. Here's my phone number," she said, handing Susan a slip of paper, "and if you'll call me after four this afternoon, I'll give you Fern's number. If you don't mind, I'll call her first and tell her you stopped by—so it isn't such a shock when you call.

"Meanwhile, about those newspapers. The editions that have news of the kidnapping and subsequent trials are in poor condition. They've been handled by so many that the papers are nearly in tatters and are under lock and key. We wear gloves to touch them and allow access only to historians. I wouldn't say you couldn't be an exception, but we have a couple of well-documented histories—pamphlets—that you can read and get the same information from. They can't be checked out, but you're welcome to read them here. Should I get them for you?"

"That would be perfect. I had no idea the kidnapping had garnered such widespread attention," Susan said. "I thought I would be doing original research. I don't need to see the newspapers; I just want to learn the facts."

"If you know none of the circumstances, Mrs. Cornell, you'll be fascinated with these accounts."

When the librarian came back with the slim leaflets she said, "Choose any table you like. There's coffee and water near the back. You'll see the signs to the restrooms back there too."

Susan found a seat where she could watch the front door .Walter would come in to fetch her if she wasn't sitting outside. She went to the coffee pot and poured herself a cup. She sat and retrieved her reading glasses out of her handbag perusing the covers of both booklets. Inhaling a deep breath, she thought as she opened to the first page, "Let the facts begin."

Walter came through the library doors more than an hour later. Susan waved at him, got up to intercept him, and steered him to the desk to meet Miss Durham.

As they got back to her table, Susan said, "There's coffee in the back if you want some. I've finished one booklet and started on the second. When you get to the second, I'll jot down some notes and dates from the first. I know Gennie will want to know everything."

Halfway through reading the first pamphlet, Walter looked up, and their eyes met. He shook his head, not believing what he read. Both had been educated to respect the silence of the library and knew that any excited chatter would be distracting.

By the time they finished reading both booklets, the library had filled with many clients. As Susan returned the informative books to the librarian, she said, "I'll call you at about five. That will give you enough time to alert Fern. At that time you can tell me if she wants to hear from me. I really appreciate all this information. Thanks so much." The two women smiled as their eyes met.

As Walter and Susan descended the library steps, Walter shouted, "Wowsee!" All that silence made him burst.

"Is that not more than you expected?"

"But that still doesn't explain why and how your mom disappeared the second time."

"That's what I hope my aunt Fern can tell us. Did you find us a better place to spend the night?"

"Yes, it's a lot nicer. Also, I saw an interesting place for dinner. They specialize in Cornish pasties—meat pies the miners used to carry in their lunches. They're a specialty of this area."

"Since it's already two thirty, why don't we get an ice-cream cone to tide us over until dinner?"

Walter drove to the old downtown section and found a confectionary store called the Sweet Shoppe. Besides homemade ice cream, they had hand-dipped chocolates, plus cakes and pies.

"Why don't we buy a box of chocolates to take to Aunt Fern if she is willing to see us?"

With black-raspberry and rocky-road ice-cream cones, they strolled along the sidewalk, looking in the storefront windows as they licked.

"Let's go back to the room so I can call Gennie and tell her what we've learned. Then I'll call Miss Durham."

Walter had chosen a rustic but recently constructed two-story hotel that had been built for the winter sport seekers as well as summer tourists. The large dining room overlooked the swimming pool, with tall evergreens framing every vista.

"It smells so fresh out here. You made a good choice," Susan said.

She dialed the hotel operator and asked her to place a long-distance call. Gennie answered and said, "Where have you been? I've been trying to call you."

"We're still gone. I'm calling you from Grass Valley."

"I didn't know you had plans to go up there."

"All very spur-of-the-moment. I tried to call you before we left, but I guess you were at work. Anyway, let me get down to the nitty-gritty—we can't talk all afternoon.

"We went to the library and learned that the trial after Mom's kidnapping was well known and controversial. There are a couple of research papers on the subject. Turns out Mom's father sold Mom to that man—Jimmy Bullock. Mom's father, Luke, made up the kidnapping story because he knew his wife wouldn't allow him to sell their child. Luke told Jimmy where Mom and her little girlfriend were going berry picking so the other child could testify that Mom had been abducted.

"What started out as a kidnapping trial—the State versus Jimmy Bullock—ended up being a trial about the legality of selling children. The state advocated for the rights of the child and also for the child's mother's rights. The two male defendants claimed that child (orphan) selling was prevalent and not considered a crime. Plus, Luke quoted multiple biblical verses about selling children—slaves—who were owned by their fathers."

"My gosh! That's an amazing story."

"That's not all. The circuit judge ruled probation for both men. They were fined an amount that had to go into a bank account for Mom to receive when she was twenty-one years old. He said the two men had shared equally in the wrongdoing but that putting Luke in jail would punish his children by denying him a way to provide for the family. So Jimmy Bullock got probation too. Besides Mom, there were four other siblings—the youngest just a year old."

"I'd like to read those accounts."

"They're only at the library and have to stay there. But there's more to this story. The librarian knows Mom's younger sister, Fern, who lives in Nevada City. I'm going to phone Aunt Fern in a couple of hours. Maybe then we can learn what happened to Mom after the trial and when and how she left town."

"Wow! Now, more than ever, I understand why she told us nothing. How can you explain such bizarre things to your young kids?"

The phone calls to Miss Durham and Fern Hart were both positive. Fern suggested that, if Susan and Walter usually got up early, they arrive at the boardinghouse at nine o'clock, when most roomers went to work. They could have privacy and quiet.

Overnight a heavy dew turned the blacktop highway into a ribbon of glistening licorice winding through the tall evergreens. Misty vapors emanated from the wet grasses between the trees. Ephemeral. Tranquil.

Walter and Susan drove through occasional wispy patches of fog floating above the road. Inside the car, they shared the bubbly enthusiasm of eager youngsters anticipating some secrets being divulged. Maybe—between the puzzle pieces of information they had and those Fern had—maybe finally they would piece together Erma's life.

Fern sat in the rocking chair on the large porch that extended across the front of the boardinghouse. She got up to greet them as they parked right in front. She extended her hand and said, "I'm Fern."

Susan realized that Fern didn't look like Erma at all. She was taller and heavier but had a welcoming smile that was only marred by front teeth that overlapped. She had gray hair- curly from a permanent wave-that encircled her head like a woolen cap.

"May I hug you?" Susan asked. "You're the only aunt I've ever met."

Fern warmly accepted the hug. "Come into the breakfast room. There's coffee and pastries there, and we'll have privacy."

Walter and Susan followed Fern into the wallpapered vestibule, then through the sitting room and into the bright breakfast room. Its windows looked out on a big shade tree with hydrangea bushes beneath. They sat at a round table where Fern poured them coffee and placed a plate of various sweet rolls, cinnamon snails and crullers between them.

"Help yourself," Fern said. They each picked a favorite.

Susan said, "Where do we start? I'm willing to tell you what we know, and then you can fill in the gaps. My mom and dad met in San Francisco. They were thirty-seven and thirty-nine years old. Mom worked as a legal secretary, and Dad worked as an architect's assistant. Dad lived at home and commuted. In the next two years, Dad's mother—a widow—died, so when he and Mom became serious, he suggested that they move to the home place in Mayfield. They married. He became a building contractor, and she happily became a homemaker. A year later my sister, Gennie, was born, and two years later I came along. They obviously loved each other very much. I've never known anyone kinder than my dad—next to my husband, of course."

"Your story makes me very happy," Fern said. "Erma's childhood was so disconnected. After the trial, when she'd learned that our father had sold her and deceived our mother, Erma became a maligned celebrity in our community. She didn't know who to trust."

"I am saddened just to think about what she went through."

"Just like you, I learned the true story from my mother only a few years ago—basically on her deathbed," Fern said, dabbing a handkerchief at her eyes.

"What was your mother's name? I've never known my grandmother's name."

"Her name was Bertha. After the trial was over, Momma—Bertha—decided that justice had not been done. She wanted to make sure that Erma received a better life. Momma worked at a bakery, scouring all the baking pans in the evenings and late at night. The bakery family consisted of a father and son. The son's wife came from San Francisco and wanted to return to the city and start a bakery business there. They had two small children. They offered to have Erma go to San Francisco with them, be part of their family, finish high school, and help with the babies after school. She would be a big sister. Bertha agreed and decided she could be just as devious as her husband, Luke, had been. She and the baker's family invented a story that Erma had run away. This, she thought, would challenge Luke's mental stability—torment him just as he had caused anguish for her—as he wondered whether Erma had returned to her 'kidnapper.' If Erma had gone back, he'd have wanted more money from Jimmie Bullock. Both Jimmie and Erma were gone, he knew, but where?"

"The bakery family was sworn to secrecy, yet in yearly Christmas-card notes to Bertha, they would mention that their 'little one' was okay, was happy, had finished school, had gone to secretarial school, or whatever. Mother knew Erma had found a new life."

"So do you think my mother, Erma, agreed with this arrangement? After all, she would again be estranged from her family."

"Yes, life here after the trial left her an object of ridicule: an immoral child. There were questions of her experiences and a lot of teasing of the kind only youngsters can do."

"So I guess you've never told outsiders about your mother's complicity in allowing Erma to escape?"

"No, by the time I learned the story, no one in our family cared anymore. I was the youngest and all my siblings had left town as soon as they'd been able, some not finishing school. We had a toxic family—lies, extreme religion, and distrust; the speculation about what had happened to Erma had long ago diminished. Chances are that Erma was the luckiest of us all—she escaped."

Susan continued to answer questions about Erma's married life. They guessed that Erma may have lived with the baker's family until she'd earned enough money as a legal secretary to have her own room in a boardinghouse for single ladies. Both Fern and Susan felt satisfied that they now had answers to most of their questions. They promised to stay in touch, exchanging mailing addresses. Susan gave Fern her phone number.

Then Walter said, "Chances are that we'll return home tomorrow, but would you be willing to join us for dinner tonight? I'd like to invite the librarian too—Miss Harriet, I believe. If Susan hadn't met her, this may not have happened."

"I think Harriet and I would enjoy that."

"Okay, I'll pick you and Harriet up at about five, and we can go to our hotel, which has a nice restaurant. Let's call her now and see if that will work."

After midnight, when Walter had delivered both guests back to their homes, he and Susan returned to their hotel room. Although the temperature was nippy, they sat on their balcony, sipping a snifter of brandy and Benedictine and looking out on the moonlight-spangled evergreen landscape. "What an amazing couple of days," Susan said.

"Has this given you a semblance of satisfaction?"

"It truly has. How about you?"

"Yes."

The next morning, over their breakfast, Walter asked Susan, "Did you jot down the name of the bank that was to receive the funds for Erma's compensation?"

"I think so." She opened her handbag and brought out a small notebook. "Comstock State."

"That's not a familiar name to me. I wonder if it went out of business or if it was bought out by a bigger bank," Walter said.

"Gosh, fifty-plus years of buyouts, mergers, or name changes might require a bit of research."

"Then again, since Erma never changed her name, she could have claimed the money when she was twenty-one. And if she didn't claim it, think of the compounded interest over that amount of time." That speculation tantalized Walter's mathematical mind.

"But wouldn't Mom have had to expose her whereabouts to get the money? And you have to wonder if those two guys—products of the devil, to be sure—ever contributed to the fund."

"By the time we're ready to leave here, the banks should be open. Why don't we stop at the two big banks on Main Street and see if either one claims to be descended from Comstock State," Walter suggested. "If we get no definitive answer, we can go home and make inquiries by letter."

"Don't you think too many years have gone by and it was distributed in some other way once the account was declared dormant?"

"Perhaps, but since it was part of a court order, you have to wonder if there isn't some record of it."

Susan said, "This mystery surrounding Mom's life just goes on and on. But I know this is just the kind of challenge you love researching: a bit of history, a little business law, and whether it was accounted for."

Chapter 36

Trying to find time together challenged John and Gennie. She juggled her part time working schedule because they had agreed to spend one weekday unfettered by work, business appointments, or pastoral visits. They traveled north to Napa Valley, south to Carmel Valley, and to all coastal towns in between. They both gravitated to the ocean and its scenic and rhythmic beauty.

Meanwhile, John met with the bishop on several occasions. Choosing a new priest can take a church a minimum of six to twelve months. John had given the bishop his résumé and his request to stay in California. The bishop continually voiced his opinion that John and Gennie should marry before going to a new parish. The logistics of relocation were daunting, and his current church should not know of his search for a new one. If John wasn't called to the first or second parish needing a priest, they could be in limbo for a couple of years.

Gennie marked items off her checklist of things to be accomplished: the stores had been sold and the house too. She'd had much of the furniture stored—especially the family heirlooms. She'd chosen a headstone and placed it on Margo's grave. Emotionally, she tried to make peace with the circumstances. At times sadness seeped in, but it no longer grabbed her in the pit of her stomach and squeezed out pleasant thoughts.

When her yearly pap-smear appointment reminder came in the mail, Gennie made an appointment with the doctor who had delivered Mason and

Margo and had seen her each year since. Gennie talked to him about the feasibility of becoming pregnant at age forty. He expressed his reservations because older birth mothers often had infants with congenital defects. Gennie explained that her mother had delivered her at the age of forty-two and her sister at the age of forty-four. He relented a little but couldn't encourage her. Because she had overall good health, he suggested that both the prospective mother and father take daily multivitamins and maintain physical activity. Before Gennie discussed the possibility of having a family with John, she wanted the doctor's okay. The doctor hadn't been enthusiastic, but he hadn't ruled it out.

When John asked her if she wanted to wear Erma's engagement ring, Gennie hesitated only because of the size of the diamond. It commanded attention, and she worried that it may cause comments in any new parish. It did represent such a blissful marriage though; she thought it brought good vibes.

John called Susan and asked her if he could give the ring to Gennie.

"That's exciting! Mom would be so proud," Susan said. "When are you going to pop the question and give her the ring? Do you want me to bring it to you?"

Chapter 37

Eight months had passed since Will's death. John and Gennie were sitting in a booth at a restaurant with panoramic windows overlooking the Monterey Bay, midway between the towns of Monterey and Pacific Grove. The restaurant was perched right on the water's edge at the end of a wide dock. Its culinary fame had been founded on abalone burgers, but now fishing restrictions had made that menu item a memory. Dungeness crab in every form imaginable now graced the bill of fare. The lunch crowd included natives and tourists, and a line had started to form outside.

Both had ordered Crab Louie and were awaiting its arrival.

"What would you think about getting married in Hawaii?" John asked.

"That sounds lovely, but you've forgotten one small question. You've always assumed we would marry, but you've never actually asked me. I'd like you to do that sometime."

"Okay, why not now?" John had been carrying the engagement ring in his pocket for weeks—trying to gauge her readiness to accept. He slid out of his side of the booth, went to her side, and knelt in the passageway. There he was—dressed in a black priestly shirt with a clerical collar, on bended knee in the restaurant aisle. Gennie could feel the eyes of the diners beginning to look at the scene.

"Darling Gennie, may your wish be always my command. Will you marry me?"

"Yes, you lovable man, I will."

He slipped the ring on her finger, and she bent over to kiss him. His lips met hers in a passionate response.

He slid back into his seat, grinning, looking like he had accomplished the coup of the year. The people around them clapped, and then some started to sing "For He's a Jolly Good Fellow," and others joined in.

Gennie and John nodded to them as they held hands across the table.

"I guess I'd better get used to your spontaneity—and beware of what I wish for, and where," Gennie said.

In a moment the waitress brought over two glasses of champagne. "On the house," she said. "Our congratulations."

As they nibbled on their seafood, exiting patrons offered their best wishes as they passed the table. Many women asked to see the ring and expressed their approval. Instead of being an embarrassment, the event had become a participatory, festive occasion.

"To get back to my original question: Would you like to hear my suggestions about a wedding in Hawaii?" John asked.

"Certainly."

"A wealthy San Francisco couple—Episcopalians—bequeathed their estate on Maui to the California diocese for priests to use for various reasons. Its use is at the discretion of the bishop. Usually he gives retiring or ailing priests a week or so to use the estate, or he allows it as recognition of superior service. The bishop has offered it to us for our wedding—the first ceremony there. His description of it was awesome: a four-bedroom house with two additional cottages, an outdoor chapel, and a staff to handle all cooking, serving, and chauffeuring duties. The donor also included a trust fund to pay for all of this. The bishop said the staff is excited about the prospect and is ready to prepare anything we desire."

"That sounds like a dream—in paradise."

"Shall we try to set a date so we can reserve it?"

"All our school-year reports at work have to be handed in by April fifteenth. Then our vacation starts, and it ends in September. Any time after May first will work for me."

"Okay, I'll try for a date between May first and fifteenth. Do you have any other thoughts?"

"Yes, I'd like Susan and Walter to be our witnesses, unless you have a choice of your own for the best man."

"No, I agree. Those two have been with you and me through many events. I'd like them to come with us to Maui and enjoy a vacation. What about Mason and Lisa?"

"They're so intent on graduating on schedule; I hate to ask them to take any time away from their studies again. Mason has an advanced art portfolio he's trying to finish. I don't think we should try to tempt them with a Hawaiian vacation."

They finished eating, paid their bill, and went out to the car.

"Let's drive around the rim of the bay. I have something to show you," John said.

They drove through Monterey, past Cannery Row, and headed east, sometimes leaving the coastline in the distance.

"This is Baytown," John announced. "The local parish is looking for a priest. They asked me to interview after they read my résumé. However, I must caution you that there are five other candidates. As you can imagine, this area is very attractive, since it's so close to the coast. There will be multiple interviews with various congregational members. Some members will come to San Francisco to hear me preach. There are negotiations for salary, living quarters, and other considerations. It's as thorough as any big corporation's search for an executive director. The vestry members and the congregation are all consulted and asked to pray for divine guidance. It is definitely a decision by committee. With so many candidates from all over the country, it may well take eight months to a year for them to decide."

Gennie said, "It appears to be a working man's town, more like Salinas, with its agricultural influence. Monterey is so centered on the bay and fishing. Carmel always attracts the artists and the rich retirees. How big a church is this?"

"About two hundred and fifty people are on their membership rolls. Also, this church attracts many servicemen and nonservice personnel from the nearby army base. That makes for a fluctuating membership. More possible changes include the fact that a small congregation in rural Salinas has voted to join this church, which would add one hundred more parishioners. They'll wait and see who this vestry chooses before making the move. So it does sound like a demanding challenge."

They drove by the Gothic stacked-stone church with a square bell tower on the corner. A wooden addition across the back contained Sunday school classes and also served as the parish hall. Grown trees surrounded it and the adjacent parking lot.

Gennie read the name on the sign: St, Andrew's By The Bay. "It has an inviting look to it. I like it," Gennie said. "Is there a rectory nearby?"

"I'm not sure—that kind of discussion comes long after preliminary talks."

"What attracts you about this specific church?"

"It's similar to the mission. The congregation is very diverse and is in a constant churn of change. Because of the huge military training base nearby, the challenge of mixing the different races of enlistees with the old farming families and the wandering homosexual community from Monterey makes for a group needing homogenization. I have no problem welcoming everyone into the fold as Jesus demonstrated, but many congregations do not feel that way. Many citizens of the community, even outside the church, feel threatened by the large influx of black military families, yet most of the newcomers are well traveled and educated and should make the community stronger. Certainly the Episcopal Church has been known for its high-society white membership. Part of this exploration for me and the church members is to see if we are on the same page. This church could be considered the poor stepsister of both Carmel and Monterey. Personally, I relate better to the working-class congregation—people who struggle with their budget, their faith, and their philosophy. I find it an interesting ride."

"Since I have no social pedigree, this type of church is more appealing to me too," Gennie said.

They continued driving on the road rimming the bay, and it again returned to parallel the edge of the sandy beach that was dotted with huge boulders. John stopped the car, and they walked along the shoreline close to the water but evaded getting wet. They found a large rock they could climb on and sat holding hands and then kissing. Their passion mounted, and Gennie realized she had finally given herself complete permission to show her love for John. In a few moments they slid down the rock and headed for the car, walking hand in hand. In the car Gennie saw that familiar errant wisp of hair on John's forehead and this time she brushed it back with her hand.

On their way northward they drove past Watsonville, marveling at the fields of artichokes, and continued toward home on Highway 101.

Thinking again of the church's potential, Gennie said, "I can see you want this type of challenge. Just to come into a sophisticated church and babysit the status quo doesn't seem to fit your personality."

"Don't get your heart set on this. I'm a long way from being called. It also may be a challenge outside of my capabilities."

"Since we're contemplating our future, I have some questions for you. When we marry, are you hoping we'll have a family? I ask this because I went to my gynecologist for my yearly exam and discussed with him the possibility of having children at my age. He discouraged it not because of my health but because of the higher incidence of Down syndrome in children born to older mothers. So if we decide to try for a family, do we put it in God's hands and accept whatever happens?"

"Yes, of course. I would pray for healthy children, but I would love whatever we were given. As long as we can discuss everything with each other and God in prayer, we will do just fine,

They rode in silence for a few moments and then Gennie said, "I'd like to share a conclusion—maybe a confession. I now realize that Margo was conceived with a job description: she was to heal our marriage by seducing Will into being a loving father. At the time I didn't recognize that fact, but she soon did and I eventually grasped that we both knew she was doomed to failure. I don't want to make that mistake–or a similar one-again. I want our babies to be loved without any preconceived motive."

"Amen to that, I agree completely."

The following week Gennie learned that John had never visited either the Japanese Tea Garden or the Flower Conservatory in the Golden Gate Park in San Francisco.

"Instead of traveling out of the area, why don't we go there? It's been years since Susan and I went to the Fleischaker Zoo with our parents; later we brought Mason and Margo to the zoo and the gardens."

The next Tuesday John went to Mission Castro's office for a couple of hours because they were not having a long drive to their destination. Gennie drove there to pick him up and then they stopped at a Mediterranean grocery and delicatessen on Mission Street. Floor length strands of beads hung in the open doorway. Inside round cheeses and long sausages were suspended on cords from the ceiling. A glut of spicy aromas permeated the air. They ordered pita breads filled with a salad mixture of feta, olives, various hard cheeses and smoked sausages. Next they picked up a squatty bottle of Mateus wine and a couple of cheap wine glasses.

Walking to their parked car Gennie said, "Looks like we're having an international adventure today: we are going to the Japanese gardens with our lunch from Italy and Greece, and our wine from Portugal. Oh, and a thermos of coffee from Brazil."

The parking lot by the entrance to the garden held few cars. Weekday visitors were sparse especially on this cool jacket weather day. A Japanese greeter dressed in a kimono stood at the entrance, Father John asked if they could bring in their grocery bags and eat lunch in the garden. She said, "Yes, it's usually not allowed but since there are few visitors, you may." Gennie had noticed how often a priest received favorable answers to his requests. The greeter gave them a map of the gardens showing the paths intertwining, crossing and traversing the streams. Studying the diagram John said, "It looks like a web made by a drunken spider."

Once inside the gates and just a few steps down a path, the green foliage surrounded Gennie and John. The precisely trimmed bushes were nestled below some tall trees next to ferns, spiky succulents, and the greenery of rhododendrons: a well-planned jumble of plants. Various water attractions intermingled alongside the paths and under the bridges. Finally they found a wooden bench in a cul de sac near a pond and decided to eat there. John opened the wine bottle and filled the glasses while Gennie read the history of the gardens aloud.

They clinked their glasses and Gennie said, "Have you read the book The Feminine Mystique?"

"No but I have read a few reviews. Did you read it and what do you think?"

"It presents challenging information on so many levels. I found I immediately compared Ms. Friedan's findings with my own experiences. And I did relate to what she wrote. Her premise is that the housewife of the forties and fifties was sent messages through newspapers and magazines that her place belonged in the home, having and raising babies, and abdicating all power to her husband when he returned from war. This, the experts wrote would provide self-fulfillment for women. If a wife provided a clean and beautiful home, clean and obedient children, submitted to and obeyed her husband, she would achieve nirvana."

John said, "After twenty years the author challenged this theory because beside feeling empty herself, her fellow college classmates also had similar complaints that they hadn't found fulfillment."

"Exactly, and although I was fortunate to have family support, many wives had struggled financially with work and children during the war and surely felt denigrated when told to relinquish all control and be submissive. One thing I remember is that the experts giving this advice backed up their theory by stating it was grounded in biblical scriptures. Ms. Friedan doesn't mention this. Instead she notes that all editors were male and in charge of what they printed. Plus she states that a whole business of products were specifically targeted to the housewife and mother intent on cleanliness, thus their advertising supported this ideology. So Ms. Friedan is advocating this is the result of male chauvinism."

Gennie opened the pita sandwiches and handed one to John. He said, "Well with the author's Jewish background, I doubt that she would be spouting biblical verses from the new testament to support her premise."

"Yes, but I was intrigued: what does a Christian marriage entail? What rules apply and would I be happy complying with them?"

"Ah-hah. Now we are coming to the crux of this conversation."

Gennie swirled the wine in her glass and her face started to flush with color. "I know that telling you what I found in the scriptures is the same as a novitiate nun announcing her findings to the pope."

"No, not at all. I admire your interest and tenacity to clarify any doubts."

"My two main readings were Genesis and Ephesians. In both places one can extract one phrase or sentence and substantiate the premise of these writers from twenty years ago. But if you read the whole chapter, one verse in Ephesians does sum up the teachings: 'Submit to one another out of reverence to Christ.' Both husband and wife have an equal obligation to the other. In Genesis the message is more confusing but it also seems to stress fairness."

"So you think you can be in a Christian marriage? Some theologians have written dissertations on this subject so I'm glad you found the answer for you. The writers of the bible would be proud."

"Yes, and I double checked the marriage vows in the prayer book—no 'submit' or 'obey' is in there either and the vows are the same for both the man and woman."

Gennie enjoyed the fact that these trips gave them a chance to discuss various prenuptial subjects.

PART VI

Chapter 38

MAY 1964

John met Gennie, Susan, and Walter at the San Francisco airport for their 8:00 a.m. departure. After the five-hour-plus flight, they landed in Honolulu, deplaned, and hopped on a puddle-jumper plane to Maui. A young man with almond shaped eyes, light brown skin and dressed in a bright Hawaiian shirt approached the group as they awaited their luggage on the tarmac. Recognizing Father John's priestly garb, he extended his hand and asked, "Father John, I presume? My name is Charlie, like in Charlie Chan—or others call me Good Time Charlie." He smiled at his own joke. "I will be your chauffeur and chief bottle opener."

John quickly introduced the group, and Charlie, with a wheeled luggage carrier in tow, asked which luggage was theirs, efficiently scooped it up, and said, "Follow me to the limo."

Once loaded and leaving the airport behind, the car passed scenery that quickly became tropical. Charlie suggested an itinerary for the day, which could be amended or changed at the guests' whims.

"This is my recommendation: meet the staff, view and approve your rooms, and unpack with the maids' help—at which time they will whisk the wedding garments away to be pressed. Change into comfortable resort clothes, and gather on the lanai for lunch. After lunch I can drive you to Lahaina for some island clothes shopping. Then we'll go to Kaanapali to the Sheraton for afternoon tea or drinks—they have excellent mai tais. I'll drive your purchases home for the staff to press and get ready for you. When I pick you up, you'll have an hour to rest and refresh. We customarily don't dress up for dinner. Island clothes are usually de rigueur."

As the limousine approached the stone pillars of their destination, the wrought-iron gates opened to a winding gravel drive meandering toward the low, rambling island-style ranch house. Lush hibiscus, gardenia, jasmine, and ferns hugged the bases of the palms trees that dotted the dense key-lime-green lawn. The spongy moss between stepping stones—so well manicured—oozed luxury.

The limousine slid up to the home's entrance, and Charlie jumped out to open the car doors. In an instant the staff swarmed to greet them: the cook, two housemaids, and the gardener/backup chauffeur. They lined up to be introduced, the ladies scurrying in dainty, short steps, even though their clothing did not impede them from having a normal stride.

The two couples went to their rooms to change into more relaxed garb. When John came out of the bathroom wearing a sport shirt, Gennie started laughing. "I don't even recognize you without your clerical collar." She couldn't help but stare. They had always met in public places, so he'd always had his priestly clothes on.

He came over and put his arm around her. "Does this mean I'm going to have to wear my collar in bed so you know who you're married to?"

"Maybe..." She smiled with a naughty playfulness.

They met Susan and Walter in the hall, and all proceeded to the lanai. The rectangular table had been set for four, and each seat had a view of the ocean or the paragon vistas of the tropical landscape. They could hear the crashing surf beyond the trees. As they stood behind their chairs, Father John said, "Shall we bow our heads as I say grace?"

Charlie, who had appeared noiselessly, said, "Can you wait just a moment, Father?" He went to the pantry door, clapped twice, and the staff quickly gathered, standing in a line with heads bowed. "Thank you, Father."

Father John said a few words of general thanksgiving and then asked for a blessing of the food. From then on, whenever John said a prayer in a public room, the staff joined in.

The foursome sat down at the glass-topped table, which had rough bamboo placemats and apple-green and white bamboo-motif napkins. Plain iridescent white plates held the entrée: white-fish crepes with beurre blanc sauce, delicate baby butter lettuce (freshly picked that morning) lightly brushed with a blue-cheese dressing, and a cup of South Pacific fruit. Tropical iced tea accompanied the meal, and dessert was a lime sherbet with coconut shortbread cookies.

John leaned back in his chair and said, "Ambrosia from the Pacific Islands' gods."

Walter agreed and joked, "I'll recommend this establishment to my friends."

When Charlie came back into the room, John told him, "The cook and her staff did a superb job with this meal."

"You'll get used to it," Charlie said. "The cook is French trained but adds her own ideas with the fresh fruits and vegetables on the island. She likes to please; I will tell her."

He added, "I'll drive the station wagon into Lahaina—easier to park. Whenever you're ready, we'll depart."

On the road to Lahaina, Charlie said, "Let me run down a list of details for tomorrow's events: one p.m., nuptials in the grotto chapel with organ music. The minister and his wife, from Lahaina, will stay for the reception and dinner. Mixed white orchids and lilies with greenery for the altar. White bridal bouquet with a Cattleya orchid in the middle and Phalaenopsis and Dendrobium orchids trailing. Matron of honor bouquet similar but smaller. A little single orchid as a boutonniere for the best man's tuxedo.

"A string quartet will play for the reception and dinner. Choice of drinks with canapés for the reception. The wedding cake will be served with champagne as the dessert for dinner.

"A photographer with an excellent portfolio has been engaged.

"I think you will enjoy the menu the cook has planned.

"Ladies, what about a manicurist or a hairstylist? Any questions?"

Gennie was the first to answer. "Sounds wonderful. What a lot of planning you've done. I don't need a manicurist or hairstylist; neither does Susan."

Father John asked, "If Gennie and I get up early and go to the chapel for Morning Prayer, will it interfere with your setup?"

Charlies shook his head no and said, "Then it is a go!"

The station wagon turned onto the main road in the shopping area of Lahaina. The shops' goods spilled out onto the sidewalks to entice customers in, but that only meant that walkers wandered into the streets and competed with the cars.

Tourists and a few locals mulled amid the slow-driving cars on the main street of this small harbor town.

"I will drop you off at a few of the nicer stores. They handle better-quality merchandise and are honest. I don't get a cut, but they know if our visitors complain about the service or quality, I won't bring any of our guests back. It's a fairly good quality-control device." Charlie winked at his passengers in the rearview mirror.

After they'd shopped at three stores and wandered into a few souvenir shops, Charlie drove them to the Sheraton at Kaanapali. The large inside-and-outside bar already had a band playing; cocktail hour was in full swing. Charlie had said that this venue always helped visitors get into the vacation spirit.

"There are always so many honeymooners and families enjoying the vacation of their lifetimes. It's fun to share the excitement."

The hotel sat on a craggy promontory overlooking the Pacific Ocean. Many visitors gazed at the water hoping to see whales breaching, but by May most of the mammals had left the area.

As the couples sipped their mai tais, the band struck up some danceable music, and couples drifted onto a small dance floor.

“”Do you want to dance?" John asked Gennie.

"There's a first time for everything—sure."

"I'm really better at boogie-woogie, but that kinda dates me," he admitted.

The band finished one number and then started the first few chords of the "Anniversary Song"—"Oh, how we danced on the night we were wed." Obviously it was a popular song with the newlyweds, and the dance floor became crowded. John and Gennie returned to sit with Walter and Susan.

In an hour they met Charlie and headed back to the estate.

Dinner again tantalized the senses: large-prawn cocktail, charcoal-grilled mixed meats with tiny roasted new potatoes, haricots verts, and bittersweet chocolate éclairs for dessert.

As they sipped their coffee with their chairs shoved back from the table, Susan said, "The only thing missing is for Ezio Pinza to come out of the bushes singing 'Some Enchanted Evening.'"

They all started discussing where they had seen *South Pacific*. Susan had seen it on Broadway, her very first show in New York. Gennie had seen it in San Francisco.

The sun had gone down, so twilight had ascended over the grounds. Scattered Malibu-type garden lights flickered on among the plants. Charlie had lit two tiki lights at the end of the patio.

"This is fantasy land," Gennie observed.

Suddenly, there was a rustle in the bushes, and then a rich tenor voice started singing, "Some enchanted evening, you will see a stranger..." Charlie stepped onto the lanai with arms outstretched like a solo performer.

He finished the three verses with "Once you have found her, never let her go."

The group clapped and yelled, "Bravo!" But Charlie wasn't done yet.

He motioned to Walter and John and said, "Come up here and make it a trio." He put an arm around each man and said, "From the top! One-and, two-and..."

The trio sounded talented: John had a booming bass voice that God evidently gave to most priests, and Walter had sung minstrel songs all through college to his own guitar-plunking accompaniment. By this time the house staff had come out to hear and joined in the applause and laughter. The theme of "Once you have found her, *never* let her go" resounded with all of them.

Walter turned to Charlie and said, "From now on, you will be 'GT' to me. You are really a 'Good Time Charlie.'"

It was time to call it a night. Charlie reminded them that breakfast had no set time and would be cooked to each individual's order. Good nights were said. It had been a long day.

In their room Gennie went to the bathroom to remove her makeup, and John followed to brush his teeth.

"Quite a domestic scene, don'tcha think?" he said, grinning through the foaming toothpaste. He looked at her, her face slathered with cold cream, and they both started laughing.

After he'd donned pajama bottoms and she a nightgown, he said, "Shall we kneel together and say our prayers?" Silently they prayed and then slid between the bedsheets.

Gennie put her arm across his bare chest and kissed him on his cheek.

"Not tonight, Mrs. Calabash," he said, certain that Gennie remembered Jimmy Durante's famous radio sign-off saying.

"What?" she asked.

"We're not consummating this relationship tonight."

"Oh?"

"I've waited five years to marry you and to do it right. I've tried to deny my love, forget you, reject you, and erase my memory of you. I've postponed my ardor while you plowed through your emotional ties and became ready to commit to a new relationship. Now, twenty-four hours from the goal, I'm going to wait to make it perfect—for both of us."

"You have been so patient, and I love you for it."

As he leaned over and kissed her on the forehead, he said, "But it doesn't mean I won't have to get up in the middle of the night to take a cold shower."

In moments they were asleep.

They awoke in the morning, dressed, and went to the chapel, which was built with stones from the nearby beach. The light cardigan over her shoulders felt good in the cool morning chill. John carried his well-worn prayer book and gave Gennie a white leather one with "Geneva Lanham" engraved in gold on the cover. They read the family morning prayers together and went to breakfast. Walter and Susan soon joined them on the lanai, and afterward all decided to go swimming in the pool.

They went inside to get ready for the ceremony, the men and ladies going to separate dressing rooms. The dresses were identical in style: sleeveless silk shantung sheaths similar to the ones Jackie Kennedy had popularized. Gennie's had a watery, pale celadon hue; Susan's was a deeper shade with a tint of blue. Both wore the pearl necklaces their parents had given them for their high-school graduations. A flat matching ribbon adorned Susan's short, straight pixie bob. A lace mantilla borrowed from Josefina covered Gennie's curly hair and acted as a veil. As they stood side by side, so similar in size and stature, Susan said of their reflection, "Simple and elegant. I approve."

At about ten minutes to one, the four walked to the living room, where the minister and his wife were sitting. After introductions were exchanged, Charlie came in with the news: "There will be a short delay: the organist called to say that she has a flat tire. Our gardener is driving to her house to fix it. Maybe thirty minutes."

Susan and Gennie exchanged looks. Gennie said, "I think Susan and I will change into muumuus while we wait. This silk fabric wrinkles, so we can't sit down without having crinkles in our skirts."

As they left the room, John asked Charlie, "Have you heard from the kids?"

"Yes, the plane had a fog delay out of LA, but the gardener just phoned that the commuter has landed in Maui. They'll be here in thirty minutes."

"And what about the organist?"

"She's sitting outside our gate in the shade. I just took her a soft drink. She's a good sport."

When Gennie and Susan returned, Charlie served them all glasses of iced tropical tea, and the couples conversed.

In thirty minutes Gennie and Susan went back to the dressing room to get rezipped into their dresses and put their head coverings on. They were not yet back in the living room when the crunch of tires on the gravel announced that the car had arrived. Expecting it to be the organist, Gennie stopped for a moment and listened in the bedroom hall.

"That's Mason's voice!" she exclaimed and started running for the living room. There in the front foyer stood Mason and Lisa.

"Surprise!" they shouted simultaneously.

Gennie grabbed Mason's neck and just held on. She stepped back and hugged Lisa.

"This is an absolute, complete surprise." She looked over at John and realized that his face did not reflect amazement. "Did you know about this? Or did you organize this?"

John only responded with a smile.

"You are a darling man for planning this, and you kids are so generous in taking time off from school."

"Hey, Mom, it was a no-brainer: School or Hawaii? It wasn't a difficult choice."

Charlie assembled the luggage in the vestibule, waiting for the first greetings to be complete.

"May I show you to your rooms? They're on the other end of the house."

When they reached the adjacent rooms, he said, "The staff will help you unpack and take your wedding apparel to be pressed."

Within twenty minutes the two were dressed: Mason in a tux and Lisa in a blue-linen cap-sleeved sheath. She wore a blue sapphire necklace that matched her eyes, and her red, shoulder-length hair was now in a French twist.

Mason looked at her with an admiring smile. "You look beautiful enough to be a bride today too. Shall we just tie the knot?"

When they reached the living room, Mason asked John if he could walk his mom down the aisle.

"Okay, but let me tell the reverend and organist of our change of plans."

They all walked to the outdoor stone chapel. Gennie turned to Charlie and asked, "Can the staff take a few moments off and come to the ceremony?" Then, when she saw the minister's wife sitting alone in the last pew, she went to her and suggested that she go up and sit with Lisa.

A few wafts of breeze tickled the jasmine and gardenia blossoms just enough that they released their perfume, and the radiant sunlight made all the landscape Crayola-bright.

As the organ music started, Susan turned to Gennie and asked, "Are you ready?" With Gennie's nod, Susan started down the aisle. Mason and Gennie followed Susan, and the minister asked, "Who giveth this woman to be married to this man?"

Mason replied, "My sister in heaven and I do."

Gennie felt her knees start to buckle, but John was quickly at her side. "Mason, you can sure throw me a curveball," she thought. "I wasn't expecting that."

After the ceremony they all gathered on the lanai, and Mason said, "I didn't mean to take you by surprise with my statement. But if you remember, that

Christmas day when John came to dinner, Margo remarked that he would be such a good dad. She said she wished she had a dad like that. So I know she approves, and I wanted to remember her."

"You are so insightful, but sometimes I wish you would give me a little forewarning." Gennie smiled at her son. "Actually I was thinking about her this morning, wishing she were here. Now I think her spirit is."

After being served drinks and appetizers on the lanai, they went into the dining room, where the elegant table setting included antique tableware and tall silver candelabras. The wedding cake was wheeled in at the end of the meal; Gennie and John cut it. Glasses of champagne ended the meal.

The next day, Charlie had a voyage planned for the group.

"Every honeymoon needs a cruise," he said.

They left the Lahaina marina in a small yacht and sailed to Lanai, the pineapple island. The boat's crew members were young college students, tanned, muscular, and enthusiastic about their jobs.

This island still remained untouched by the resort developers and had remains of the original housing for the Mormon kids who'd come and harvested the crops each year. They toured the old pineapple farm in a couple of jeeps and returned to the beach for lunch—a barbeque cooked by their tour guides and served on picnic tables. They arrived back in Maui by midafternoon.

Charlie had planned a drive to Hana—an all-day trip—the following day.

They got up early, had juice and coffee, and piled into the station wagon. A thermos of coffee and iced soft drinks accompanied them as they set out. Two hours later, Charlie pulled off the road by a waterfall.

"I've got some malasadas and mini pork sausages for breakfast," Charlie announced. The Portuguese donuts were still warm. Lisa grabbed her camera to film the energetic waterfalls. They stood around the station wagon munching food and drinking more coffee.

"If you want to see more waterfalls, there are a few that require a ten-minute hike off the road, but they're awesome," Charlie announced.

All six of the passengers were familiar with the California coastal highway that followed the seashore the full length of the state. It was known for its crooked route and beautiful vistas—except when a sudden fog could obliterate the view and even the road. They were not prepared for how beautifully different this road to Hana was. Lush with greenery and waterfalls on either side, the two lanes twisted and had several hairpin turns that required slowing down to fifteen miles per hour. If one had a propensity for motion sickness this would not be an enjoyable trip.

Charlie knew the best stops to overlook the crescent beaches or to watch the surfers. They were overwhelmed by the diversity and endless beauty.

Gennie also appreciated that they had the time to discuss with Mason and Lisa their ideas about the ranch and stable property. Walter inquired about their business plan and how they would acquire investors.

Mason said, “One of our instructors asked me if he could use the property as a model assignment for our whole class to study. Lisa and I will be interested in their different visions for this project and in the instructor’s opinion.”

By noon they reached Hana and stopped, putting a picnic quilt on the ground. They ate the lunch that had been packed for them and then returned home via the same road. Once back at the estate the six raced to the pool for a pre-dinner swim.

That night—actually in the early morning—Gennie awoke with a start. A dream had aroused her into an anxious wakefulness. John’s arms were still wrapped around her so she carefully extracted herself and went to sit in the chair by the window. Already the early light of dawn had started to erase the dark night skies, She watched John patting the mattress and when he realized she wasn’t beside him, he sat up. He saw her across the room.

“Anything wrong?” he asked.

“No, a disturbing dream awakened me.” John came over and sat in the armchair opposite her.

She continued, “I’ll work it out.”

"Tell me about it. In this marriage we are going to share our hopes and fears. There will be none of this 'facing problems alone.' What was the dream?" He got up and offered his hands to hers. "It's chilly here, let's get back under the covers."

In bed they intertwined their cold feet.

"Well, in the dream I was surrounded by a forest of tall white marble columns. They were close together but a person could have slipped in between. These pillars were endless, no horizon-- just light from above with no shadows. Was there a way out or would one just walk in circles? I've deciphered this as a depiction of my fear of my role as the wife of a clergyman. It's been on my mind recently as the time draws nearer."

"I hope your assessment is correct and not that you already feel trapped in this marriage." He smiled and plumped up his pillow so his face could be close to hers. "I planned to discuss your possible duties on the flight home. I didn't want anything to distract us from this glorious island experience while we are here but let's do it now.

"The rules of being a pastor's wife are loose and sloppy. You can do as little or as much as you want. It's like being the first lady in the White House. One can be as aggressive and active as Eleanor Roosevelt or as quiet and retreating as Bess Truman. And everything in between.

"Since our little mission hasn't had a minister's wife in years, I doubt they will have expectations or be demanding."

"You make it sound so easy."

"I am not belittling your anxiety but let me tell you what I plan. I just asked for vacation time and did not reveal I was getting married so we will definitely take them by surprise." John grinned as if this shock would be fun to watch. "I will introduce you during the usual announcements before the sermon. I'll mention that you are a widow with a son in college and that we will live in San Bruno so you'll be close to your work in Palo Alto as a registered nurse. I might add that we met at All Saints Hospital years ago. We'll let them surmise that I met you when you worked there. I'll ask you to stand You can smile at the congregation and sit again. After the recessional you can join me to greet everyone."

John moved closer to her and gave her a hug. "See how simple that will be?" He looked at her, "It doesn't look like I've convinced you."

"You make it sound effortless but my knees will be knocking."

"As the weeks go by we'll evaluate any requests for your time. Having a full time job will make it easier to decline invitations. We can also plead that we are newlyweds and need more private time.

"I also thought we'd invite Father Stanley and his wife Miriam to join us for dinner in the next few weeks. She can answer your questions from a female perspective and introduce you to other wives she knows. And any Sunday you want to visit your old church and friends in Redwood City, you're free to do so. I don't want you to feel like you have signed up for servitude."

Their eyes met and he kissed her. "I doubt if there's much more sleep here tonight. Do you want to go down to the chapel for Morning Prayer?"

After breakfast Walter and Susan went snorkeling. Mason and Lisa took the jeep and rode up the road to Mount Haleakala. They planned to stop at the horse farms nestled in the hills on the route and talk with the foremen and owners.

Gennie and John chose to stay on the estate and enjoy it. They wandered single file down the trail from behind the chapel leading to the beach. The ocean tide was coming in. They watched as each wave started way out in the deep water and then grew. Parallel to the shore, it would crest and crash upon itself with a dramatic crescendo. As a final farewell, the foaming froth bathed their toes. Repetitive, relentless, mesmerizing.

"The energy and the magnificence—it reminds me of the power of the Almighty," John observed.

Gennie stayed silent for many moments and then said, "Power alone can be a bad thing. Thank goodness God's power is gloved in mercy and dispensed with grace."

John bent down to kiss her and then said with a smile, "I didn't realize I was getting such a philosopher and sermon critic in this marriage deal."

On their last afternoon, they gathered for their evening meal. Afterward John went into the kitchen to give each employee a stipend. By this time they felt like family, and hugs were exchanged. The week had been glorious. Such a happy conclusion made them wonder, "Why does this have to end?"

Chapter 39

"This is our first Christmas as newlyweds," Gennie thought as she put the next day's dinner preparations in the refrigerator. She planned to get the table set and ready before she went to the midnight services. John had been home earlier and now conducted the children's seven o'clock Christmas Eve service. After the ten o'clock services the next morning on Christmas Day, they both could relax.

It had been a whirlwind of activity since they'd arrived at Baytown on the first of November. John had received the call from the congregation in the middle of August. Before he accepted, he'd had long discussions with Gennie about the history of race in this town.

Baytown did not have its own industry and this led to the town being buffeted by the decisions of other towns and the military base In the eighteen hundreds northern European emigrants farmed the land. At the turn of the century an entrepreneurial real estate developer persuaded the Southern Pacific railroad to build a streetcar line from its railroad tracks to a luxury hotel he was building. His vision had been to have a cluster of summer homes surround the resort. This endeavor brought in many Asians and Hispanics to work in his inn. The advent of mass automobile ownership and the burning of the lodge led to its demise.

The population of Baytown had declined until World War I brought a military training camp nearby. A sudden influx of people and business erupted and then disappeared after the war when the army downsized. During the thirties the depression and dust bowl victims flooded into the area to the fishing and canning industries. Again in the forties the second world war required the army base to train thousands of service men. When the army was desegregated many of the men and their families decided to establish homes in the community. The majority of new settlers were African Americans.

Father John learned during deeper question-and-answer sessions with the vestry that the city's racial balance seemed to be headed toward being half-white and half-minorities. Historically Negros had a rich religious experience in the African Methodist Episcopal Church. It combined Methodist doctrine with episcopal structure. Many new residents in Baytown gravitated to St. Andrew's because it had been welcoming.

"These changing demographics affect the whole area. We will all need to work together: the community leaders, the elected officials, and the churches." John told Gennie.

Gennie replied, "If you think, with God's help, you can make a difference and want to, go for it. I'll be with you."

The church did not have a permanent parsonage, so the couple had to find a home. Gennie and John hoped to find a place close to the church, within walking distance. Baytown as a community had grown in reaction to the needs of the canneries and the military base. For many years it had been unincorporated, so no organized plan had existed. A few blocks of older—turn-of-the-century—nicer homes were by the church, but most needed repairs. One of the elderly parishioners offered her home for the price of the tax evaluation, but it needed updates. Did the neighborhood merit the monetary investment?

The vestry approved the acquisition and funding so the remodeling began. The kitchen, two bathrooms, and a powder room were all ripped out and rebuilt. Hardwood floors were refinished, and new carpeting was put in the bedrooms. Rotting wood in window sashes needed to be replaced, and everything had to be repainted. Meanwhile, Gennie packed up their San Bruno apartment, picked out some of her furniture in storage, and had their belongings sent to Baytown.

This Christmas Day dinner would be the first opportunity for the family to come and visit. Lem and Margaret, Walter and Susan, and Mason and Lisa were all expected about one o'clock. Although the church tradition dictated that the tree not be decorated before Christmas Eve, Gennie had decorated hers but hadn't plugged the lights in. She couldn't figure out how to be in the church and at home at the same time.

Letters and telephone calls had been exchanged among family members in the previous six months, but no personal visits had taken place; it had been too hectic.

Lisa and Mason arrived with wrapped packages and a bottle of wine. Lisa showed off her engagement ring—gifted on Christmas Eve. The couple's radiance filled the foyer. The ring combined a round European-cut diamond from Lisa's grandmother with the sapphire-and-diamond ring that Erma had left. They all huddled around admiring the new setting, which had been created by a local jeweler. They also announced their June wedding date, two weeks after graduation.

Hearing that information, Gennie looked at John with a questioning glance. He nodded, and she announced that in June she would be eight months pregnant.

"Won't the two of you be embarrassed to have an enceinte mother of the groom?"

Lisa immediately said, "Nonsense. We're thrilled for you and John. Actually, this is very exciting." She walked over to hug Gennie. "We'll want you front and center in every photo."

It took a moment for everyone to absorb the revelation: Gennie was pregnant.

Susan came over with a congratulatory hug and asked, "Are you feeling okay?"

Gennie said, "Yep, great." She realized how difficult this news probably was for Susan. Maybe hearing it in a group helped to soften the announcement. Susan and Walter had wanted children and in their early years of marriage had sought advice and looked into adoption. Now, again, Gennie had become pregnant quickly. If Susan saw the unfairness of it, Gennie would not blame her.

Margaret came over and said, "I almost feel like I'm having another grandbaby."

"Mama M, I hoped you would feel that way."

"I came to the conclusion that if God had wanted me to die with Margo and Will, I would have. Since I'm still alive, I must choose to act lively and embrace every opportunity. You know how I love babies. Hopefully, I'll have the inside track to visit and care of him or her." Margaret smiled and added, "Gennie, you will always be our daughter; we love you."

During dinner Mason revealed that the spring semester schedule had just been printed. The senior art show would be the first week in May. He had talked with Jeff, the heir apparent to his uncle's ranch. Jeff and his uncle planned to fly out in their private plane for the event because Mason had named his collection "A Year at a West Texas Ranch." Two other couples from nearby ranches and a representative of the Albany Old Jail Museum were coming too. Lisa would also display a portfolio of her photography.

Walter counseled, "With all those moneyed buyers there, I hope you put aside a couple of paintings for your personal collection. You may never have the luxury of so many hours to commit to your painting again. I would hate for you to sell something and regret it."

In May the exhibition proved successful. Even a gallery from Santa Fe came to look at Mason's work. The art grapevine was alive and well.

PART VII

Chapter 40

JUNE 1965

Gennie invited Lem and Margaret to drive down to Baytown and spend the night before both the graduation and wedding.

Lisa wanted their wedding to be at the Methodist church in Paso Robles. Gennie wore a two-piece maternity suit in a pale champagne color, with a brighter-colored scarf at her neck. She stood with John in the vestibule waiting to be escorted to their seats after Margaret, Lem, and the bride's grandparents were seated.

Gennie dreaded the next few minutes. She knew that implicit in the marriage vow Mason would agree to was God's instruction in Genesis that said "...a man shall leave his father and his mother and hold fast to his wife." Although she admitted this was fair and proper, the fact remained that she was losing Mason to another woman: Lisa. She was happy for her son but sad for his mother. A bittersweet moment.

While she indulged in this self-imposed pity, the baby in her abdomen kicked and Gennie's thoughts were shifted.. She couldn't help but smile; though not yet born it was already vying for attention. The usher approached her and offered his bent arm and John followed behind her to their places.

When Gennie sat next to her sister, Susan leaned over and whispered into Gennie's ear, "You aren't the only one in this pew who's pregnant." Gennie looked at her sister and let out a loud, enthusiastic squeal. John tugged at

Gennie's arm in a gesture of admonition. Such a sound was inappropriate as the bride's mother walked down the aisle with her escort.

Gennie turned to John and whispered the news. He nodded his understanding and then whispered back, "I'm afraid they'll think you're going into labor." Gennie wanted to giggle but didn't.

Lisa started down the aisle and the congregation stood. When she reached the front pew, she stopped, pulled a rose out of her bouquet, and gave it to her mother.

Mason bounded down from the altar and presented Gennie with a small bouquet of greenery with three short stems of silk almond blossoms tied with a ribbon.

"This is from me and Pops," he said and kissed her on her cheek.

"Mason! You rascal," she said, stifling tears. "Thank you."

Mason went back to his place at the altar.

The organist stopped playing, and the minister said, "Dearly beloved, we are gathered together here in the sight of God…"

Gennie felt overwhelmed with happiness upon hearing Susan's news. It wiped out her melancholy thoughts of losing Mason. She remembered the saying: "When one door closes God opens a new one." Their new baby would soon have a cousin. Happy days were ahead. She grabbed John's hand and squeezed it.

ABOUT THE AUTHOR

Anne Kane worked as a registered nurse for forty-three years. Her career gave her ample occasion to witness family tragedies, pain, and joy, which informs her writing with poignant realism. She earned a BSN from the University of Texas at Arlington at age forty-five.

Married with three children and three grandchildren, Kane lives in Texas. She is the author of the memoir *Elusive Joy*.

41310883R00163

Made in the USA
San Bernardino, CA
09 November 2016